HUSK

HUSK

Dave Zeltserman

This first world edition published 2018
in Great Britain and the USA by
SEVERN HOUSE PUBLISHERS LTD of
Eardley House, 4 Uxbridge Street, London W8 7SY
Trade paperback edition first published
in Great Britain and the USA 2018 by
SEVERN HOUSE PUBLISHERS LTD

British Library Cataloguing in Publication Data
A CIP catalogue record for this title is available from the British Library.

ISBN-13: 978-0-7278-8802-0 (cased)
ISBN-13: 978-1-84751-927-6 (trade paper)
ISBN-13: 978-1-78010-983-1 (e-book)

All Severn House titles are printed on acid-free paper.

Severn House Publishers support the Forest Stewardship Council™ [FSC™],
the leading international forest certification organisation.
All our titles that are printed on FSC certified paper carry the FSC logo.

MIX
Paper from
responsible sources
FSC
www.fsc.org   FSC® C013056

Typeset by Palimpsest Book Production Ltd.,
Falkirk, Stirlingshire, Scotland.
Printed and bound in Great Britain by
TJ International, Padstow, Cornwall.

To Peter Kanter, my good friend and occasional chess nemesis.

ONE

L abor Day weekend is always a good time to pick up students hitchhiking, but that wasn't why I pulled into the rest stop on the Massachusetts Turnpike. While I had fourteen empty burlap sacks in the back of the van that needed to be filled before heading back home, along with more than enough rope and gags to take care of things, I didn't expect to be picking up any of *them* here. While there's always the chance of finding a hitchhiker at a place like this, it's a small one and I was expecting that most of the stragglers I'd be getting would be in cities off the Turnpike. Hartford, Bridgeport, and if need be, New Haven. For this trip I hoped to get mostly students. They were generally healthier and leaner than the usual types – the prostitutes, drifters, homeless, and other such stragglers that I'd often have to collect. Students also tended to carry more books, clothes, and money on them than those others, all of which was good to bring back to the homestead. If I ended up needing those others to fill up the back of the van, I would. But I was hoping for mostly students.

Another reason I didn't expect or care about getting one of them at this rest stop was it's safer and easier to collect them at night when it's dark and you don't have to worry about prying eyes. But it's not impossible to collect them during the daylight. It's not even that hard, and I've done it plenty of times in the past. You just have to be careful. So why did I stop? Only because I'd been traveling for over five hours, and I wanted to get a bite to eat and stretch my legs.

As you'd expect on the Saturday before Labor Day, the building housing the small food court and restrooms was teeming with travelers, even though it was only a little after ten thirty in the morning. I stood among them fantasizing how much simpler things would be if I could just pick fourteen of them out, take a club to them, and load their unconscious bodies into the back of the van. If I could've done that, I'd be heading home shortly afterwards and arriving at the homestead well before sundown. But these trips are never that easy. Not hard, exactly, but they take time. Almost always at least a full twenty-four hours, and there have been times when it's been double that.

I purchased a newspaper and then searched the food kiosks until I found the one I'd frequented the last time I came this way. At the kiosk I bought a large black coffee and what was advertised as a vegan chocolate-covered doughnut, and took it to a small table in the back. For the next twenty minutes I stretched out my legs fully, read the newspaper all the way through, ate my doughnut, and sipped my coffee. After that I sat with my eyes closed and listened to the hubbub *they* made, letting my mind drift. What knocked me out of my daydreaming was realizing there was a heated argument going on nearby. Lovers were fighting. From their raised voices, the man was angry and getting angrier, and the girl tearful.

I glanced casually in their direction. They were two tables away. The girl's back was to me, so I couldn't tell much about her other than that she had long yellow hair and seemed to be a slight thing, at least from her slender shoulders and how narrow her back was. The man I was able to get a good look at. Red-faced, beefy, cruel mouth, eyes even angrier than his voice. He looked young, but that didn't mean much. The healthy ones always look much younger than we do because of the soft, pampered lives they lead. Even after all the forays I've made into *their* world, I still have a difficult time judging their ages.

I glanced away, but soon after that my ears perked up when he told her in a strained and lowered voice that he was done with her. This meant there was a chance of me being able to get him safely, assuming he had been a passenger in her car and now needed to find another ride to wherever he was heading. He'd be a good one to pick up. The women back at the homestead would get a lot of meat off of him when they stripped him to the bones. But it was more than just that. Because of his cruel mouth and the way he left that girl sobbing, I wanted him to be the first one I left trussed up in the back of the van.

I kept him in my peripheral vision and watched as he left the table. Soon he was crossing diagonally in front of me as he made his way toward the exit. I found myself holding my breath, hoping he'd put out a thumb and start hitchhiking. I could see him through the glass as he stepped outside and moved doggedly in a straight line as if he knew exactly where he wanted to go. That didn't mean he wasn't going to be hitchhiking. He could've quickly decided where he was going to try to flag down a ride.

I decided to give it three minutes before heading out after him, and was still counting down to zero when a small green-colored sedan pulled up in front of the entrance. That same man I'd been hoping would be my first pickup got out of the car, walked to the trunk, opened it, and flung a duffel bag toward the door. After slamming the trunk closed, he got back into the driver's seat and sped off.

I couldn't help feeling disappointed as I glanced over at the girl, and it wasn't because of how much less meat we'd be able to get off of her.

TWO

Even though she had to know her duffel bag was lying unattended on the pavement outside, she didn't bother getting it, or even looking in its direction. Instead, she sat as if in a daze for the next forty minutes before slipping a backpack on and finally leaving the table. She must've been hoping her boyfriend would have a change of heart and come back for her, and it took that long for her to finally accept that he wasn't. Or maybe the ordeal had weakened her to such an extent that until then she lacked the strength to stand on her feet. Whichever it was, the rush of travelers entering and leaving the building during that time all stepped around the duffel bag, with none of them bothering to locate who it belonged to or check whether that person needed help.

I didn't want her to notice I was watching her, so I looked away as she wandered somewhat aimlessly toward the door. I then waited five additional minutes before following her outside.

She sat cross-legged on her duffel bag, her face buried in her hands. She looked so tiny it again made me think there just wouldn't be enough meat on her to justify the bother. But I had already invested time in her, and I knew the elders in the clan would've expected me to collect her if possible. They might not be able to trim more than forty pounds from her, but it would be high-quality meat, leaner, tastier and more nutritious than much of the meat I brought back. I stood in front of her making up my mind before telling her that I had been sitting nearby when she had her fight with her boyfriend. She didn't move at all, and I wasn't sure she heard me or realized I was there. I tried again.

'That was rotten what he did to you,' I said. 'Abandoning you like that. Where I come from, we'd skin a boy alive doing something that mean to a pretty gal like you.'

I made sure I was smiling, so when she looked my way

she'd think I was joking about the skinning alive part. She slowly lifted her head, and as her eyes caught mine I felt a hitch form along the side of my mouth. Even as red-rimmed as her eyes were from crying and as blotchy as her skin was around those eyes for the same reason, she looked younger than I expected, much more so than her boyfriend. She also struck me as very pretty. Usually I don't think of them in any particular way – pretty, ugly, or otherwise. They're just *them*. Something different from my kind, and certainly not something to think of as anything other than the meat we can trim off of them. But in her case I thought about how pretty she was. I also realized that for a few heartbeats I'd been somewhat mesmerized by her blue eyes and all her blondeness. That was easy to understand. I'm not used to blue eyes or golden hair, especially hair that looks like it could be finely spun silk. In my clan, and all the other clans I know of, all of us have brown eyes that are so dark they look black in most lights. Likewise, we all have coarse black hair.

Her lips turned upwards slightly so she could return me a frail smile. 'This is embarrassing,' she said. 'But thank you. And yes, that was pretty awful what Ethan did.' She shook her head slightly. 'I still can't believe it.'

'You look like you could use some help. Anything I can do?'

'That's awfully nice of you, but no. I'll be OK.'

'I don't know.' I rubbed the back of my neck in a folksy sort of way to put her at ease, which seemed unnecessary given how relaxed her smile had become and the way her eyes held steady on mine. 'It looks to me like he left you stranded out here, and where I come from we don't walk away from someone in need of help.'

'I don't know . . .'

I turned my smile up a notch. 'People tell me I have a friendly face,' I said.

That was the truth. Many of them I've picked up in the past have told me that. She broke out in a soft laugh. 'True, that,' she said. She stood up and offered me her hand. 'My name's Jill Zemler.'

Seeing her standing in front of me, she was every bit the

slight thing I'd thought earlier, the top of her head barely reaching my chest. Maybe ninety pounds soaking wet. Her hand quickly disappeared in mine as I took it. Her flesh felt warmer than I expected it to be.

'Charlie Husk,' I said.

I felt a sudden dryness in my throat that I couldn't quite explain, and it caused my voice to crack a touch. I also realized that our handshake had gone on longer than it should've. She didn't seem to mind, but I released her hand anyway.

'Nice to meet you, Charlie,' she said. Her smile had turned into something impish that also showed in her eyes. 'Where are you heading?'

I must've been too distracted by the way she was smiling at me, because I should've gotten her to tell me first where she was going. From where we were on the Massachusetts Turnpike, it was likely she'd be heading in one of two directions, at least if she was a college student as I suspected. Either somewhere along the way to New York or Amherst, Massachusetts. I took a gamble and told her New York.

'Well, it must be fate,' she said. 'I'm heading there also. I'm a student at Queens College.' A flash of hurt momentarily dulled her smile. 'It wasn't much fun being dumped here, and you really are rescuing me, Charlie Husk. I didn't know what I was going to do, other than try to get an Uber ride to a bus station.' The little that remained of her smile turned into something brittle as she said, 'I hope you understand, but my mom would kill me if I didn't ask to see your driver's license.'

'Sure, of course.' As good-naturedly as I could manage it, I pulled a leather wallet out of my pocket, dug a driver's license from it, and handed it to her. Like the dungarees, flannel shirt, and work boots I was wearing, the wallet came from one of *them* I had picked up on an earlier run, and it was in good shape, not too worn. The driver's license was a fake, but to my eye looked every bit as genuine as any others I've seen from the state of New Hampshire. The name on the license, Charlie Husk, is my real name and I do live in New Hampshire, but while the address on it was a real street address in the state's largest city, Manchester, my clan lives eighty miles from there, deep in the wilderness – an area nobody, other than us and other clans, knows about. Occasionally we get lost hikers stumbling upon us, but ever since the advent of handheld GPS devices we get far fewer of them, which is one of the reasons my clan needs me to make these runs more often than I remember anyone ever doing when I was a child, even though there are fewer of us now.

Her eyes and smile brightened as she handed me back my license. 'I must be a mess,' she said. 'Do you mind if I go back in there and wash up before you leave?'

'Not at all.'

She disappeared into the building leaving me to stand guard by her duffel bag. I knew she wasn't going to just be washing her face, she'd also be calling someone, probably her ma, so she could give that person my name and address. Others I'd picked up in the past had tried that same safety precaution – at least they claimed they had before I choked them into unconsciousness. Of course, with those others I had shown different driver's licenses – I was always collecting licenses from pickups who physically resemble me, at least enough so their license photos could pass for me. I had several of those with me now, and I wondered why I gave her my real name and showed her the license I did. I'd never done that with any of them before. It didn't matter, though. When the person she's calling now later calls the authorities about her disappearing, it will be a dead end, as always.

It didn't take her long to finish up whatever she was doing and rejoin me. Before she could reach for her duffel bag, I hoisted it up and pointed in the direction where I left my van. She squinted toward it, but couldn't see the van because of the larger vehicles surrounding it. It was no accident that I parked where I did.

'I'll be paying for gas,' she said.

'That won't be necessary.'

'I insist.'

I didn't argue any further. It didn't matter. She followed me as we squeezed between cars until we reached the back of the van. I didn't drag her inside of it like I had planned to. Instead, I threw her duffel bag into the back and closed the door before she had a chance to see the burlap sacks and rope. As I made my way to the driver's side door I tried to understand why I didn't take care of her then. I'd made sure nobody was watching. It could've been handled quickly and without any fuss. Now I was going to have to take care of her while she was sitting in the passenger seat. This meant grabbing her by the throat while she was unaware and choking her into unconsciousness, then pushing her body to the floor of the van, and driving someplace where we'd have privacy so I'd be able to move her to the back and take care of her properly. It wouldn't necessarily be difficult to do that – I'd done it plenty of times in the past. And with her being such a little thing, it wasn't as if she'd be able to put up much of a fight. I have a surprising amount of strength in my hands and arms, even for someone of my own kind, and I've easily subdued men bigger than myself. Still, it didn't make any sense for me not to take advantage of the opportunity I was given, and it left me confused. But that was only because I was still lying to myself.

THREE

'Is anything wrong? You look so . . . preoccupied.'

'What? No, nothing like that,' I lied, because I was very much preoccupied, enough so that I'd been scowling without realizing it. The reason for my consternation was that I had gotten off the Massachusetts Turnpike over forty-five minutes ago, was now on Interstate 84, and I'd had plenty of opportunities where I could've taken care of her. I was also beginning to accept the reason why I hadn't. I had stopped thinking of her as one of *them*, and was instead thinking of her as a very pretty girl with a sweet smile. Maybe I'd been thinking of her that way ever since she'd looked up at me and our eyes met outside that rest stop. That could've been why I'd been feeling this uneasy anxious fluttering in my chest almost from the moment I led her into the passenger seat of the van. I'd also pretty much decided she wasn't going to be one of them I brought back to the clan. Instead, I would drive her to New York like I'd promised, and from there work my way home filling up the burlap sacks along the way. If the elders ever found out about this, the consequences would be severe. But I just didn't see how I'd be able to do anything other than that. I said to her (and while it wasn't the whole truth, there was still some truth to it), 'It bothers me thinking of how that boy treated you.'

'Please, don't waste another second thinking about him. I'm not going to.'

The tone of her voice caused me to glance in her direction. Because of what I'd said, she was now brooding as she stared straight ahead out the windshield, her body stiff, her jaw clenched. I wanted to ask her what their argument had been about, but instead I asked how long she had known that boy.

'Long enough to have known better.' There was a heavy breath from her. Then, 'Let's not talk about him anymore, OK?'

'Sure.'

A silence fell between us, which was fine with me. I had a lot on my mind trying to come to terms regarding how I was thinking of her, because I'd never thought of any of them in that way before. We're not supposed to ever think of them in that way. From a very early age we're taught to think of them only as *them*, and that they have only a single purpose. The elders reinforce these teachings by bringing us to the slaughtering rituals once we turn nine years of age.

Maybe part of why this had left me so shaken was that I'd always believed we'd feel the same about *them* even without the elders' teachings. That our attitude toward them was simply something instinctive. The natural order of things. After all, we're different than they are. Our eyes are darker than any of their eyes I've ever seen. There are other differences, too. It might be too subtle for them to notice, but the shape of their eyes and mouth marks them as a different breed. Also the scent they give off and the texture of their skin. But none of that matters. Even if we were blindfolded and had our nostrils plugged up with mud, we'd still know. There's something unspoken that we pick up on right away. Maybe it's akin to how bats instinctively use radar so they can know about objects they can't see. It could be that way with us – that we pick up a frequency of some sort that tells us when we're with our own kind. And when it's one of *them* – when we're not picking up that frequency, or we're detecting that unusual scent they give off, or noticing the subtle physical differences – we find ourselves unable to think of *them* in any way other than that one way, which is how it needs to be because of our cravings. Except now. Because I wasn't thinking of this girl next to me in that way. That was why I welcomed the silence. I needed to understand what had happened to me – at least that was what I told myself.

I'm not stupid or thick. I knew what the truth was even though it was something too big for me to acknowledge, at least at that moment. So I instead went through the fruitless activity of trying to figure out something I already knew, and I told myself the half-truths and half-lies that I needed to so I could avoid the real answer. That maybe it was only because of how pretty she was, even though I must've picked up dozens of other girls in the past whom I also would've thought of as pretty if I'd let myself think of them in that way. Or, that her needing rescuing had triggered something inside me, which I knew made no sense since most of them that I pick up are in trouble and need help. I was in the midst of trying to fool myself with another of these half-lies (or half-truths, depending on how you look at it) when she interrupted me by asking whether I was married.

That question drew my attention back to her. She must've worked past my asking about that boy who had abandoned her, because she was no longer brooding and instead was smiling in this impish way, sort of like the Cheshire Cat illustration from the badly battered copy of *Alice's Adventures in Wonderland* that I used as a child to learn to read.

'Don't look so surprised,' she said, her smile inching up. 'You know my relationship status. *Recently broken up*. It's only fair that I ask about yours.'

'I'm not married.'

'Girlfriend?'

I shook my head.

'That doesn't make sense. You're too good-looking in that tough masculine sort of way.' There were several beats as she waited, hoping I'd answer the unasked question about whether I liked girls, but before the silence between us could grow into something uncomfortable she asked whether I'd ever been married.

'No,' I lied, because I was married once. The elders had arranged for me to marry this small, furtive girl from the Webley clan, who make their home deep in the Appalachian mountains between Pennsylvania and West Virginia. All marriages between our kind are arranged with other clans, to bring in new blood. Or at least stir up the blood, since I suspect we all originated from a single people. Whether or not it kept us from inbreeding, that's what we did, with custom having the bride always traveling to the groom's clan. In my case, my wife was named Patience. I never much liked or trusted her, and was relieved when she died of complications from a tooth abscess eight months into our marriage.

All at once I felt fidgety, my palms sweaty as I gripped the steering wheel. My voice echoed thinly in my head as the words leaked out of me, 'Maybe things would be different if there were girls as pretty as you where I'm from.'

Since I was still not ready to admit the truth about her, I was left confused about why I'd said that. But before I could puzzle over that too much, she laughed. It was a soft, gentle laugh, and I found myself liking the sound of it.

'Come on! There must be plenty of girls in Manchester prettier than me.'

'Not that I've ever seen.'

I could sense her body relaxing. That's something we're able to do. Just by being in close proximity to them we can pick up on their tension and fear. At that moment she was completely empty of any fear or wariness. Without looking at her, I knew she was smiling a little brighter than before.

'Charlie Husk,' she said playfully. 'That's an odd name. *Husk*. Of course, I shouldn't talk. Not with a name like Zemler. Is Husk a common name in New Hampshire?'

'The only Husks I know are blood relations,' I said. 'But it's an old name. We've been there for a long time.'

She didn't ask me how long we'd been there, which was just as well. From the stories the elders told, she wouldn't have believed me. Of course, I wouldn't have told her those same stories. I would've changed things.

Another silence grew between us, but it was OK. It was a comfortable silence, one that didn't need filling. A lot of *them* that I've picked up in the past plug in their ear thingies right away so they can listen to their music and act as if I wasn't there. I always had mixed feelings when they did that. In a way I'd feel that was rude, but in another I'd be grateful for them doing that because it kept them distracted from what was going to happen to them. I would've been OK if she'd plugged herself into her music the same as those others did, but she didn't, and that made me even more convinced I couldn't make her one of *them*.

I'd never needed to go past New Haven before in order to fill up the van, so once I passed the city I was in new territory, which left me searching for signs that would lead me to

New York. She noticed that and told me she'd give me directions.

'Have you ever been to New York before?' she asked.

I shook my head.

'Are you going to be there long?'

'Maybe my whole life.'

FOUR

I thought it would be harmless to tell her that I was moving to New York. That if I told her that, then I wouldn't have to come up with a clumsier reason for why I was driving there. What I did though was open myself up to more questions, the first one being what I planned to do once I moved there.

'I'm not sure. I'm what you call a jack-of-all-trades. Carpentry, masonry, automotive repairs, electrical, plumbing. I can do a passable job with all of that. I'll see what I can find.'

That was pretty much the truth. The winter months are different, but during the other seasons the women and children and the elders in the clan spend their days working the fields using crude farming instruments that aren't much different from what must've been used two hundred years ago. We grow wheat, barley, oats, and vegetables, since our diet is grains and stews made from ground meat simmered with vegetables. Most of the able-bodied men perform the heavy labor that's needed. My days are spent differently. I've brought electric generators, fuel, power tools, and other building materials to the clan, and when I'm not going on these pickups or doing other business in their world, including selling our excess vegetables, the elders have begrudgingly allowed me to build new homes that are a marked improvement over the primitive structures the clan has used for hundreds of years. So far I have seven of these new homes completed, all with indoor plumbing.

After that, Jill (I had probably stopped thinking of Jill as simply *her* long before I was ready to admit it) peppered me with questions about my family and upbringing, while volunteering information about her own. I tried to stick as closely to the truth as I could – telling her that my ma and pa were still alive, that I had five brothers and three sisters, and that I had a very large extended family (Jill, on the other hand, was an only child with fewer living relatives than she could count on one hand) – and I only lied when I had to. When she asked whether I'd been to college, I didn't mention that I'd never had any schooling – only that I hadn't had the opportunity for college but read a lot.

'A self-made man,' she said without any hint of meanness or insult, only genuineness, like she firmly believed the statement. 'What do you like reading?'

'Anything I can get my hands on,' I said, which was the truth. The elders have always believed that those of us with my duties need to be able to fit in among *them* as best we can, and because of that they have saved the 'frivolous' books gotten from wayward travelers. Since I've been doing these pickups, I've more than tripled our library, bringing it to almost four hundred books. While the others are discouraged from reading (although none of them that I know of have ever shown any interest), it's still tolerated from me, and I've read every book we have, many of them several times over. (Though more recently I've been receiving disapproving looks from the elders, as if they feel I've read enough by now.) On past forays into *their* world, I've even bought books at used bookstores, although I've kept that secret – I have little doubt the elders would not be happy if they knew I'd done that.

I rattled off to Jill the titles of my favorite novels, while not bothering to mention our more obscure books, such as the one on dentistry written in 1908 and or the one on bee farming published in 1887.

'Twain, Dickens, Faulkner, Hemingway, Tolstoy, Hawthorne, Dumas . . .' Jill said, nodding approvingly as she repeated the authors of the books I'd mentioned. 'The classics. I read many of those when I was in high school and as an undergraduate. The last few years I've been on a kick where I've been sticking mostly with more modern literature and quite a lot of genre stuff.'

Shortly after I'd picked her up Jill had mentioned that she was working on a graduate degree in psychology, and now she was telling me how she had almost majored in English literature and that books were one of her early loves. This led to a discussion of some of her favorite recent books. (Mostly a one-sided discussion, but I didn't mind.) I'd only read one of them – an allegorical fable about a man who takes on an ancestral duty of weeding a field each day by hand, believing that if he doesn't the world will end. I'd gotten the book from a man I'd picked up while driving through Boston. He'd been walking alone on a darkened street, and at the last second I took the opportunity to swerve the van up on to the sidewalk, crippling him. In less than a minute I had him in the back with the others that I had already picked up, and less than three minutes after that I had him secured in a burlap sack and was driving away without anyone being aware of what had happened. Much later, when I got around to reading the book, I discovered from the photograph on the book jacket that the man I'd taken was the author. Maybe he was walking around Boston with a copy of the book he'd written because he was planning to give it to an acquaintance, or maybe he had another reason. Whichever it was, I never had a chance to ask him, same with missing my opportunity to question him about several things in the book that had left me wondering about their true meaning. I was so absorbed listening to Jill's insights that I only half paid attention to her as she directed me through the maze of streets once we entered Queens, and it took me by surprise when she pointed out the three-story brick building up ahead and on my right as where she lived.

'This is home,' she said. 'My apartment's on the top floor, in the back.'

I pulled over so I could park in front of the building, and was further surprised at how disappointed I felt that my journey with Jill had come to an end. Up until then I was still telling myself it was only because I'd never had the opportunity before to talk about books with anyone, or really have a discussion about anything. My clan is not a talkative lot. Usually a few words is all we'll say to one another. Even though I was married to Patience for eight months before she succumbed, most of our time together was spent in a cold uneasy silence where neither of us had much to say to the other. And I certainly never said much to any of *them* that I'd picked up in the past, nor gave them much time to say anything to me.

This was the first time I'd ever had a chance to carry on any conversation at length, at least outside of my head, so it wasn't hard to convince myself that that was the only reason I was disappointed.

After I put the van in park and turned off the ignition, we both sat awkwardly for several moments as if we both had something we wanted to say to the other. I wasn't sure exactly what it was I wanted to say. It was more of an uneasy feeling working its way into my stomach. But then I remembered the burlap sacks and rope in the back of the van, and I moved quickly so I could get her duffel bag out without her being able to look back there.

I brought the duffel bag to Jill as she waited for me on the sidewalk. I was still trying to figure out what it was I wanted to say to her when she moved quickly to me. It wasn't so she could take her duffel bag from me, but so that she could stand on tiptoes and kiss me. With her being so short, she didn't make it to my cheek and instead kissed me on my jaw, which was free of any whiskers. If she'd had the opportunity to kiss me yesterday, that wouldn't have been the case. I learned long ago that my kind blend in better in their world – and they trust you more – if you don't have long whiskers or shaggy hair that falls past your shoulders. So any time I'm going to be entering their world, I first have my hair shorn short and my face shaved clean. My own people have never appreciated the reason I do this and always give me odd, even hostile, looks until my whiskers and hair grow to a more acceptable length, but it can't be helped.

She stepped back and smiled at me in this secretive, amused sort of way. 'You really did rescue me today,' she said.

I was too flustered to do much more than grunt out something unintelligible to her, which made her smile all that more secretively and got her blue eyes sparkling that much brighter. I wasn't even sure myself what I said. Feeling flustered like that was a new experience for me, and it left me even more confused about what I wanted to say to her.

'Let me buy you lunch,' she said. 'It's the least I can do. After all, it's not every day a gal gets rescued by a handsome stranger.'

The idea of eating with one of *them* was crazy but, as I said earlier, I had stopped thinking of Jill that way. Without fully realizing I was doing it, I nodded OK to her. The look she gave me made me feel weak in my knees. Her smile became something mischievous as she turned so she could lead the way to her apartment, letting me carry her duffel bag.

'You guys from New Hampshire look nice when you blush,' she said as she walked in front of me.

FIVE

Jill thought my first meal in New York should be in Manhattan, so after leaving her duffel bag in her apartment we took the subway to the West Village. I'd been traveling in their world for the last six years, but I'd never experienced anything like I did on the subway with Jill and later as we walked through the overly crowded West Village sidewalks to the restaurant she had picked out. When I ventured into their world to sell vegetables or to buy fuel or building supplies I'd only have to move among a small number of them, and during my other trips I'd be alone in the van most of the time and the ones I picked up would be by themselves. Saying that being amongst so many of them was unsettling wouldn't come near what I experienced. It was at times maddening, and it was a struggle to keep my composure. I'm not a savage. It wasn't as if I had a compulsion to grab one of them and take a bite of his flesh. That's not something any of my kind would ever have a desire to do. As strong as our cravings might be, there first have to be the slaughtering rituals, then the meat must be prepared according to custom before we can accept it. While the thought of doing something that outlandish and savage never occurred to me, I was still left on the verge of a panic. How could I not be with so many of them so close to me? Their scent so overwhelming? Or standing packed among them in that subway car? Somehow I kept my wits about me, and even though my legs were shaky we made it to the restaurant. It was better after that, with fewer of them around and our table far enough away from the others that I could barely smell them. At least I could start breathing more normally and unclench my fists.

Jill sensed something had been wrong, and asked if I was OK.

I reached for the water glass. My throat had become drier than if I had swallowed a handful of dirt, and I wanted to drink some water so I could answer her without my voice cracking. But I was still too jittery, and with how badly my hand was shaking I was afraid I'd spill the water all over myself. I pulled my hand back and hid it under the table so she couldn't see the tremors running through it.

'I'd never been in crowds like that before,' I said, my voice surprisingly mostly normal. 'But I'm feeling better already.'

I was, too. I wasn't feeling as funny inside as I was earlier, and my heart was no longer racing so fast that I thought I might expire. It was soothing looking straight into Jill's face, especially her soft but brilliant blue eyes. I found myself touched in a way seeing her brow wrinkled with concern.

'You must've been having the beginnings of a panic attack,' she said. 'Has that ever happened before?'

'No, I can't say it has.'

'Hmm. It could be agoraphobia.'

I stared at her blankly. In the roughly four hundred books I'd read, including the copy of *Webster's New International Dictionary* dated 1909, I had not come across that word.

'Fear of being in crowded places,' she explained. 'Also the opposite. It can also mean fear of being in wide open places.'

'I can tell you I don't suffer from that. I've been in many wide open spaces in my life. Places as desolate as anything you could imagine. I've never felt anything like that before. But sitting here with you like this is making me feel better.'

A light pink flushed her cheeks. She made me promise to tell her if I felt any of that panic again.

The restaurant she'd brought me to served Indian and Chinese food. When Jill asked me earlier what type of food I wanted, I told her it didn't much matter as long as they offered vegan dishes. I had learned the hard way that there was a difference in their world between being a vegetarian and being a vegan when I bought myself an apple muffin at one of the markets where I sold vegetables. I'd first warned the wrinkled gray-haired woman selling me the muffin that I was a vegetarian, and she'd promised me I had nothing to worry about. All it took was one bite of that muffin for me to be knocked to my knees by chills and nausea, and when I could stand again I went back into the market to complain that the muffin had to have been made with either eggs or cow's milk. That same gray-haired woman listened patiently before explaining to me about vegans and vegetarians.

Our waitress was a short, plump foreign woman with eyes almost as dark as my own. I asked her for an Indian dish with lentils and eggplant after being assured that it was vegan, and Jill ordered a vegetable stir-fry dish that was on the Chinese side of the menu. She waited until the waitress left with our order before asking me how long I had been a vegan.

'As far back as I can remember.'

'Your parents raised you that way?'

I nodded.

She seemed to appreciate that with the way she smiled. 'They sound very enlightened. I've been thinking for some time that I should become a vegetarian for moral reasons, and you inspired me today to order what I did.'

I didn't correct Jill about how enlightened my parents or any other member of my clan truly were. Morality has nothing to do with why we don't eat animal, fowl or fish meat, or animal milk, or chicken eggs. It's because our bodies can't tolerate any of that. If we could help it, we wouldn't live the way we do. We'd gratefully find a way for animal flesh to satiate our cravings so that we could live among *them*. But that option just doesn't exist for us.

My food was served on rice, which I'd never tasted before. Same with lentils. I'd eaten eggplants, though, plenty of times in the past, since we grew far too many of them. I didn't know quite what to make of the meal since I'd never had anything like it before, especially the spices. I wouldn't say that I disliked it entirely, just that it was different from what I was used to. But then again, I'd felt the same way about vegan chocolate doughnuts the first time I tried one and now I liked them quite a bit. The same with coffee.

Jill suggested that I try the chai tea, so I did. In my clan, those experienced in the art make tea from flowers, mushrooms, and roots. This was very different, but once I'd added three packets of sugar to it I liked it almost as much as the chocolate doughnut I had earlier. We talked some more over our tea, and Jill rightly guessed that this was the first time I'd had

Indian food. Beaming and clearly proud of her city, she added, 'Here in New York you can get anything.'

That wasn't true. I wished it was, but I was certain that no restaurants here served the stews I was familiar with. But I saw no reason to correct her on that point.

When the bill came, I made only a token effort to pay it. Fortunately, since I didn't have the necessary money, Jill was adamant about treating me. At the beginning of the trip I'd spent most of the money I'd brought with me on fuel for the van, and I'd planned to get more money from the ones I picked up. Once Jill'd successfully battled me for the bill, I sat back while she triumphantly handed the waitress a credit card. We talked some more while we waited for the waitress to bring back her card, and I realized I was feeling different than I'd ever felt before. Lighter in a way I couldn't quite explain, and nervous too in a way that I didn't understand since I was still not being fully honest with myself.

Jill noticed the lighter part of how I was feeling. She told me I looked much better than earlier. 'Most of your color is back.' She hesitated before adding, 'You had me worried before with how pale you had gotten and how much you were perspiring.'

'No need to worry. My family are a hardy sort. I'm sure I'll be fine.'

'If you're up to it,' she said, 'I'd like to take you to the most touristy thing you can do in New York. If you wait even a week, you'll be like the rest of us New Yorkers and never do it, which would be a shame since it really is such a worthwhile experience.'

I told her I'd be up to it, no matter what it was.

Jill's credit card was brought back. As we got up from the table, concern weakened her eyes. 'You'll let me know if you feel any more of that panic? If you do, I can call for an Uber to take us back to my apartment.'

'I'll be fine. I won't be feeling any more of that.'

She didn't seem completely convinced, but she didn't argue it any further. Once we stepped outside, her hand found mine. I'm not a fool. I knew this gesture of hers was more to comfort me than anything romantic. Still, as her delicate and fine hand disappeared within mine, I was grateful for the touch of her skin.

All of my kind have a strong sense of direction, and without needing to ask I knew we were heading north. Jill leaned in closer to me and asked if I'd mind if we walked to where she wanted to take me. 'It's probably about a two-mile walk. But it's nice out, and after all the driving earlier a walk would feel good.'

I told her I'd like that, too. The sidewalk was as crowded as before, but being among *them* didn't affect me like it did earlier. I couldn't ignore their heavy scent or the heat from their bodies, and their presence caused my senses to be heightened, but it didn't bring about the panicky feeling I'd had earlier. I think what kept me calmer was partly getting used to having so many of them around me and partly the feel of Jill's hand in mine. I was able to keep most of my thoughts centered around Jill and how nice it was having her body so close to mine, but after we had walked four blocks another thought entered my mind. Everything in their world costs money, and wherever Jill was taking me was going to cost more than I had. I had little doubt she was planning to pay for me, but I didn't like the idea of that or the thought of her finding out I had no money. I waited until we were approaching a coffee shop and asked Jill if she wouldn't mind waiting inside the shop for me.

'There's something I need to do. It will only take ten minutes. Maybe twenty at the most. I'll be back then.'

She gave me this confused, uncertain look, like she wasn't sure she'd be seeing me again, but told me she'd get a coffee and would wait for me inside. Once she was inside the shop with her back turned away from me, I moved quickly and retraced my steps to where we had come from.

After two blocks, I turned down a side street heading west. This street wasn't so crowded, although there were still plenty of *them* on the sidewalk. I found it interesting how little attention they paid to one another as they went their way. It was as if they felt completely safe and didn't realize there was a predator among them. I couldn't blame them for that. While my kind is as old as theirs, we separated from them almost a thousand years ago, invading their villages and towns only when necessary. For as far back as I could remember, my own clan had been able to make do by taking no more than eighty of them each year. The other thirty-eight clans I know of probably take close to that same number. When you add it all up, not enough of them go missing in any one year for the rest of them to pay attention, and the ones that do go missing are mostly the ones the rest of them don't care about. So it's not surprising that they had long ago forgotten about us.

Thirty feet ahead of me I spotted what I was looking for. He was walking in the same direction I was. Well-fed, with carefully combed thick orange-yellowish hair. His suit expensive, fitting him as if it had been custom tailored. When his suit jacket rode up, I saw the bulge that his wallet made in his back pants pocket, and I quickened my pace to make up the distance.

As I mentioned earlier, none of them were paying attention to me or anyone else, so none of them bothered looking my way when I lengthened my stride to where I almost stepped on the back of his shoe and at the same time drove my fist into his kidney. His body seized up, and I grabbed hold of him with one hand while deftly removing his wallet with my other. As if I were simply a concerned member of the public, I carefully lowered his body to the sidewalk while yelling out for help, all the while making sure to keep his wallet hidden from the others.

'This man's ill,' I yelled. 'I think it might be his heart.'

Others slowed down, and some of them gathered around us. The man I had struck a minute earlier would normally have looked wealthy and aristocratic. But that wasn't how he looked as he lay crumpled on the pavement. I had tried to hit him only as hard as needed to immobilize him, but it was likely I had caused serious injury, given how his eyes had rolled up into his head and the sickish-yellow pallor of his skin. He was still alive, though. I could tell that from the way his feet were twitching.

I backed away from the crowd. More of them were gathering to look at him. I said something about trying to find a doctor. They weren't paying attention to me, at least most of them weren't. One of them was. This girl who was probably the same age as Jill. She looked at me in a way that made me think she had seen what I'd done. But she didn't say anything, and she made no attempt to follow me as I made my way away from the crowd.

SIX

J ill appeared tense when I spotted her through the front window of the coffee shop. I don't think I'd been gone more than the twenty minutes I promised her, but I guess she didn't fully believe I'd be returning. Her attention was focused on her cardboard coffee cup, so she didn't notice me entering the shop, or as I approached the table she was sitting at. When I sat down across from her, the look she gave me had a little bit of hurt and indecision mixed in.

'Did you get done what you needed to?' she asked as if she didn't truly believe there was anything I needed to do.

I nodded and handed her a pin in the shape and color of a yellow rose. The pin was made of glass and silver and had cost me $54 at a store a block and a half away.

'When I saw this in a store window, I decided more than anything I wanted you to have it.'

The lives of my kind are filled with hardness and drudgery, and we've never developed the custom of gift-giving – the idea of it is completely foreign to us. The clothes, money, and other useful items we get off of *them*, we keep. Anything else of value, especially jewelry, we sell; or more specifically, I sell, usually at one of three pawnshops I've learned about who don't ask any questions. Anything else, we bury.

The first time I encountered someone giving a gift in a book, the concept was difficult for me to fully understand, especially since this book had a father giving an expensive train set to his young son. In my clan, and I'm sure all the others as well, children at a very early age are expected to do for their parents, not the other way around. But as I read more books, I realized how prevalent that custom is, especially for a man to give jewelry to a girl that he favors. So while I'd hoped Jill would be pleased by the pin, I didn't expect her eyes to moisten with tears like they did, nor for her to leave her chair so she could kiss me on my cheek. Since I was sitting down, she had no problem this time kissing me higher on my face than earlier.

'This is so sweet of you!' she said. She used a knuckle to wipe away some wetness near her eye. The smile that broke over her face was brighter than any I'd ever imagined from the stories I'd read. 'After being with Ethan for two years, I'd forgotten what it's like to spend an afternoon with someone with a good heart.'

Her cheeks blushed a deeper shade of pink, which was a nice color in contrast to her honey-colored hair. I might've blushed myself if I hadn't been paying attention to the wailing cry of a siren. I braced myself as the caterwaul grew louder. But the noise just as quickly began fading, letting me know that the police car had already driven past the shop. I found I'd been holding my breath, and let it out in a slow exhale. When I first heard the siren approaching I thought that girl might've followed me to this place and had sent the police after me, but that wasn't what had happened. The girl might still have told them her suspicions and described me to them, but it was doubtful they'd be looking for a man walking leisurely with a pretty little thing like Jill. If they did find me, it would be a shame, but I was pretty sure I'd be able to handle them.

I told Jill, 'That was the way I was taught to be.' This wasn't exactly a lie. I might not have been taught that way from the elders, or my ma and pa, but I had learned it from the books I read. 'And I thought it would look nice on you.'

Jill attached the pin to her shirt, and indeed I did like the way it looked on her. It was as delicate-looking as she was, with the rose's yellow petals matching her hair nicely. It was fortuitous that I needed to buy it for her as a way to excuse my absence. Even after its cost, I still had over eleven hundred dollars from what I took from the man I'd robbed and possibly killed.

'I was right. It does look awfully pretty on you.'

Her eyes lowered. She might've blushed more, but if she did I couldn't tell, given how pink her cheeks had already become. 'We should continue on with our adventure,' she said. 'I need to get you there while it's still daylight.'

We both got up, and once we were back on the sidewalk her hand found mine again. Maybe it was still partly to provide comfort, but there was more to it now.

There was a cacophony of other noises outside, but the only sirens I could hear were far away. That didn't mean I was safe, and before too long a police car slowly approached us from behind. Out the corner of my eye I could see that both police officers in the vehicle were searching the crowds on the sidewalks, and I could feel one of them staring straight at me. I knew it would be a mistake to show that I was aware of this or to let my pace quicken, and I concentrated on keeping from doing either. Still, I was expecting the car to pull up next to me and for a confrontation to occur, but neither happened. The police car drove on past us, and I kept an eye on it as it continued on out of sight. If that girl had given the police my description, either she'd done a poor job of it or Jill was doing a better job of allowing me to escape their notice.

We continued walking for a spell, and Jill ended up taking me to the Empire State Building. I was right about everything in their world costing money. Thirty-five dollars a head to ride in an elevator. The greed in their world amazes me, and I couldn't help smiling, thinking of how many hours of fuel that would buy for the generators back at the clan. But I insisted on paying for our tickets, even though Jill fought me tooth and nail over it.

'It was my idea that we come here. Please, let me treat!'

I refused, and I kept refusing, and eventually Jill had no choice but to give in. We took the elevator to the eighty-sixth floor, and I'll admit it took my breath away looking out over New York from that height. They certainly could build impressive structures and machinery. After a while, though, as I looked out into their world it made me bitter thinking of the primitive shacks that most of my clan still live in. But how could it be any different? There are so many more of *them* than there are of us. We have no choice but to hide in the wilderness and to live almost the same as we did hundreds of years ago. These and other such thoughts were darkening my mood when I became aware of Jill standing next to me. Without looking at her, I knew she was staring at me intently.

'Awe-inspiring, isn't it?' she said.

Her hand found mine again, and my dark ruminations calmed.

'I had to take you up here before it was too late,' she said. 'It's like a virus that invades us New Yorkers. It makes us think it's too lame and touristy to ever come up here, which is a shame because this is such an amazing view. It makes you fully appreciate how incredible this city really is.'

'Is your family from New York?'

'Yep. I was born and raised in Staten Island. My parents are still in the same house I grew up in.'

'You had me fooled,' I said. 'I thought you might've been from Massachusetts since I found you at that rest stop.' Somewhat stubbornly, and I guess as a way to explain myself, I persisted, adding, 'It just made sense given it's Labor Day weekend and you were traveling from your home somewhere in Massachusetts to school in New York.'

Jill shook her head. 'I was visiting my jerk ex-boyfriend at his parents' house. We were driving back to the city together, and you know the rest.'

Her mood had darkened just as mine had earlier. Her hand slipped free of mine, and we stood silently for the next several minutes staring out at the city below. She didn't let her dark mood last. Before too long she asked, 'You couldn't tell from my accent that I was a New Yorker?'

I turned to see that she was grinning at me. The truth was I couldn't tell *their* accents apart. It was only that some of them were harder for me to understand than others.

'You had me fooled.'

'Gawd, I hope I didn't pick up any sort of Massachusetts accent from spending time with that jerk. That would be wicked awful!' Her grin grew into the mischievous kind I'd seen earlier. 'It's funny, you don't have a New Hampshire accent.'

I shrugged. 'I can't help it. I've been there my whole life, but I'm not sure what a New Hampshire accent is supposed to sound like.'

She thought about that and shook her head. 'Now I think of it, I can't really say either. I know what a "Bahston accent" sounds like, and a Maine one, and even a Rhode Island accent.

But I have no idea what a New Hampshire one is supposed to be. Maybe you have the prototypical one, and I just never realized it until now.'

We stood where we were for several minutes, and then I followed Jill a quarter of the way around the observation deck. Where we were standing now, we were facing north, and Jill pointed out a large area of greenery and trees that lay straight ahead and told me it was Central Park. She pointed out a winding body of water to my right as the Hudson River, and another to my left as the East River. Dusk had arrived, but we continued to stand motionless, looking out at the sights before us. Before too long Jill's hand found mine again, and not much after that lights began to turn on throughout the city below us. As it grew darker, I looked up and was amazed at how few stars were in the sky. I'd never bothered to notice that about their world before.

I'm not sure exactly how long we stood like that. Without the sun to guide me, I have a hard time judging time. Maybe it was an hour, maybe longer. But the whole time we stood in silence, until at the very end Jill told me in a soft, dreamy voice how much she loved being up there at this time of night. 'The city just looks so peaceful and calm right now. But I've hijacked you long enough. It's been a long day, and I'm sure you need to be heading back.'

After we took the elevator down to the ground floor and left the building, we continued north, the sidewalks almost as crowded at that hour as they had been during the day. Jill took me next to Grand Central Station, and walked me through it so I could see the stars they had on the high curved ceiling overhead. There were more there than I had seen in the sky.

From there we navigated through the station and got in a subway car. Unlike the sidewalks, the car at that time wasn't nearly as crowded as the one I'd been in earlier. Even if it had been, I don't believe I would've felt the panicky uneasiness that I had earlier. I was getting more used to feeling their heat close to me and being inundated by their scent. Jill was very different from the rest of them, though. From almost the very beginning, I found her scent exotic and pleasant. The same with the closeness of her body to mine.

We didn't stay long on the subway car we had taken, and soon had to get on a different one after walking almost half a mile to a different part of the station. After a forty-minute ride, this one took us to where we had a short walk to Jill's apartment building. I felt a heaviness well up in my chest as we approached it. When we reached my van, which was directly in front of her building's entrance, both of us hesitated as if we had something we wanted to say to the other.

I spoke first, telling Jill how much I'd enjoyed spending the day with her. I felt light-headed as I blurted out, 'Can I see you again? Maybe take you out for a meal?'

She smiled brightly. 'I would really like that.'

I nodded, confused in a way because I was still deceiving myself; and because it didn't make sense that I would ask her what I did. All I could think then was that it was something that must've been building up inside me and had just burst out. I stumbled as I turned toward the van, still trying to sort out why I'd asked her something as impossible as that.

Jill's voice made me turn around again. 'Where are you staying?' she asked.

I stared at her blankly before fully making sense of her question. Because if I was asking to see her again, that meant I was planning to stay in New York and not drive off so I could start to fill up the burlap sacks with stragglers and any others I could find before starting my journey back home. 'I'll be sleeping in the back of the van until I find a place to stay,' I said.

'Uh-uh. That's way too dangerous.' In the glare of the streetlight I could see the determination hardening her slender face as she came to a decision. 'You rescued me earlier today, I'm rescuing you now. You're going to sleep on my couch until you find a place. And I won't take no for an answer.'

Since I still wasn't ready to accept the truth, all I could think was that this had gone too far. *That I had let it go too far*. But I couldn't keep myself from nodding.

SEVEN

I lay on Jill's couch fully awake, my nerves on edge the same as if I were smelling out a kill-crazy catamount skulking about the room. Even if earlier I hadn't come to the realization that I had, I wouldn't have had a chance of falling asleep that night. To be fair to Jill and her apartment, I'd never slept in their world before, never even attempted to, even the times when my trips had lasted more than forty-eight hours.

Back at the clan, when the fires are extinguished it's so utterly dark at night that you're unable to see your fingers an inch from your eyes, and the only noises in the night's air are animal, bird, and insect sounds, and the wind rustling through the trees or rain pattering against the thatch of our homes. Here it was two hours after midnight, and it wasn't much darker than dusk and the noises drifting in from cars, sirens, horns, dogs barking, and even some of *them* shouting and laughing as if nobody else mattered, were enough to keep any of my kind awake. Even if all that hadn't been a problem, the air here would've kept me from sleeping. Back home the air is clean and soothing; this city air made my eyes itch and left an unpleasant taste in my throat. And while I was sure the couch Jill offered was a fine piece of furniture, it was far softer than the bed I was used to.

But there was far more to it than those problems, and no matter where I was sleeping it wouldn't have been possible – not after finally accepting the truth that my spending the day with Jill wasn't a lark, as I'd earlier tried convincing myself, and I wasn't just playing out a peculiar fantasy of being one of *them* for a day.

Hours ago I'd finally accepted what I must've known early on, at least deep inside. That I would stay in New York with Jill as long as she would let me be near her. That for her, I would abandon my clan and kind. And what was more, I was pretty much powerless to do anything other than that.

This realization was staggering, and it left my mind bombarded by worries, guilt, and questions, so much so that it was hard to stay on that couch. As tempted as I was to bolt from it, I didn't want Jill waking to find me crazily pacing her apartment.

As far as I knew, none of my kind had ever tried living among *them*. So I had no idea whether what I was planning to do was even possible, though it didn't seem so.

I never bring our food with me when I travel into their world. It seems too reckless to do something like that. It would be bad enough if the police stopped me, especially if they looked in the back of the van after I had already started filling up the burlap sacks. If they were ever to find a meat stew that I'd brought from home and they realized what it was, that could be disastrous for the clan. When I was given my responsibilities, I would have cold sweats worrying about something like that happening, thinking that if it did it might cause *them* to search deeper into the wilderness to root out my clan. Since I never brought our food with me, the cravings would leave me jittery the times I was gone for two days. Even now, when it has been less than twenty-four hours since I last ate one of our meals, I was feeling the cravings stirring inside me.

As I worried myself more about how the cravings would affect me, I remembered a year when we'd had an exceptionally harsh winter that had brought snow and ice deep into the spring, leaving us snowbound almost two months longer than the elders had expected. This was well before I had taken on my current responsibilities, and for many years I, like the rest of the clan, had tried to forget about this nightmarish time. Now I tried to remember as much of it as I could. I was a teenager then, probably no older than thirteen, and my great-uncle Jedidiah had the responsibility of collecting *them* for the clan. We ended up running out of meat and had only our vegetables and grains to eat, and it was almost three weeks before Jedidiah was able to bring more of *them* back to us. The cravings near the end of those three weeks had gotten so bad that it left us on the verge of lunacy. I remembered the elderly writhing on the ground in agony, womenfolk rocking back and forth as they gripped their knees and screamed out gibberish, my own ma and pa with their eyes squeezed tight, their hands clutching at their faces as if at any moment they might start ripping apart their own flesh. In my own situation, I remembered how feverish I was and how it seemed like I was looking out into a blood-soaked fog.

It was only the day before Jedidiah returned with his pickups that we decided we couldn't wait, and in our madness chose one of our own for the slaughtering ritual. This is the only shameful occurrence I know of where a clan has done this, and in this case it was a slow-witted boy who was a fourth cousin of mine, who I believe was the same age as myself. It was all for nothing, though. Once the slaughtering and the preparation were complete, the smell of the simmering stew made many of us nauseous, and those who tried to eat it found themselves violently ill after only a few minutes. Three of the clan who'd been poisoned by the stew, including a direct aunt of mine, ending up dying within the week. Whatever the physiological differences are between us and *them*, we learned then that it makes it impossible for one of our own to be chosen.

I sank into despair as I thought more of that dark period in my clan's history. If this was the way we were after three weeks, how could I possibly hope to stay with Jill in this city? Soon my thoughts began drifting again and again to what seemed like the only answer. That I would need to find a place where I could continue the slaughtering rituals and prepare the meat on my own. After ruminating more deeply on the matter, I decided I couldn't do that. If I were ever discovered, which was likely in a city like this no matter how careful I was, the knowledge of what I was and what I was doing would ruin Jill. She would never be able to understand it, and would look at me as some sort of blood-crazy maniac, and I couldn't fault her if that happened. No, if I was going to live with Jill as I hoped, I was going to have to live as one of *them*.

That was the conundrum torturing me. If I stayed, the cravings were going to become something awful; but as long as there was a chance I could be with Jill, I couldn't leave.

Before this day, my lot in life seemed cast in stone: until I died, I would be with my own kind and do what the clan required of me. My path had seemed simple and unalterable.

While I'd come across romance in novels, the concept of romantic love had eluded me, appearing even more foreign and puzzling than their custom of gift-giving. There certainly was never any romance between Patience and me during our short-lived marriage. As required by the clan, we had sexual relations each night while she was capable of conceiving, but it was a joyless and at times distressing activity where I felt as if I were forcing myself on a feral creature who despised me. There was never any tenderness between us. Never any trust. We barely spoke to one another, and looked at each other even less. All I felt when she died was relieved and grateful.

That's not to say it's impossible for tenderness to exist within the marriages in our clan. After enough years a small degree of tenderness might possibly develop between a husband and a wife, but I've seen scant evidence of it – and certainly nothing approaching the romantic ideals I'd read about. My own ma and pa have as little to do with one another as possible, and even though they share a bed I can count on one hand the number of times I've heard them speak to each other when it wasn't necessary, other than ill-tempered words. It makes sense for it to be this way. Women are uprooted from everything they know and everyone they are close to so that they may move to a foreign part of the country and become the wife of a man they've never met and live among strangers. Because of the distances and the risks of having our kind travel within their world, there's never any visiting between clans, so these women are never going to see any of their blood family again unless one of them ends up being married off to the same clan. And while customs within the clans might be similar, there are still differences that, understandably, may seem foreign and discomforting to these unhappy new members. From what the elders have told us, only the slaughtering rituals and meat preparation must remain unchanged among the clans; everything else could be altered to suit the circumstances of the individual clan. It's no wonder that our women are so miserable when they're married off, and why the men in our marriages end up being no happier.

I'm twenty-eight, so I'm still young enough for my clan to arrange another marriage for me, but there is little likelihood of that happening. My kind can be a suspicious and superstitious breed, and with Patience dying so young and so shortly after our marriage the other clans would be wary of sending me another of their daughters. I had nothing to do with her death. It really was from a tooth abscess, and if she had ever told me that her tooth was aching I would've made sure it had gotten yanked out. But she never trusted me, just as I never trusted her. And so she died, and I became someone unworthy of marriage, even if those words went unspoken. I accepted that and grew to greatly prefer the idea of a solitary life, especially understanding that another marriage could very well be more wretched than the one I had with Patience. But today everything had changed.

Love at first sight. I'd read about that in several of the novels, and when I was informed that I would be marrying a girl from the Webley clan I indulged myself in the fantasy that I and this Webley girl would fall in love at first sight, even though I wasn't quite sure what that would be. No surprise that the opposite happened, and I bitterly told myself that these books were lies, just as the ideal of romantic love had to be a lie. Now I knew otherwise.

I can't say I fell in love with Jill immediately upon seeing her, but I know that I did the moment she looked into my eyes, even if at first I refused to believe it. But it's what happened. From that moment, I couldn't think of her as one of *them*. It was far more than that, though. This dizzying sensation overtook me and made my knees weak, and it was unlike anything I'd ever experienced. And each time she smiled at me, it took my breath away and made me feel almost as if my heart might stop. When I finally stopped lying to myself, I accepted that her smiling was the most beautiful sight I'd ever seen, or could hope to see.

When we held hands that first time, I became hers forever. I might not have been willing to admit it at that time, but at some deep primordial level I understood that as long as she wanted me I would never leave her. That I needed her as much as I needed to breathe air, and that I would suffer whatever I had to for her happiness. Even the cravings.

I knew my feelings for Jill weren't one-sided. I had seen it in her eyes and in her smile, and felt it in the warmth of her touch. And I had sensed it in her as strongly as wolves might sense fear. Her feelings for me might not last, though. I knew there was the possibility that she might grow cold to me. It could even happen the next time I saw her. She might wake up and leave her bedroom and look at me as if we were strangers – or worse, see me as the predator that I'd been in their world – and act as if yesterday had never happened. It would be cruel if that were the case. To give me a taste of something so wonderful and intoxicating and joyful only to just as quickly take it away. But if that were to happen, I still wouldn't look at Jill as one of *them*. I would leave her unharmed. Somehow I'd find a way to continue with the responsibilities required of me by the clan, and I'd try to forget how different life could be.

So I lay there and worried that in the light of the new day Jill would look at me differently, and that the romance I believed existed between us would be dead. And I worried equally about how bad the cravings would get if she continued to look at me the same and I stayed. I also worried (or I guess I should say it was more that I was sickened with guilt) about how I would be betraying my clan if the latter happened, because I understood fully the hardships I'd be bringing on them. I tried consoling myself that as difficult as my disappearing might be for the clan, at least I wasn't damning them or leaving them in dire straits. But that was little comfort.

When I'd left on this latest trip, there was still a month's supply of meat remaining. There was also another van, not too different from the one I was driving, filled with burlap sacks and rope. It was mechanically sound last time I checked it out, and in good running order. In several days, maybe a week, assuming nothing changes between Jill and me and I am able to stay with her, they'll come to the conclusion that something has happened to me – either that I've been caught or killed by the police or some other calamity has befallen

me. My ma and pa will be saddened by this, at least as much
as any of us are saddened by any of our deaths. My brothers
also, though to a lesser degree. Same with my little sister
Olive, and possibly my other sisters if they hear about it at
the clans where they were sent for marriage. It's hard to grieve
much when you live the hardened lives we live. But there's
more to it than that. There's an additional weight that we carry,
knowing what we do to survive. We might work hard to
convince ourselves that *they* only have one purpose, and that
we're doing only what nature requires of us, but the knowledge
still weighs on us and coarsens us to death. Still, I was sure
it would sadden my immediate blood, though it would be far
better for them to think of a tragedy befalling me than to know
the truth, that I had betrayed them.

The elders will have to choose either my younger brother
Daniel or my third cousin Clement to carry on my responsibilities. My great-uncle Jedidiah is still alive, but he has become
simple-minded and feeble since I took over from him, so it has
to be one of those two. Other than myself, they are the only
ones young enough who've been taught to read, although neither
of them've developed any interest in reading. Still, both of them
should be capable of reading street signs and able to navigate
in the outside world. And they both know how to operate the
vans, it being sport for them to drive the vans around the empty
field where I kept them parked. It's a shame the elders never
had me train one of them so there'd be a replacement ready in
case anything ever happened to me. But they are both cunning
in their own way, and they'll figure things out. They'll have to,
if the fate of the clan is going to be resting on them.

I began wondering what it would be like, assuming I was
able to stay with Jill, to never see any of my kin again. The
thought of it wasn't as distressing as I might've earlier
imagined. I felt no heaviness in my chest, or any sorrow other
than a nostalgic longing. When I tried imagining my kin, I
was left with only vague images that were fading quickly. Like
night-time phantasms disappearing in the light of day. I was
sure the idea of never seeing my kin and family home again
would've been harder if it wasn't for Jill and the excitement
I felt over a possible life with her.

I decided I couldn't just continue to lie there and stew in my worries. It had gotten hazy in the room, but still light enough for me to read. I swung myself off the couch and walked over to the treasure trove of books that lined almost half a wall of the room. Jill must have had over a thousand books, and my worries faded quickly as I greedily searched the titles. I only made it halfway through the first shelf before picking out a book that Jill had told me was one of her favorites. This was a book written in the early eighteen hundreds, written even earlier than the book I'd read by Charles Dickens, *Great Expectations*, which had absorbed me completely. This book was *Frankenstein* by Mary Shelley. Jill had told me a number of things about it, but what stuck in my mind was it having a monster who was hated and hounded as it tried living in *their* world. The book was a slender paperback. I brought it back to the couch and quickly lost myself in it.

EIGHT

I was nearing the end of *Frankenstein* when Jill emerged from her bedroom wrapped in a green-and-white flannel nightgown that went down to her ankles, her long golden hair tied back in a ponytail, her feet enclosed in fuzzy red footwear. It was a little after seven in the morning and her face appeared craggy from recently waking, but every bit as beautiful as the previous day. When she smiled at me brightly and said 'Good morning!' I knew nothing had changed between us.

She squinted as she looked at the book I was reading. 'Ah, *Frankenstein*. How are you liking it?'

'The monster is more intelligent and compassionate than I would've expected. Overall, I find myself not caring much about Victor Frankenstein's plight, but I find the monster's fate tragic. While Frankenstein's demise seems inescapable, I still have over a dozen pages before finishing and I'm hoping the monster might somehow be given a happier ending.'

'I'm not going to let slip any spoilers, but you're not alone in finding the monster the more sympathetic of the two. Many other readers do too, including myself.' Her brow furrowed as she squinted harder at the book. 'You're almost done with it? Charlie, you must've been reading it for hours. You should've put a light on.'

'It wasn't necessary. I have good vision, especially in the dark, and had enough light to read by. I didn't want to turn one on and risk disturbing you.'

She frowned at the idea of that. 'While you're here, don't worry about something like that. I can sleep like the dead. Feel free to turn the lights on, or anything else.' She added, 'I hope the couch was comfortable enough and didn't keep you awake?'

'Your couch and the apartment are paradise compared to the back of my van,' I said, smiling. 'They're not why I didn't sleep. I was too excited about being in a new city and starting my life afresh.'

That wasn't so much of a lie. I was excited and anxious about starting a new life with Jill wherever she lived, and that did outweigh all my worries. She accepted what I said, and asked if I'd like some coffee.

'That would be good.' I remembered that in their world 'thank you' was frequently expected, so I added that. Back at my clan, we do what's required and the concept of thanking one of us for it is as foreign as gift-giving.

Jill went into the modest open kitchen that was off to the side of the living room and built up along one wall. It consisted of four cabinets, no more than two feet of counter space, a small sink, a refrigerator, and an oven-and-stove combination. (I'd read enough of their newspapers and magazines when I traveled into their world to know about the equipment they use.) This kitchen was about the same size as the ones in our many century-old shacks, even though during Jedidiah's time we'd moved away from cooking over hearths and instead outfitted most of the shacks with wood-burning stoves. The seven houses I built all had roomier kitchens than Jill's, partly to accommodate the indoor plumbing I added, which allowed the water to be pumped into a stone sink directly from a well, and partly because of the large pantries that they house – spacious enough to hold half a year's worth of canned vegetables and glass jars of fruit preserves (sweetened with honey, which is the only animal by-product that we are able to consume without becoming ill).

I watched as Jill removed a small coffeemaker from a cabinet, measured out water to add to the reservoir, then added a filter and spooned ground coffee beans into it. I had no trouble recognizing what it was, since over four years ago during one of my travels to sell off our excess vegetables I had bought a similar type of coffeemaker and smuggled it, along with packets of coffee filters and cans of ground coffee, into the first of the new houses I built and resided in. (After tasting coffee for the first time during one of my trips and dreaming about it for several months, I had to do this the first chance I had even though I knew the elders would be furious if they ever discovered it.) Since this house was outfitted with a generator, I could run small appliances like coffeemakers. When I first built the house, I expected one of the elders to claim it, but being superstitious they didn't trust anything that went contrary to custom, even if it was only a new style of shelter – at least not until they were able to witness me living in it unharmed. After six months of seeing no illness befall me, they begrudgingly accepted my claim that these shelters would be an improvement for the clan, and they grabbed for themselves and their closest blood kin the next six houses that I built. I was surprised that they let me stay in the first one once they'd overcome their fear of it, but they did. It wasn't difficult sneaking the coffeemaker and the accompanying supplies into my house. I hid them in the van, and waited until the dark of night while the rest of the clan was asleep before trekking the four miles to where the vans were kept so I could bring all of it unwatched into my home. After Patience arrived, I had to be more careful and make sure the coffeemaker and supplies were well hidden, because if she'd ever found them she would've made sure the elders knew about them – no doubt in the hope of having our marriage dissolved so she could move back to her own clan. There were times I'd catch her sneaking around, trying to find something, but fortunately she never discovered my secret hiding places.

Once the coffee finished brewing, Jill brought it to a small table that was set up in the living room near the kitchen. There, I drank my coffee with two heaped spoons of sugar, while Jill drank hers without anything added to it, and we chatted about the novel I'd been reading. Jill appeared completely relaxed, a soft glow warming her skin. She was so beautiful it brought a lump to my throat, which was something I'd never experienced before. (And yes, the first few moments the lump occurred it concerned me, but I quickly remembered reading about this phenomenon and enjoyed the experience after that.) At one point she asked me about my favorite television shows. I was familiar with television from the newspapers and magazines I'd perused whenever I entered their world, and had also seen television sets of all sizes at gas stations and rest stops the last several years.

'I've never watched much television.'

She seemed to like that answer. 'Your parents raised you to be a vegan and to read books instead of watching TV! They sound very enlightened.'

I didn't correct her on the fallacy of that assumption, and instead simply shrugged since I'd decided I didn't want to lie to her unless necessary. She mistook my gesture as a sign of modesty, and the smile she showed me made the lump in my throat even larger. We sat silently after that, but it was a comfortable silence and as we were finishing our coffee Jill suggested we go out for brunch, which was a term I wasn't familiar with but assumed was something they called one of their meals. 'I'm sure we can find plenty of vegan options,' she said.

'I would like that,' I said. 'But I need to go out and look for work and a place to live. I would've left earlier, but I didn't want you finding me gone.'

Jill seemed taken aback, and also disappointed by what I'd said. 'Come on, Charlie, it's the Sunday before Labor Day! Don't you think you could wait until Tuesday before any job and apartment hunting?'

'No, I can't.' I swallowed, feeling the lump in my throat still present. I added, 'I'd like to date you, and I can't do that while I'm a guest in your home. It wouldn't be proper.'

My answer caused her to blush lightly, and also brought back a shy smile. From the way her eyes softened, she told me without words that she favored the prospect of that.

'I understand. And please, let me help you with your apartment search. But I don't want you moving out until you have your first paycheck, OK?'

I nodded, deciding it wouldn't be advisable to argue with her. If I was going to live as one of *them*, I was going to live mostly by their laws, which meant earning my money. Besides, I'd been working every day of my life since I was seven years old when the clan had me and others my age helping out in the fields and, during the late fall and winter, chopping and canning vegetables, and doing any other duties they needed us to perform. The thought of idleness did not appeal to me, even if it were only for a few days. But just as I got eleven hundred dollars from that well-fed and expensively dressed man, I'd be able to get more money from others like him – and I'd be more careful how I struck them, so that I didn't needlessly kill them, since I was fairly certain I'd left that man dying the other day. That would only be until I got enough to be able to get my own home in this city. It was important that I do that soon, as I didn't want to wait to start dating Jill. After I obtained the necessary money, I would go back to following their laws and not do anything that could risk separating me from Jill.

When we'd finished our coffee, I nodded farewell to Jill and got up to leave, but she asked me to wait and then dashed off to her bedroom. Less than a minute later, she returned and handed me a key. 'So you can come and go while you're staying at Abode Zemler,' she said. 'If you can get back by seven, we can go to dinner together. As friends. Dating won't start until you get your own place.'

I told her I'd make sure I returned by then. That a pack of hunting wolves wouldn't be able to keep me away. From the way she scrunched her nose, it was clear she found that an odd choice of words, and she asked if that's what people said in Manchester, New Hampshire. I remembered that that was where I had told her I was from, and admitted it was more a saying among my own clan. I also reminded myself to be more careful about the expressions I used in *their* world.

NINE

I needed to get rid of what was in the back of the van. The reason is easy enough to explain. If the police were to find the burlap sacks, they'd be curious about why the sacks were large enough to hold a large person, as well as why there were holes cut in them so if someone was put inside that person would be able to breathe. And the same police would be more than curious, probably downright hostile, if they found dried human blood on the burlap. If they examined the sacks carefully enough, I'm sure they'd also find hair and skin and other debris left behind by those I'd picked up. Likewise, the cut pieces of rope. During one of my trips several years ago I'd found a scientific magazine that had an article about DNA and forensics, and I knew the police would be able to use blood, hair, skin, and dried saliva and piss to identify some of those I'd taken who had long since been missing. I'd never bothered to wash out the sacks or replace the rope because it never seemed to matter much – since if the police had ever stopped me and found those sacks, most likely they'd have found them stuffed with those I'd already picked up. Now, though, it mattered.

As I thought more about it, I decided I needed to get rid of the van too. While I didn't know whether there was blood and other damning evidence inside it, that was more than likely. I could've used a bucket of water and soap to scrub the inside of the van clean, but there were other dangers with keeping it. I'd gotten the current license plates from a disabled car I found on the road only a few miles from where our hidden dirt road intersects with a little used road that's part of *their* world. The driver of that vehicle (a ravaged, nervous man dressed in dirty clothes who blinked incessantly from the moment he first spied me) was soon added to the back of the van as my first pickup of that trip, and after exchanging his license plates with the stolen ones the van had previously used,

I disposed of his car in a way that made it unlikely ever to be found. While I could replace them now with other stolen license plates, there'd still be a chance they'd bring the police to me. And as careful as I might've been with my pickups, it was possible that someone had spotted me taking one of *them* and had given the police a description of the van. Since I'd never driven as far as New York before, let alone done any pickups there, it wouldn't make sense for the New York police to be looking for it (if, in fact, police anywhere were looking for it) but still I didn't see a reason to take a chance with something like that now I'd decided to live as one of *them*. The idea of getting rid of the van saddened me, though. I'd spent many hours repairing it and keeping it sound mechanically, and I took pride in how well it ran after all these years.

After making these decisions, I bought a map of New York City at a nearby store. In the past I'd studied maps for New Hampshire, Massachusetts, and Connecticut, so I was familiar with the use of a map, but when I sat down to study this one I found it more confusing and difficult to decipher than those others. After several minutes it started making more sense, and I began feeling more comfortable with the idea of navigating the city.

I could see three ways of getting rid of the burlap sacks and rope: burning them all, throwing them away as garbage, or dumping all of them in one of the nearby rivers. Even in this crowded city, the map showed there were woods nearby where I'd be able to set the pile on fire. The odds were by the time the police were notified about the fire, the sacks would be burnt enough to destroy all blood and DNA material on them. Unless some do-gooder stumbled on the fire and put it out. If that were to happen, it would make the police even more suspicious about what they found. I didn't see how they'd ever be able to connect the burlap sacks to me, but it still seemed a better idea for them not to find them. This also meant it wouldn't make sense to throw them away as garbage, since they might be discovered if I did that. I studied the map some more, and decided to look for an isolated place where I could dump all this stuff in the Long Island Sound.

I went back to the van and got into the back of it. I had

little problem stuffing thirteen of the burlap sacks into the fourteenth, then I added all the rope except for a single piece into this sack too. Before tying up the sack, I tested it and decided it would be heavy enough to sink without adding any rocks.

The point I'd picked out to drive to was called Dosoris Island. It didn't take me long to drive there, no more than forty minutes. I stopped at an isolated part of the road, walked to the water's edge, and flung the sack into the sound. It quickly sank and disappeared under a wave. I got back in the van, turned it around, and drove back toward Jill's apartment building.

Several miles from Jill's address, I saw a CASH FOR CARS sign. I pulled up in front of a small lot of what looked like cars for purchase. I walked up to the small single-story brick building beside the lot. A sign on the glass door proclaimed that the business was closed. The lights were on inside though, and I peered through the glass and spotted one man who looked like he was readying the shop for business, while two others sat drinking coffee with bored, sullen expressions on their faces.

I tried the door. It was locked. One of the bored coffee drinkers heard the rattling, looked my way, and got up from his chair. After unlocking the door, he opened it a foot and, showing me a slick smile that left his eyes as dull as dirt, told me they didn't open for another half hour. 'Come back then and I'll be happy to help you,' he said in a voice even slicker than his smile.

'I've got a van parked out front I'd like to sell.'

He squinted as he peered out toward the van. 'How old is it?' His smile faded into something unfriendly, as if he were blaming me for wasting his time. 'It looks ancient.'

'I bought it used seven years ago,' I said. 'I rebuilt the engine and carburetor three years ago, and have fixed everything else. It runs the same as if it were new.'

It did run well but, although I did rebuild the engine and carburetor as I said, as well as making many other repairs, the rest wasn't exactly true. The van was being used during Jedidiah's time, and maybe even during the time of old Eli before him.

He gave me an annoyed look. 'That's not saying much,' he grumbled. A heavy put-upon sigh escaped from him. 'I'll take a look.'

He joined me as we walked back to the van. Once we got to it, he peered through the windshield before commenting that the VIN had been removed. 'Do you have a registration for this relic?'

'I did, but I lost it.'

Another deep sigh. 'I can't buy it without a registration,' he said. His eyelids lowered halfway, and the way his eyes glazed made me think of a snake. 'I know a guy who might be able to make use of it. He probably wouldn't give you more than two hundred for it, though. Want me to make a call?'

I nodded. He took out a cellphone and turned his back to me, then walked several steps away so I wouldn't be able to hear his conversation. Whoever he called, he only needed to talk to that person for less than two minutes before putting his phone away. He signaled with his fingers on his right hand for me to come over. When I did, he told me he'd been able to talk the buyer up to two hundred, then gave me the name of a restaurant and said I should ask for someone named Sergei. 'It's on Neptune Avenue in Brighton Beach.' When I looked at him blankly, he smirked and added, 'In Brooklyn.'

I turned away from him so I could return to the van. He yelled at my back, 'That's right, you dumb hick! Don't bother thanking me for the favor I just did you.'

That one of *them* thought he could insult me and make any sort of demand on me got my blood rising, especially understanding that he wasn't doing me any favor out of the kindness of his heart but, rather, would be paid later by this Sergei. In the heat of the moment, I let my guard down as I turned on my heels to face him. He saw my true predatory nature unmasked then. The color drained from his face, and he stumbled as he hurriedly walked back to the shop.

It was both unnatural and a challenge hiding my true self from *them*. It tired me out more than any hard labor ever could. But seeing how he had reacted (as well as others in the past), I resolved that I would need to try harder. That it would be dangerous to let more of *them* see me that way. It was funny how I didn't have this problem when I was with Jill, even when we were surrounded by a large crowd of *them*. It was as if her presence made that part of me shrink to nothing.

I got back in the van and studied the map until I understood how to drive to Neptune Avenue in the part of Brooklyn called Brighton Beach.

TEN

The restaurant I needed to drive to was south of where I was, and when I plotted my route I saw that I could go through a large area of greenery and trees, so that was the route I chose. I was feeling a little homesick for the wilderness where I had lived, and this small piece of tamed wilderness would provide a bit of comfort.

While I drove, I held the part of the map I needed flat against the steering wheel so I could look from it to the road as needed. It didn't take me too long to navigate to the Jackie Robinson Parkway, which took me through a heavily tree-lined stretch of road that was very different from the other areas of the city where I'd been driving. Before long, this stretch of roadway ended and I was back to the more familiar, uglier city driving.

It was maybe half an hour later when I was stuck in traffic on a road called King's Highway that I felt my neck hairs rise. Instinctively I looked out my driver's side window and immediately spotted him as he walked along the sidewalk in the opposite direction to where I was headed. He was stockier and shorter than the men of my clan, but his hair was as coarse as ours and the same coal-black color. I couldn't get a good look at his eyes or much of his face, given the way he was walking, slouching and with his head bowed, but I had the sense that he had hardened features and a thick and powerful jaw. A shiver went up my spine as I had the thought that he was one of my kind. If I could've caught his scent, I would've known for sure. He never looked my way, though, seemingly oblivious of me.

I wanted to follow after him and know for sure, but by the time the other cars started moving again and I was able to turn around he was nowhere in sight. I decided it was only my mind playing tricks on me. It was possible that other clans might hunt in this city. Maybe even probable. With the staggering amount of people this city held, it wouldn't be hard to fill up a van with stragglers. But it wouldn't make sense for one of my kind to be walking along a sidewalk here. If anything, he'd be driving a van similar to the one I was in, looking for those that would be safe to pick up. Unless – and the thought made my heart race – it was someone like me who'd decided to abandon his clan and live as one of *them*, maybe even for the same reason I had. And if that was what it was, he must've found a way to keep the cravings from becoming something awful.

I found a place along the street to park, squeezed my eyes shut, and tried to picture every detail I could of this person so I could decide whether he was one of my kind as I first thought. After several minutes, I gave up without being able to figure out whether he was one of my kind or not.

I accidentally veered off my planned route several times before finding the restaurant, but it didn't cost me much time as my instincts for driving in this city were getting better and I was quickly able to get myself back on track.

The front entrance of the restaurant where I'd been told I could find Sergei was locked. After pounding on the door without any results, I walked around the building until I found a back entrance. When I knocked on this door, a rosy-cheeked young man with blond hair and heavily-lidded eyes answered and uttered something I didn't understand.

'What?'

He gave me a disgusted look. 'I said, what you want?'

I had to concentrate to understand his words, as he mumbled more than talked and his accent made his words thick and peculiar.

'I have a van to sell to someone named Sergei.'

'Where is it?'

'I parked it out front.'

He showed me another disgusted look, which I didn't like. I had an impulse to snap his neck, but fought it off. 'Bring it back here,' he said, and he disappeared back into the building.

I went back to the van and drove it down the narrow alley that led to the back of the restaurant. When I knocked on the door, a different man opened it. He was older, more lines in his face, his hair slicked back. He smiled at me the way a fox might smile at a rabbit.

'You're not a cop?' he said.

He had a heavy, mumbling accent similar to that of the other man, but his words were easier to understand. I shook my head.

'No, you are no cop!' he said, laughing softly to himself. He pointed a thumb toward the van. 'Run the engine.'

I did as he asked, leaving the engine purring contentedly as I stepped out of the van. 'Two hundred dollars,' I said.

'Sure, sure.' He winked at me. 'Two hundred dollars for the delivery. Vehicle will be returned to you.'

This confused me. I didn't understand what he was saying. I started to ask him what he was talking about, but he held up a hand to stop me.

'You are not stupid, right? Just like you are not a cop. It would be illegal for me to buy a stolen van from you.' He winked at me. 'So just in case I am wrong and you are a cop trying to entrap me, I am only buying a delivery. Understand?'

'Yes.'

'Good, good.' He took a wallet from his back pocket. He made no attempt to hide from me how thick it was with money. Nonchalantly he took two $100 bills from it, folded them, and reached over so he could stick them in my shirt pocket. There was far more money in his wallet than what I had gotten from the well-fed man I had robbed – more than enough to give me what I needed so I could afford my own place to live and start dating Jill. I considered beating him unconscious and stealing his wallet. It would be easy enough to do, and given his condescending manner, I'd enjoy it. The problem was the van. He'd report my description and the van to the police. The newspapers might then print a story about it, which Jill could end up seeing. If it was only my description, it wouldn't matter. She might find it a coincidence, though I doubt it would've occurred to her that I was the same person. But she might recognize the van.

If I was going to rob him, I was also going to have to kill him. The same with the younger blond man who had first answered the door. And even the man at the shop advertising CASH FOR CARS, though if I went back to that shop he might no longer be there. The truth was I'd never killed any of *them* before intentionally, for my own ends. The well-fed man I robbed might be dead, and some of those I'd picked up in the past were found to be dead inside the burlap sacks, which was a shame since we then couldn't use them. For us to make use of *them*, they had to be alive for the slaughtering ritual. So while choosing the ones I picked up I might have brought about their deaths, I didn't think of myself as a murderer. That was just the way it had to be, and I wasn't sure if killing any of them intentionally for my own ends would make me feel as if I were a murderer.

All these thoughts flashed through my mind as I stood there and let him push the folded bills into my pocket and then pat the front of the pocket. As much as I wanted the rest of the money in his wallet, I couldn't risk robbing and killing him, even if I decided I had no moral qualms about bringing about their deaths for a purpose other than our natural use of *them*. Not now, anyway. If I still needed his money a week from now, I knew where to find him and the odds were he'd still be carrying a wallet stuffed with $100 bills.

ELEVEN

From a market, I bought an apple, a pear, shelled walnuts, and a banana – which was a type of fruit, like many in the market, that I'd never eaten before. But I liked its smell and made a meal of it. As I ate, I thought more about the man I'd seen who I believed might be one of my kind. If he was indeed one of my kind and was now living in New York, then perhaps I could track him down and he would give me the secret of how to keep the cravings from crippling me – unless his secret for survival was to continue the slaughtering rituals and meat preparation while living in the city.

After I finished eating I searched for one of the city's train stations – or subway stations, as Jill called them – and after finding one and studying a map of the train lines, I figured out how to get back to the area in Manhattan where I'd robbed that well-fed man yesterday.

There were still a great many of *them* on the sidewalks and in the subway car that I rode, but less than yesterday when I was with Jill. While I was overly alert to them, as any predator would be, I didn't feel any of the intense anxiousness or uneasiness that I had when Jill first took me to Manhattan.

I tried walking the same path as I did with Jill, looking for more well-fed, expensively dressed men to rob. I focused on men for two reasons. Firstly, it would be easier to remove a wallet from a back pants pocket than from a pocketbook unnoticed; and secondly, although in the past when choosing stragglers to pick up I'd never cared about their gender, now the idea of robbing a woman made me ill at ease. While I spotted a few people who seemed worth robbing, I also spotted some who were trying to be inconspicuous as they watched for that type of behavior. These must've been police disguised to blend in among the others. After the robbery yesterday, they must have been alerted to look out for other robberies of the same type. I soon quit the area and tried walking north toward the Empire State Building. And while I saw other people who appeared to be good targets for robbing, I likewise spotted what must've been police watching for this. Today, I decided, would not be a good day for robbing more of *them*. That would need to wait until the police lowered their guard.

I found a subway station so I could travel to the station close by Jill's apartment building. I wasn't going to hunt for robbery victims near where she lived, but I decided to try to find work close to her since I hoped to find a home in that area also.

After I got off at the Parsons Boulevard subway stop in Queens, I walked in the direction of Jill's building, and after only three blocks came across a fenced-in construction site where a group of workers were building a new house. I slipped in behind the fence and it didn't take me long to get the attention of the one who looked like he was in charge. He was half a foot shorter than I am, with a thick stumpy body and a round bald head, his facial features rubbery like a bullfrog's. He gave me a hard look, without his expression betraying what he thought.

'Yeah?' he inquired, his voice a raspy croak.

'You look like you could use another worker here,' I said. 'I'm good at carpentry, but I can build anything. I enjoy hard work.'

He made a face that I recognized from seeing it far too often on the elders. It was the face of someone who didn't want to be bothered with what I had to say. Just as quickly, though, he changed his mind and gave me a look up and down.

'You like hard work, huh? Alright, I'll give you a chance to show me that you know what you're talking about.' He told me to stay where I was, and left so that he could bring me back the same sort of helmet he was wearing, which I later learned was called a hard hat. After I put it on, he led me to a table saw and handed me a large board and told me how he wanted me to cut it.

'If you saw off any of your fingers, that's your hard luck,' he said, frowning as he watched me.

I'd brought a similar, but smaller, table saw back to the clan, and so had no trouble doing as he asked. After that, he handed me a nail gun (another tool I had brought back to the clan and used in my home-building) and told me where he wanted the board attached, which I did easily.

'OK,' he grunted, nodding. 'I've seen enough to know you can do the job. You can give me back the hard hat.' After I did that, he asked what my name was. I was surprised he hadn't asked me to do anything more challenging than cut a board and nail it, but I didn't suggest that he do so.

'Charlie Husk,' I said.

He held out his hand and I shook it. This was a custom that my kind didn't partake in, but I was well familiar with it – even many of the hitchhikers I'd picked up had offered me their hands before I had a chance to get them into the back of the van and into a burlap sack.

'Carl,' he said. He dug a card out of his pocket and handed it to me. 'Go to that address 7.00 a.m. on Tuesday, ask to speak to Elaine. I'll make sure she knows you're coming, and she'll have you fill out the necessary paperwork. Come here right afterwards and I'll put you to work. Thirty-six dollars an hour, plus time and a half overtime, and there'll be plenty of overtime. Don't worry, I'll call ahead and make sure they're expecting you.'

I thanked him, as I knew he was expecting me to do, and as I turned to leave he cleared his throat to get my attention. He gave me an apologetic look and asked if I was legal. I didn't know what he was asking, and stared back at him, confused.

'If you're from Ireland, or elsewhere, you got the necessary paperwork, right?'

'I was born in New Hampshire and lived there my whole life, until moving here yesterday.'

'So you got a social security number?'

I didn't know what that was. His expression soured as he understood my confusion. 'This is a legal shop,' he said. 'We don't pay under the table. If you're legal like you're saying, get a social security number and bring it to that address. If a job's still open, it's yours.'

I was going to ask him how to get a social security number,

but he had already turned his back to me. As far as he was concerned, we were done talking.

Over the next five hours I found other construction sites and automobile repair shops that were open and where people were working. Some of these had no interest in talking with me, the ones that did tested me like the first construction site did and all seemed satisfied and wanted to hire me until they found out I didn't have a social security number. It didn't matter to them that I was born in New Hampshire and had lived there my whole life until the other day. I tried asking one of them how I could get a social security number. He seemed to be growing unnecessarily impatient with me, but said if I had a birth certificate I could get a social security number.

'I was born in a small town. All of our births are done in our homes. None of us get birth certificates.'

'Then go back there,' he spat out, his impatience boiling over into anger. 'Or find the social security office and talk to them. There's got to be an office here in New York. But quit wasting my time.' He clamped his mouth shut, his face growing beet red, then before turning his back on me muttered loud enough for me to hear, 'All you fucking illegals think we can hire you off the books.'

At the last place where I was tested, an automobile repair shop, the man in charge was more patient when he found out I didn't have a social security number.

'Son,' he said, 'I wish I could hire you, I really do, but the city's been cracking down on our shops hiring illegals. You've done nicely ridding yourself of your accent. If I didn't know better I'd swear you were born here, but you're wasting your time trying to find this type of work without the proper work visa. No shop is going to take the chance of hiring you. Fine's just too big if we get found out. My advice, try the restaurants. Dishwashing is still honest work, and they're more likely to pay you cash under the table.'

By now it was five o'clock, and I'd pretty much come to the decision that I was wasting my time looking for either carpentry or auto repair work. And that my arguments about being a legitimate worker and having been born in this country were falling on deaf ears, and would continue to do so until I got myself a social security number, which I had no idea how I'd be able to do.

I had an hour and a half walk ahead of me to get back to Jill's apartment. As I made my way, I tried not to think of how much I wanted to round up all those who had treated me with scorn that afternoon, so I could put them in burlap sacks and make one last delivery to my clan.

TWELVE

'd knocked but got no answer, and as I was working the key into the lock the door swung open and a blonde girl stood grinning at me. She was slender and the same height as Jill, but she wasn't Jill. Her hair wasn't the same golden color, her eyes slate gray instead of blue, her face rounder and fleshier. The way she grinned at me left me cold. She might've been pretty in her own right, but I couldn't tell because when I looked at her I saw only one of *them*. If I had picked her up at that rest stop in Massachusetts instead of Jill, I would've had her quickly in a burlap sack and by now would be either driving back to the clan homestead or already there. In any case, I stood blinking at her, wondering whether I had somehow gotten confused about which was Jill's apartment and had ended up at someone else's.

She let out a short braying laugh before putting a hand to her mouth. 'I'm sorry,' she said, her voice husky and very different from Jill's. 'You look so startled. You must be Charlie. I'm Brittany, Jill's BFF. Come on in and I'll explain what's going on.'

I didn't know what BFF meant, but it was easy enough to guess she was a friend of Jill's. I followed her into the apartment, and she made a beeline for the couch that was my bed at night and sat with her right leg tucked underneath her. She patted the spot next to her for me to join her, her grin reflecting her amusement. She could've sat further toward the end of the couch so there would've been comfortably enough room for both of us, but instead sat in the middle of it, which would force me to sit closer to her than was proper, especially given that the skimpy material she was wearing left her thighs completely revealed. I hesitated briefly, but if she was Jill's friend, I didn't want to insult her, so I reluctantly joined her even though I was sitting so close to her that I could feel her breath on my face. She might've appeared short and slender, but a glance of her exposed thighs had me thinking how the women back at the clan would've been able to trim a nice amount of meat from them.

Since she was close enough to do so, she reached out and touched my arm. She said, 'Jill told me how you rescued her yesterday after that major league a-hole stranded her during their drive back to New York.' Her grin tightened. 'I'd like to thank you for that, but it's too bad you didn't punch that bastard out.'

I knew what a bastard was, but wasn't sure what an a-hole was, although I assumed it was a profanity of some sort. 'You don't seem to have any problem speaking bluntly,' I said.

'You bet I don't, especially when it comes to talking about what a dirty, rotten bastard Ethan is.'

I accepted that. 'Where's Jill now?'

'I'll tell you in a minute. Let me pour us some wine first.'

On a small, low wooden table in front of the sofa was an open half-full bottle containing what must've been wine. Also on the same table were three glasses, two of them used. I'd never drunk wine or any other fermented beverage before. While these types of beverages were shunned by my own clan, that wasn't necessarily true of all the clans of my kind. I'd never heard of any of them fermenting grapes, but I had heard that the Carlisle clan in Ohio distilled beets and the Pachett clan deep in the Kentucky hills did the same with corn.

This girl, Brittany, reached for the bottle, and as she poured wine into both glasses I looked at her in profile. Since she was a friend of Jill's, I tried to think of her as something other than one of *them*. But I just wasn't able to trick my mind into doing so.

The wine was poured, and she handed me one of the glasses. I knew it was made from red grapes and I'd been smelling it from the moment I stood on the other side of Jill's apartment door, but the taste of it still surprised me. It had a smooth, almost velvety, texture and a rich earthiness to it that I didn't expect. I took another taste and decided I liked it.

'A fairly inexpensive, but decent Malbec,' Jill's friend said, nodding slightly as she recognized that I was enjoying the taste of the wine. 'You're supposed to be able to taste dark cherry, plum, and coffee flavors. I'm not sure I can pick out any of those. Well, maybe the cherry. But when Jill called me to tell me what happened yesterday and how jerk-faced Ethan'd come by this afternoon to try to pull his usual tricks, I had to bring over whatever wine I had lying around.'

'What usual tricks?' I asked, my voice sounding cold and unfamiliar as it echoed in my head.

Her eyes partially glazed and her lips puckered as if she were tasting something unpleasant. 'What Ethan does every time he acts like a total asshole and does something really rotten to Jill. He came over here with his tail between his legs, apologizing, but at the same time trying to convince Jill that it was her fault and that she'd egged him on and brought about his bad behavior. Fortunately, this time Jill didn't buy it. Stranding her on the highway was a new low for him, but I think you being in the picture may have given her the strength to, hopefully, give old Ethan the heave-ho for good. For that, I thank you.'

'Where's Jill now?'

She shrugged. 'A glass of wine wasn't enough to settle the girl down, not after the way that bastard wound her up. She had to go out and blow off some steam. A four or five mile walk ought to do the trick. She wanted me to let you know she'll be back in time for the two of you to go out to dinner as planned.' She reached over to touch my arm again. 'This will give me time to get to know you better, which I believe is more than prudent given that you're in her life now, at least as long as she's putting you up—'

'I didn't ask Jill to do that.'

'I know. Jill's an amazingly kind-hearted girl, far too kind-hearted at times, and no doubt you couldn't resist her invitation.' She smiled as if this were all a joke, but from the intensity sparkling in her eyes I knew she was dead serious. 'Not that I can fault you for that. But this is why I need to make sure you're not another asshole like Ethan. Expect to be grilled, Charlie Husk.'

She questioned me as she had threatened, delving into all aspects of my life, and I submitted to it with as much good humor as I could muster. What choice did I have? She seemed to hold some influence over Jill and, besides, I couldn't fault her for looking out for Jill's best interests.

Whenever I could answer her honestly, I did; otherwise, when possible, I stretched the truth only as much as necessary. Surprisingly I only had to lie outright half a dozen times. When she asked about my family and upbringing, I was able to answer her truthfully, omitting certain details. When she asked about my work, I was able to tell her honestly about my home-building, while not mentioning what my other duties for the clan had been. When she asked about my hobbies, I simply told her reading, keeping the van mechanically sound, and gardening. The last was an exaggeration, but I had spent many hard days working in the fields between the ages of seven and fifteen before the clan gave me other responsibilities and decided gardening would sound less suspicious than farming, given that she had already asked me about life in Manchester, New Hampshire, and the times I'd driven through that city looking for pickups I had never seen any working farms.

She seemed skeptical of my answer when she asked if I had a girlfriend back home. With an accusing eye, she said, 'A total scumbag might latch on to someone vulnerable like Jill so he can have a free place to stay in New York for a few days, plus a pretty girl to screw around with, before heading back home to his main squeeze in New Hampshire.'

I could only guess what she meant by the word *squeeze*. 'That may be true, but that's not the case with me,' I said. 'Jill is far more than pretty, she's the most beautiful girl I've ever met. But assuming she's willing, I will not allow myself to become romantically involved with her until I've found work and got my own home. In fact, I spent all day today searching for work.'

'That's a good story,' she said, not believing me.

I handed her the three cards that were given to me at different construction sites before the man in charge at each site realized I didn't have a social security number.

'All three of them are interested in hiring me in the future when positions become available,' I said.

While she studied the cards, I took the money out of my

wallet – what I had left of the eleven hundred dollars I stole from the well-fed orange-haired man, plus the $200 Sergei paid me for the van. I handed her the money, which she counted before giving it back to me.

'That should prove to you that I'm looking for work here. I've also sold my van. Which is why I now have that money, and it should further convince you I have no intention of returning to New Hampshire.' I clamped my jaw shut as I glared at her, the indignation I was feeling and showing genuine. My voice strained, I added, 'I do not have a girlfriend waiting for me in New Hampshire. The truth is I have never had a girlfriend.'

I thought this latter statement would impress on her the seriousness of my intentions regarding Jill. Instead, her eyes narrowed and she looked at me as if I were a liar.

'You're twenty-eight, right? That's what you told Jill. And you're telling me you've never had a girlfriend?'

'Before yesterday I'd never met anyone I felt strongly enough to want to court,' I said, which was both the truth and a deception. I'd never had the chance to court any of my kind, since the only untaken womenfolk back at my clan were my own kin, and Jill was the first and only one in their world whom I didn't see as one of *them*. Of course, there was Patience, but she was never someone I would've willingly courted, nor was she someone I ever felt any friendly feelings toward.

'So you're trying to tell me that someone who looks like you is a virgin!' she said, her tone incredulous.

'I did not say that,' I said.

'So you prefer meaningless hookups instead of relationships? No surprise there.'

I had finished the glass of wine she had given me, and I realized it had made me talk more freely, saying things I normally wouldn't have. As well as draining her own glass she had drunk additional wine before I arrived, and most likely it had had the same effect on her.

'You have had too much wine,' I said.

'Really?' An angry burst of laughter escaped from her. 'I don't think so—'

'You must have, if you believe you have the right to ask me about such private matters. I'd rather rip out my tongue than ask a woman I've just met how many boyfriends she has had, or whether she's had meaningless sexual hookups.'

Red peppered her cheek. Fortunately, many months back during one of my journeys into their world I had read a newspaper article which'd familiarized me with the term 'hookup' (at least in the sense she'd used it), so I was able to understand her accusation.

'You're right,' she said. 'I was out of line. Let's blame it on the wine. But my heart's in the right place. I'm only trying to protect my girl. You got to admit, those girls in Manchester must have ridiculously lousy taste if none of them ever nailed down a good-looking stud like you and planted their flag.'

Outwardly my countenance showed little, but inwardly I smiled as I thought about telling her how I'd picked up enough girls in that New Hampshire city to know that they tasted the same as everyone else. Fortunately I hadn't drunk enough wine to slip up and say something like that out loud.

She smiled as if to show that her insulting manner toward me had all been a misunderstanding.

'It's so easy to get jaded living here in New York and think all men are devious scum, and forget that they might grow them differently in places like New Hampshire. Jill insisted that you're one of the decent ones, and I'm beginning to think she might be right. Friends?'

That wasn't much of an apology, but I saw no advantage to not taking the hand she offered me. Her skin was cool to the touch. I wasn't sure of the proper etiquette involved in shaking hands and how much time was too little or too much, but after only a few seconds a key sounded in the door. I released her hand and watched as Jill entered her apartment.

As soon as Jill saw me she smiled in a way that made me smile myself. Next, she gave her friend a curious look. Her friend bounded off the couch and gave Jill a hug, which Jill reciprocated.

'Charlie's been a good sport,' this Brittany girl said, after the hug had ended. She winked at me (and I briefly saw her as Brittany and not as one of *them*) and added, 'I've been giving him the third degree, asking him stuff I wouldn't have stood for. He's a good guy, I think. I like him.'

Jill's cheeks reddened. 'Thanks, I guess.' She turned to me. 'Charlie, I swear, I didn't ask or want Brittany to do that. Though I should've known better. I'm sorry.'

'That's a hundred percent true,' Brittany said to me. Then to Jill, 'And what's also true, Jill, darling, you should've known if you gave me the chance I'd be cross-examining the witness.' She let out another short burst of her braying laugh. 'I don't want to interfere with your dinner plans. I'll call you later.'

The two of them embraced again, and after they'd separated Brittany waved at me and I awkwardly waved back. (Waving goodbye is not a custom my clan is familiar with, but I had encountered it in my readings, so I understood the expected response.) While my thoughts were too scattered at that moment to understand why, I knew as I watched her leave that Brittany was someone I had to be careful of. That she had the potential of bringing me trouble.

THIRTEEN

J ill had chosen a vegan restaurant nearby, and as we walked to it her hand found mine.

'I know we're not officially dating,' she said. 'But it doesn't feel right walking like this without holding your hand. You don't mind, do you?'

'No, I don't mind.'

I was staring straight ahead so wasn't looking at Jill, but I could sense that she was grinning. It was probably over the gruffness of my voice and the way my words almost stuck in my throat. Her body softly bumped against mine, and for a moment I could barely breathe.

'Thank you for putting up with Brittany.' Jill laughed, and it was nothing at all like her friend's braying noise. Instead it was light and lyrical, and it warmed my heart to hear it. 'She's in law school, and sometimes forgets she's not a prosecutor yet. I should've known she'd cross-examine you, but I wasn't thinking.' There was a pause where I could feel her mood darkening. 'She must've told you that Ethan came over. The jerk who stranded me on the Mass Pike yesterday.'

'Yes, she told me.'

'He put me in such an awful mood. I needed to bitch to someone, so I called Brittany, who's been my best friend since forever. But a glass of wine and bitching didn't help. I needed to walk off my emotions.' She laughed again. This time it wasn't as lyrical, and there was an angry edge to it. At the same time, her grip on my hand tightened. 'But again, I apologize for leaving you to Brittany. I swear, it wasn't a setup on my part. I didn't want her digging into you like that. It couldn't have been much fun.'

'I didn't mind,' I said. 'She was only looking out for you.'

We walked the next block without either of us saying anything. Jill broke the silence by commenting that she didn't see my van parked near the building. 'I hope it wasn't towed.'

I knew the word 'towed', but I wasn't sure what she meant. Was it possible that strangers in this city attached chains to vehicles and hauled them away? I didn't ask Jill for an explanation, and instead told her that I'd sold the van. 'I didn't need it any longer. I'm where I want to be.'

I felt her body stiffen. Her hand slipped free of mine. 'What happened to your stuff?' she asked, her voice different than earlier. 'You didn't bring any of it up to my apartment.'

'I didn't take anything with me when I left.' I hesitated before adding, 'I wanted to come here and start life over.'

She stopped. I turned to her and saw that a hint of fear showed over her face, which made me feel weak inside. And I heard that same fear in her voice as she asked whether the police were after me.

'No, nobody's after me. That's not it.' My head was swimming over how nervous Jill had become. It was as if at any moment she might take flight and run away from me. I told her how I hadn't lived in Manchester for more than a few years. I despised every lie I told her, though I had no choice. But then I came clean, at least as much as I could.

'I grew up in a small community in New Hampshire,' I said, my voice hollow in my ears. I shifted my glance so that I stared blindly past Jill, afraid to look at her face any further. 'It's a forgotten-about place that few know exist. I might not eat animal meat, but my kin aren't enlightened. They're backward folks, living in many ways like people did hundreds of years ago. They tolerated me reading books, but they weren't happy that I did so and before I left many of them thought I'd read enough books already. I don't want that type of life. And I didn't want to bring any of those memories with me. Manchester was still too close to them, but New York is far enough away.'

I'd betrayed my kin. I'd pretty much ripped a knife through all their hearts. But I didn't care. All I cared about was Jill not running away from me. And not being afraid of me. I was deceiving her in what I said, omitting important details. I wasn't about to tell her about what my kind needs to do to survive, or about the nearly two thousand of *them* who during my lifetime had been abducted and brought back to the clan, or how their crushed bones help fertilize our fields and filter our well water. And I didn't tell her about the cravings, about how bad I knew they were going to get, and how I had no idea what I could do so that I could live with them. Still, as deceptive as I was, there was a good amount of truth in what I said. I didn't want that life anymore. Not as long as I had a chance of being with Jill. Even if the cravings become something intolerable.

For a long moment neither of us spoke. The sound of the cars passing by and all of the other city noises surrounding us grew into such a deafening clamor that I could barely stand it. My neck had hardened like stone, not wanting to allow itself to move even an inch, because if it did I might find myself looking down into Jill's face and see fear flooding her eyes. Or worse, see that she was lost to me. But then her hand sought out mine, and that gave me the courage to look at her again.

There was no fear anymore. Instead, her face had softened, her eyes large and liquid. 'I can't even imagine what you must've gone through,' she said, her tone hushed, her voice raising that lump once more in my throat. Whatever danger might've existed of her fleeing me was gone. I felt a wetness around my own eyes, which confused me before I realized that for the first time in my life I was crying. Not so that I was sobbing or making undue noises. But still, tears were leaking from my eyes. I was ashamed, but I wasn't going to turn away. More than anything I needed to look into Jill's eyes and the breathtaking beauty they provided.

'None of that matters, because everything in my life has led me to being here with you right now,' I said.

That was maybe the truest thing I'd ever said or will ever say, and Jill recognized that.

'Let's go eat,' she said.

The restaurant Jill took me to was much smaller than the one we'd eaten at the other night. I counted only eight tables and there was little space separating them, leaving me and Jill crowded among *them*. Both tables next to ours were occupied, so I had other eaters sitting on both sides of me, leaving less than a foot between us, even though they were both thinner than many of *them* I'd seen. (Thin enough that I might not have stopped to pick them up if I was still collecting *them* for the clan.) While their scent was ever-present and I could feel a moist heat from them, having *them* so close no longer caused me any undue anxiousness. I was getting used to having so many of *them* around me. Jill was also well aware of the other eaters' close proximity, and it caused her voice to be more guarded as she thought of additional questions to ask me. Her first one was whether I'd really been building houses as I had told her.

'Yes, of course. So far I've built seven of them.'

'How did you learn to do that given your, um, upbringing?'

'I taught myself. The same with how I learned to read. The same with fixing an automobile.'

She had other questions about my childhood, some of which I was able to answer honestly, others where I needed to lie. At no point did the fear and distrust that I saw earlier resurface. If anything, the look she favored me with was more endearing. At the end of her questions, which were interrupted only by our server (a bony man who wore jewelry in his ears and had his arms and neck covered with peculiar ink symbols) coming to take our order, Jill, lowering her voice so no one else could hear her, told me she found me remarkable.

'The way you overcame your early environment is so impressive. I can't even fathom the inner strength required to do what you've done. No wonder the crowds here freaked you out as much as they did yesterday. Charlie, I am so happy I met you. It was worth having Ethan mistreat me the way he did if it ended with us meeting.'

She reached out across the table (which didn't require much of a reach given how small the table was) so that she could rest her hand on top of mine, and the look she gave me let me know that words from me weren't necessary. There was no longer any risk of her fleeing me.

I had guessed right that I needed to explain about certain oddities she must've been noticing about me. My traveling to a new city without any belongings was only one of them. Even though she didn't say anything about it, I'd caught a fleeting look from her when she asked me this morning for my cell-phone number, and I told her I didn't have one. Although that look lasted barely a heartbeat, it haunted me for much of the day. I knew also that she must've been finding my manner of talking unusual. I'm not stupid. How could it be anything other than that, given how few conversations I'd had in my life that had lasted more than a dozen words? Even though I had read all I could and had spent many evenings studying the dictionary in the clan's possession, my vocabulary and the manner of talking that I'd learned from my books were different from how Jill and others of *them* talked. I knew this simply from the idioms and slang they used. Jill's use of 'freak' as a transitive verb was an example, although I reckoned I was able to guess its meaning – to cause someone to act as if they'd been turned into something aberrant. Even if Jill hadn't admitted to herself her suspicions about me, I knew she had them, and thankfully I realized before it was too late that I needed to address the matter.

Her hand rested on mine until the food was brought over. On Jill's recommendation, I ordered the refried bean, grilled onion, and green pepper burrito once the server'd assured me that the cheese used in it wasn't made from cow's milk but from nuts, oils, and spices.

Jill had ordered the same meal. When it arrived, I sniffed my food cautiously before trying it (which caused Jill to laugh, in a good-natured way, her eyes sparkling as she did so, and then to quickly apologize), and decided right away that I'd be happy eating that kind of food every day of my life, as long as I was able to figure out how to keep the cravings at bay. (It hadn't been two full days yet and the cravings were already causing a dull, persistent ache in my teeth and jawbone.) While I'd had plenty of onions, green peppers, and corn from what my clan grew in the fields, I'd never had refried beans before and certainly never tasted anything like guacamole. Jill could see how much I was favoring my meal, and she commented about how glad she was that I was enjoying the burrito. I grunted something back in response, but I couldn't say exactly what.

We were still eating when music of some sort came from

Jill's pocketbook. She made an annoyed face and told me that was Brittany's ringtone. 'I should've turned the phone off,' she said. She removed her cellphone from her bag and presumably did just that. A short time later our server came to our table and sheepishly asked Jill if she was Jill Zemler. When she nodded, the server told her that she had a phone call from someone named Brittany Hennessey, who claimed it was urgent she speak to Jill. Jill sighed in exasperation and accepted the phone handset from the bony long-haired server.

'I should never have told Brittany where I was planning to take you for dinner,' Jill whispered to me, her hand covering the mouthpiece on the handset. 'But if I don't talk to her, she'll probably be storming the restaurant in minutes. She's a very sweet girl, but she can go overboard at times.'

A look of patience settled over Jill's face as she greeted her friend. I have learned during my ventures into *their* world that my kind's hearing is exceptionally strong compared to theirs, and even over the din of the restaurant I was able to hear what Brittany was telling Jill. I wasn't surprised that what she was saying appeared to be having no impact (in fact, Jill told her friend that what she was saying was pretty much what she already suspected, given what I had told her), nor when Jill told me about the call once she'd ended her conversation with her friend.

'That was Brittany freaking out after discovering that you have zero presence on social media,' Jill said, smiling sadly at what she considered her friend's unnecessary alarm.

I'd read about social media in magazines and newspapers during past trips and knew it had to do with cellphones, computers, something called the web, and other things called websites, tweets, and blogs, but the concept remained unclear to me. Still, I recognized that in some way Brittany had spied on me, and suspected this wouldn't be the last time if I left her alive.

'I told you earlier today that I never owned a cellphone,' I said, trying to act as if I fully understood what Jill had told me. 'But I'm not a Luddite. I used power saws and other modern tools in my home-building. And you know that until today I drove a van. But given the way my ma and pa and others of my kin raised me, I never developed any interest in using computers.' (I was proud of myself for remembering the term 'Luddite'. I think I came across it over a decade ago, although I might've also seen it while studying the dictionary.)

Jill said, 'I know, and that's one of the things I find so cool about you.'

That was it. That Brittany girl's attempt to drive a wedge between us had failed. If anything, all she had accomplished was to make me more endearing to Jill. Of course, I was fortunate that I'd earlier told Jill what I did. If I hadn't, Brittany's call might've had its desired effect.

When we later walked back to Jill's apartment, instead of holding my hand like Jill had done earlier, she took hold of my arm with both her hands and kept her body touching mine. The closeness of her made me nearly breathless.

Once we were back inside Jill's apartment, she told me it was about time I watched my first movie. I didn't object, whatever she wanted was fine with me. She chose what she claimed was her favorite movie from a small library that she kept. It was called *The Shop Around the Corner* and she told me it was an old movie, made in 1940. Which didn't seem all that old to me given the publishing dates of many of the books I'd read.

We sat together on the couch as we watched the movie. I was well aware of what a movie was from my reading, but it was a strange experience watching one unfold. It had a different kind of power than a book. Maybe part of the excitement was having Jill so close to me, but I still found myself absorbed in the story, which seemed to be an account of love at first sight, even though initially the couple bickered worse than my ma and pa ever did. It stunned me when I realized that I wasn't considering the participants in the movie as *them*, but more in the same manner that I viewed Jill and my own kin.

We'd watched a fair amount of the movie when Jill moved closer to me, and then without any notice swung her feet on to the couch and curled up with her knees almost to her chest, lying on her side so that her head rested on my leg.

'It just feels natural for me to be on the sofa like this with you,' she said, her voice the very definition of the word sultry – at least, as given in the clan's dictionary that I had studied. 'That's all this is.'

A dizziness overwhelmed me, so much so that I could barely pay attention to the goings-on in the movie. Later I realized that while Jill was lying like that, and maybe for as much as an hour afterwards, I wasn't aware of any of the aching that the cravings had brought on. We sat like that for a dozen minutes or so (although the time seemed to stretch into something far longer) while my heart pounded so heavily that it seemed to be beating in my ears. Then Jill tilted her head so that she was looking directly at me, her eyes larger than I'd ever seen them.

'You can kiss me,' she said.

'I want to more than I've ever wanted to do anything,' I forced out, my voice heavy and catching in my throat. 'But I can't. It wouldn't be right. Not now. Not until I move into my own home and we start dating properly.'

Her head titled back so that she was looking again at the movie. 'Is it OK if I lie like this when we're on the sofa together?'

I nodded, not sure I would've been able to get any more words out of my mouth. Even though Jill couldn't have seen me nod, she knew I had done so. So we remained like that until the movie ended, with me sitting nearly breathless, my head and heart pounding, while Jill lay curled up, her head resting lightly on my leg. I had told Jill the truth about how badly I wanted to kiss her, but I lied about my reason for not doing so. I did want to court her properly, which meant waiting until I wasn't a guest in her home, but if that was all there was to it I would have weakened. What kept me from doing so was that I was afraid. It was partly because I had never kissed a girl before. Even though Patience and I had engaged in marital relations, we never once kissed. She would never have put up with it if I had been inclined to try to do that with her, and she probably would've bitten a chunk out of my lip or tongue if given the chance. But that was only part of the reason. It had been almost two days since I'd last had one of the clan's stews, and even though I'd used the toothpaste and mouthwash that Jill made available to me, as well as having other meals since that stew, I couldn't help worrying that if we kissed Jill might taste the meat used in it. I needed more time to pass before I could risk kissing her.

FOURTEEN

I accepted that I wasn't going to be able to sleep that night, not with all the thoughts whipping about in my head, and not with the intense longing that I felt for Jill. After Jill had disappeared into her bedroom, I tried reading the rest of *Frankenstein*, but I was unable to concentrate on the words, and I knew I'd have no better luck if I tried choosing any of her other books.

Once the lights went off in Jill's bedroom, I waited a spell and then slipped out of the apartment. I had warned Jill that I might be too restless for sleep, and if that turned out to be the case I would wander outside for a while, hoping the cool night's air would help. She seemed concerned by this (as evidenced by the way her brow wrinkled and she bit her lip), but she told me she understood and warned me that I needed to be careful when walking around her neighborhood late at night. I listened to her warnings as if they were genuine, but the idea of any of *them* individually or even in small groups posing a threat to me was absurd. There was the same chance of that as of rabbits posing a threat to a wolf.

After I left her building, I stared up at the sky, but it was starless and the moon was hidden by haze and clouds. My sense of direction, though, was still strong enough to direct me north. There were far fewer of *them* outside at that hour, but there were still occasional stragglers roaming about, as well as cars and taxis on the streets, although far fewer than earlier. If I had still been collecting *them*, this would've been the hour for it. As I walked, I spotted one of the predators Jill had warned me about. He was hiding in the shadows and eyeing me, but as with most predators he recognized that I was a more dangerous one than himself – even though I was keeping my true self hidden – and he remained in the shadows.

I let my instincts guide me, and it wasn't long, no more

than several miles of walking, before I entered an area of greenery, and not long after that I reached a small lake.

I found it soothing to a degree sitting on grass among trees beside this body of water. Perhaps it would've been even more soothing if I had heard more animals rustling about or other noises from animals, but there were almost none, which made the setting seem both familiar and foreign to me. Still, as I sat there I was able to slow down my thoughts and was better able to untangle and study the problems weighing on me. First and foremost were my worries about the cravings.

After two days the cravings were only a discomfort, nothing more. I could easily live with them if this was how bad they were going to get. But I knew from that black time when my clan was driven nearly into madness that the cravings were going to get much worse, and I couldn't just ignore what was going to happen. Ever since I spotted that man in Brooklyn with the heavy jaw, I'd been trying to decide whether he was one of my kind, and I had pretty much came to the conclusion that he was. So I needed to find him. It was that simple. I needed to have him tell me his secret for keeping the cravings at bay, which meant I had to hope he lived near where I spotted him.

Resolutely, I decided I would search the area of Brooklyn where I'd seen him walking. Either I'd find him or I'd discover another way to fight the cravings. Or alternatively, the cravings would end up destroying me. With that problem settled in my mind (at least as much as was possible at that time), I moved on to the next issue troubling me, which was finding work.

My evening with Jill had made me doubly anxious to court and marry her, but that wasn't the only reason I needed to start working. Even this one day of mostly idleness left me feeling uneasy, and I didn't know how many more days of it I could stand. But that was still only part of it. When the cravings maddened my clan, we were snowbound, and icebound, and were more idle than during the other seasons. The thought stuck in my mind that if I was spending long hours each day building houses or doing carpentry or fixing cars, that would lessen the cravings. Although I knew I might turn out to be wrong about it, I kept thinking that would be the case. I therefore desperately needed to find work, but judging by my experience earlier that day it seemed as if I would be blocked from doing so unless I was able to obtain a social security number. And from what I'd been able to gather, it didn't seem as if I could get one unless I had a birth certificate. Which I didn't, and I didn't see any way I could.

It was maddening. Despite having been born in the New Hampshire wilderness, because I didn't have an official document proving it I would be unable to work in *their* world, even though I was able to prove that I could do the work required. I considered telling Jill about my quandary and seeing if she could help me find a solution, but I soon realized the dangers in doing that. After what I'd already told her about my upbringing, she'd believe that my ma and pa had never obtained a legal document from the authorities regarding my birth. But she might question how I had worked in the past without the necessary social security number. And even if she believed that I had been able to work without one, it could very well lead to a disastrous outcome, such as Jill or others wanting the whereabouts of my kin so they could verify my birth. I soon accepted that I couldn't tell Jill about this, nor anyone who might end up wanting to find my ma and pa. So it appeared that I was stuck as badly as a fly in molasses, and I didn't see any way of getting unstuck.

I remembered one of *them* telling me that I should look for work as a dishwasher. That restaurants were willing to hire workers illegally. The thought of seeking out that kind of work was highly distressing. Back at my clan the women were responsible for scrubbing the pots and cleaning the plates and eating utensils, and no self-respecting man would do such a thing. I brooded on this for a while, unable to arrive at a decision. On the one hand, I was in *their* world, not my clan's; and if men in *their* world were willing to do such work, then I should not hold myself above it even if I found the chore utterly demeaning. On the other, I enjoyed the physical labor of home-building and carpentry and repairing cars, and I very much wanted to be employed in that manner of work. But I just didn't see how I could do it unless I was able to get a social security number, which didn't seem possible.

After a while, I felt drowsy and quit worrying about that problem since no solution seemed evident, at least not then. I started thinking once again about how that Brittany girl had spied on me. Because that was what she had done, even if I didn't understand how she had done it. But for her to call Jill while we were at that restaurant, sounding as excited as she did because she believed she had discovered something damning about me, showed that she wanted to cause me trouble. As I lay on the grass, I replayed in my mind the questions she had asked me and the answers I provided, and tried to decide if she could cause me any additional trouble from this. I couldn't see any way she could, which was fortunate for Brittany. Soon, though, my thinking became fuzzy and I found myself closing my eyes. As much as I tried focusing on other problems the Brittany girl might cause me, my mind kept wandering to nonsensical areas.

I must've drifted into sleep. I hadn't realized I'd done so, but I woke with a start as something kicked the bottom of my foot and a harsh, bright light flooded my face.

'Hey, you can't sleep here! Move your ass!'

I was too startled and enraged to remember that I needed to keep my predatory nature hidden. Unmasked, my true self showed before I could control it. The man who was shining an electric lamp into my face stumbled back several steps. I could see fear dancing wildly in his wide open eyes as he recognized what I was. And then he was reaching for the gun that he had holstered on his hip.

I had little doubt that in his panic he was going to shoot me. It was too late to hide my true self. He'd seen that part of me, and the terror that drove him was something primordial, something dating back more than a thousand years to when my kind lived among *them* instead of hiding in the wilderness. He wasn't capable at that moment of reasoned thought. At some deep instinctive level, he believed he needed to kill me so that he could survive.

I had moved into a crouch by the time he started to bring his gun out, and I leapt at him before he could level the gun at me. With a quickness that must've surprised him, I grabbed his gun hand with my left hand and gripped his throat tightly with my right. His legs gave out under him, and he fell backwards into the water with me on top of him.

He was helpless as he thrashed about, unable to scream out for help because of how I held his throat. I could've beaten him unconscious and left him alive, but I'd read enough to understand how *their* world works. He had flashed his lamp on my face while I was asleep and had gotten a good look at me. If I let him live, a drawing of me would appear in the newspapers and on television, and soon afterwards Jill would be lost to me.

I crushed his windpipe, leaving him dead, with his head mostly submerged in the water and only the tip of his nose and his chin sticking out. The water was clear enough that even in the night's darkness I could see his eyes bulging and his mouth gaping open. I didn't regret killing him. He was only one of *them*. But I regretted the wastefulness of his death. His body could've provided necessary meat for my kin or one of the other clans, but instead his death would be meaningless.

I didn't bother searching for his wallet. He wouldn't have had much money on him, and whatever he had it wouldn't have been worth the time to look for it. I quickly moved away from his body and soon saw an empty police car parked no more than thirty yards away in an area illuminated by a street-lamp. The road he was on appeared to snake around the lake, and he must've spotted me when he was driving by, and made the bad decision to harass me even though I was sleeping peacefully and not bothering a soul. Was sleeping outside, on grass, a crime in their world? Was something like that possible? Such a law seemed as outrageous as needing a special number in order to work.

Other police could be coming soon. If they found me nearby in my wet clothing, they'd guess correctly that I was responsible for that policeman's death. I started running in the direction of Jill's apartment, keeping my body low and as much in the shadows as I could. I was able to run a mile without passing any stragglers, and I doubted that the people in the few cars that passed were able to get a good look at me in the darkness. I slowed down to a walking pace, knowing that if I kept running any further I would risk attracting undue attention. While I passed a few of *them* after that, they not only avoided eye contact but seemed unwilling to look in my direction. From what I could tell, they were outside for their own nefarious reasons. There was no reason for any of these stragglers to inform the police about me, so I left them alone.

I was able to return to Jill's apartment building without incident. Earlier, Jill had shown me a room in the building's basement where there were machines for washing clothing. The room was empty of other people, and after emptying my pockets I stripped myself of what I was wearing. The machines had operating instructions printed on them, and there were vending machines for buying soap and for changing dollar bills into the coins that the laundry machines required, so I had little trouble using them.

FIFTEEN

I went into a small market, bought a large coffee and, having added three packets of sugar to it, sat at the sole remaining empty table so I could read the newspaper that I'd purchased at a nearby market. Several hours earlier, after my clothing had finished drying in the machine and I was at last able to stop sneezing from the heavily artificial flowery smell the soap had left on my shirt, I had snuck back into Jill's apartment and scribbled a note saying I would meet her back at her apartment at five o'clock that evening, a time we'd arranged the night before as she was going to be busy for most of the day at her college.

I was sure the body of the policeman whose throat I had crushed would have been discovered hours ago, and I searched the newspaper to see what they had written about it and to find out if anyone had spotted me. There was no mention of it yet, but I did find a story about the well-fed orange-haired man whom I had robbed. As I suspected, he had died from the blow I struck. It turned out that he was well-known and was the head of some sort of organization that people cared about. The newspaper printed both a photograph and a drawing of a man the police were looking for, and it wasn't me. The photograph had this man in profile, while the drawing showed what the police believed he would look like if he were facing front. His head was round and heavy, and his face covered by a beard and mustache that were a light-brown color and cut so short they looked almost like animal fur. He also appeared to have small eyes and a flat nose, and he was wearing a cap of some sort. I was curious as to how this man had become a suspect, and I read the story carefully. The same witness who took the photograph claimed that she saw this man strike the orange-haired man I'd robbed. There was no mention that this well-fed man's wallet had been stolen, and from what I could gather, the police didn't yet know the name of this wrongly accused man and were asking the public for information.

As I thought about what I had read, I realized how lucky I'd been. So many of *them* carry cameras and someone could've taken a photograph of me, instead of the man who was being falsely accused. I had no idea why this witness was claiming he was the guilty party instead of myself, but I was fortunate she was so unobservant. I also realized that I couldn't rob any more of *them* the way I did that well-fed man, no matter how careful I thought I was being. There was too great a chance that next time it would be my photograph that was taken and printed in the newspapers.

I sat for a while drinking my coffee and reflecting on my good luck in the matter, and then read more of the newspaper. There were other murders and crimes that were written about, but none of them seemed to have the police's attention as much as the death of the well-fed man. Finding the wrongly accused suspect seemed to be their top priority. A thought struck me that perhaps other witnesses had taken photographs which the police might have, and I might appear in one of them. I tried to think if that could have happened, but I wasn't able to imagine what it would've looked like if it did. I knew they used their cellphones now to take photographs, and not the large bulky cameras I was familiar with from my reading. So if someone had taken my photograph, I probably wouldn't have known it. I worried some more about that possibility, but in the end decided that the incident happened too fast for any of them to have done so. Only seconds had elapsed from the time I yelled out that the well-fed man needed help to my fleeing the circle that had formed around his critically injured body.

Before leaving the coffee shop, I studied the map of New York that I'd bought the previous day and was able to identify the subway stop in Brooklyn I needed to travel to so I could search for the thick-jawed man who I thought might be one of my kind.

I had more than learned my lesson from the other night and made sure to keep my true self well-hidden, both as I walked among *them* to a nearby subway station and later as I took two different subway cars to get to the East Flatbush neighborhood of Brooklyn.

I spent the rest of the morning and a good part of the afternoon searching without any luck for the thick-jawed man. During my search, whenever I came across a construction site where people were working, I sought out the man in charge, even though I didn't hold out much hope of a happy outcome. The ones that tested me seemed eager to offer me work until they discovered I couldn't provide them with a social security number, and then I was treated the same as I was the other day. It was hard to take, and I struggled to keep my true self masked as I found myself growing increasingly bitter regarding how *their* world operated. One of them appeared more patient and kinder than the others, and explained that he wished he could help me but was unable to for the same reason others had given me. In my frustration, I told him what I'd told the others, that I wasn't illegal, and then confided to him that my kin didn't have their births in hospitals and never bothered getting legal certificates. 'My blood family's all in New Hampshire. I swear, that's where we were all born and raised. There must be something I can do.'

He gave me a confused look, his eyes squinting the same as if he were staring at the sun. 'Is your family part of some sort of anti-government group living off the grid?'

I wasn't sure what he was asking, but I nodded, since it sounded most like the truth, at least in a way.

'Your parents still around?'

'They are.'

'I don't know,' he said. He clasped the back of his neck and rubbed it as he continued to give the appearance of trying to be helpful and sympathetic. 'I guess you could try contacting a lawyer. I'm sure if your parents were willing to sign the right forms this problem could be taken care of. Good luck.'

He offered me his hand and I took it, trying hard to hide the despair I was feeling. I accepted then that I was going to have to do work that was considered illegal. Either something demeaning, like washing dishes, or something that could lose me Jill forever. Such as robbing more of *them* like I did the well-fed man, except being more careful about it and making sure no one was around to take my photograph.

Later, as I rode a subway car back to Jill's apartment building in Queens, I continued to debate the matter, undecided which I would do. All I knew for certain was that it would be calamitous if I called on a lawyer, as that would certainly lead to questions that I wouldn't want anyone asking or, worse, taking it upon themselves to solve. I found myself thinking about several magazine and newspaper stories I'd read in the past about people called 'hit men' who were paid a lot of money to kill people. If I was going to do illegal work, maybe that would be the right kind for me. While I'd regret the wastefulness of it, I wouldn't have any qualms about killing some of *them* to make money if *their* world was going to prevent me from working legally. That type of work could be done in the shadows, with no one around to take photographs. And really, who would be more suited for it than a predator, like myself? I started warming to the idea, and even had the thought that the man named Sergei whom I sold the van to would be able to help me find that type of work. He clearly worked as a criminal, and had planned to use the van in the commission of a crime. Or, if not him, he'd be able to point me to someone who could.

After I left the Parsons Boulevard subway stop, I continued to debate the matter in my mind as I walked toward Jill's building. I was three blocks away when a HELP WANTED sign in a restaurant window stopped me. The thought of spending my days scrubbing pots made me feel ill, but I was struck by the realization that I'd already been lying far more often to Jill than I ever wanted to. And if I found work killing *them* for money, I would need to lie to her about what I did for work every remaining day of my life. Resigned to my situation, I headed inside.

The restaurant had a scattering of customers and smelled heavily of grease. It looked dingier inside than the restaurants Jill and I had eaten in. I didn't know it at the time, but it was a style of restaurant called a diner. I approached a heavyset older woman who stood behind the cash register, and told her I was there seeking work. She continued to stare at me in a blank, uninterested way before telling me to wait at one of the empty tables and she would have Chris speak to me.

I sat at one of the empty tables, as she had directed, and several minutes later a short, stocky man who must've been Chris came over and sat across from me. He had his hands resting on the surface of the table, and I noticed that they were stubby, but strong hands. His other most prominent feature was that his head seemed much larger than it should've been for his body.

He gave me an accusatory eye for a long moment as if he was trying to decide if I was worth talking to, and finally said, 'I'm looking for a short-order cook and a dishwasher.'

'I'll work as a dishwasher,' I said. Then using the vernacular I'd heard from the men in charge at the construction sites I'd spoken with, I added, 'But I need to be paid off the books.'

'Are you in law enforcement? You have to tell me if you are. It's entrapment if you don't.'

'No, I'm not in law enforcement. I'm just a man who needs work.'

His eyes narrowed as he gave me a cautious look, and I knew what he was doing. He was trying to decide if I'd lied to him. He smiled thinly as he made up his mind that that couldn't have been the case.

He leaned closer to me and, keeping his voice low so others couldn't hear him, said, 'You fooled me. I would've guessed you were an American.'

I didn't bother correcting him, and instead stared back at him. His eyes hardened as he nodded to me. 'You'll be here six to four Monday through Saturday, and I'll pay you two fifty a week. If you're late once, that's it, you're fired. No second chances. Same if you come here too high to work. Or you break too many dishes. Or you loaf. Or you steal from me. OK?'

'Yes.'

'OK. Good.' He got up from the table, and leaned so close to me that I couldn't help smelling the sourness of his breath. 'Be here tomorrow morning at six sharp. One minute late, and that's it. Kaput.' He made a sweeping gesture that started at the middle of his stomach, using both hands, one on top of the other and each going in a different direction. 'You get two fifteen minute breaks each day, no lunch break. If you want to eat scraps off the plates, I don't care. Those are the rules. And don't loaf around anymore by these tables. They're for paying customers.'

He watched me while I got up and headed for the exit. He had hired me without even bothering to ask me my name. The decision I'd made to do this kind of work left me with a choking despair in my chest that seemed to grow as I walked back to Jill's apartment. A dishwasher. That was going to be my lot in their world. Even though I had the skill and desire to build houses and do other carpentry, because of the way their world operated I was going to have to spend my days scrubbing pots, working for someone who openly sneered at me.

I heard music coming from Jill's apartment. I stood listening for voices and, after not hearing any, knocked on the door and announced myself. Light footsteps padded toward me from inside the apartment, and then the door was swung open and Jill stood in front of me smiling brightly.

'Charlie, you don't need to knock. You have a key. Just use it to come and go as you please.' Her smile dimmed as she looked at me. 'Is something wrong?'

'No, nothing.' I hadn't realized how low I was feeling until then. I was ashamed to tell Jill about the work I was going to be doing. But the reason I made the decision I did was so that I wouldn't have to lie to her about work, so I steeled myself and told her I was going to be washing dishes each day at a nearby restaurant. 'I still hope to be building homes again, but for now this is what I need to do,' I said.

Jill laughed in her soft, gentle manner, and while I couldn't say it lifted my spirits it did make me feel less morose. She took my hand, and her eyes sparkled as she grinned at me. 'I'm proud of you for finding a job this quickly,' she said. 'And come on, Charlie, we've all had to take shit jobs at one time or another. I've had my share of them. I worked the last two years as a cocktail waitress at a dive club before getting my teacher's assistant position. And hey, it wasn't all bad. The tips were good and it gave me a unique perspective on the human psyche, which should come in handy in my future career as a psychologist. It's all good. You'll find a way to kick ass at this job. I'm positive you'll persevere, and before too long you'll get the kind of job you want, doing carpentry.'

I forced a smile. There wasn't any point in telling her that the maddening rules of her world would prevent me from ever doing that. She sighed, recognizing that my smile wasn't genuine.

'Keep the faith, Charlie. It will happen. I promise.'

She gave my hand a squeeze, at least as much as she was capable of with her small, slender fingers, and led me into her apartment. She stopped, tilting her lovely head slightly to one side. 'Mozart's Piano Concerto Number Twenty-Four. I confess, I'm a bit of a classical music junkie, and this is one of my favorite pieces. I find it so soothing and meditative.'

I knew Jill was talking about the music. I had read about Mozart in one of the clan's books long before the elders chose me to replace Jedidiah, and knew that he composed music during the eighteenth century. At the time I couldn't quite grasp the concept of what music was, although I reckoned it was organizing an assemblage of sounds that was similar to what the birds sang. After I started entering *their* world, early on, while the van's radio was still functional, I used to hear music playing over it that mostly involved voices, usually screeching or yelling or uttering unintelligible words. I found much of this music little more than jangling noise, but at least hearing it allowed me to understand what I had read about and to realize how wrong I had been thinking it might sound like a chorus of birds. This concerto from Mozart was different from that other music. There were no voices disturbing it, and I found the sounds of the instruments clean and pleasing – as well as soothing, as Jill had mentioned. I told Jill that I liked this Mozart music, and she seemed pleased.

It took only six steps to pass through the small hallway and enter the living room. Letting go of my hand, Jill pointed out the carrots, onions, mushrooms, green pepper, and squash piled up on the kitchen counter.

'I was just about to start cutting up vegetables for a stir-fry

I'm making us for dinner. Why don't you relax and enjoy Mozart in the meantime?'

I shook my head. While I wasn't sure there'd be enough room for the two of us to work in her kitchen, I told her that I'd help her chop up the vegetables.

'Certainly not. I'm guessing you walked all over Queens in search of employment. You look beat.'

I didn't tell her that most of my hiking had been in Brooklyn. Nor that, although I took the opportunity to inquire about work at ten construction sites or so, I had had a very different purpose for trekking about that area. But Jill was right, I did feel tired. It was partly because the only sleep I'd had since leaving my clan early on Saturday morning was roughly two hours, when I'd dozed off by the lake, and partly because I found it far more tiring walking among *them* and interacting with *them* than being engaged in solitary labor.

'I'll wash the dishes after dinner,' I insisted. 'After all, it's going to be my new profession.'

'I won't fight you on that,' Jill said, smiling thinly. Her smile soon grew into a wide grin. 'Charlie, I've been sitting on some good news, and I've been trying to decide whether to tell you now or over dinner. How about over dinner?'

'Sure. That would be fine.' I had no idea what kind of news she could have for me, but I didn't pester her about it. Jill left me to start scraping the skin off the carrots, which seemed wasteful, but I kept that to myself. I took a step toward the couch that I had become very familiar with, but had a change of heart and instead turned and headed for the door. I told Jill there was something I needed to do, and that I would be returning soon. She gave me a questioning look, but simply nodded.

I remembered seeing a market not far from Jill's building, and walked quickly to it. I needed to keep some food of my own at Jill's apartment, but I had another purpose in mind too.

I picked out an assortment of fruits, vegetables, nuts, and seeds, some of which I was familiar with and others that I'd be trying for the first time. I was amazed to find a whole section of the market dedicated to vegan food, and chose a number of items from it. I was further amazed to come across milk made entirely of nuts, and selected a carton of that also. I picked out a few other items, including a bar of dark chocolate made with espresso beans, and a bouquet of daisies. (Daisies grew wild around my clan's homestead, but I was aware of many other types of flowers too from a botany manual published in the nineteenth century that was part of my clan's collection.)

The cashier didn't bother to look at me as I brought these items to her to tally. She moved at a slow and uninterested pace, and when I told her that I had wanted to buy wine at the market but couldn't find any, she at first acted as if she didn't hear me and only after I repeated myself did she tell me that they didn't have a license to sell wine. If I were still collecting for the clan, I would've gladly thrown her into a burlap sack.

'Where can I buy wine?' I asked, not bothering to mask my impatience with her.

She finally consented to look at me, and sighed heavily as if I was the one trying her patience. 'There's a liquor store two blocks over, on Main and Sixty-Ninth.'

The tally for my food was more than I was expecting (everything in *their* world cost far more than I expected), but I paid for it without comment. After consulting my map, I carried my bundles out of the market and walked to where, in her extreme exasperation, this woman'd told me I could purchase wine. I knew from firsthand experience that *they* had an abundance of food and goods in their world, but I still found it staggering when I entered the shop and saw row upon row of different wine bottles, and realized that purchasing wine wasn't as simple a matter as I had imagined. The sales clerk, a thin man who had grown a small patch of whiskers only on his chin, recognized my distress and asked if he could be of help.

'I'd like to buy wine.'

'Of course. What type, sir?'

After the rude treatment I'd received from the woman at the market, I wasn't in the mood to be made fun of by any more of *them*. From what I knew of their world, I certainly wasn't someone to be addressed as 'Sir', but I couldn't tell from his demeanor if he was making sport of me. Grudgingly, I gave him the benefit of the doubt and decided that he had me confused with someone he was supposed to address as 'Sir'.

'Something inexpensive, but decent,' I said, remembering how Brittany had described the wine that she had poured me the other day.

'Red, white, rosé?'

I didn't know what he meant by 'rosé'. Could that be a fancy way of saying rose? The wine Brittany had given me was more purple in color than red, but I knew there were roses that were a similar purple. I was trying to work out whether that was what was meant by 'rosé', when sensing my consternation he asked what the wine would be served with and then offered me the choices of meat, poultry, or seafood.

'Vegetables,' I said.

'Let me suggest a Chardonnay then.'

Before I could say anything, he turned down one of the rows and after a quick study of several bottles picked one out. He held it for me to look at since my hands were full with the bundles I was carrying.

'A very nice Chardonnay from Chile. Crisp and clean, with subtle pear and peach aromas. On sale for eighteen dollars, normally twenty-five, making it inexpensive and one of the best bargains we have.'

Again, everything in their world seemed to cost more than I expected, but I grunted, told him I'd take it, and followed him back to the cash register. As he handed me my change, he asked where I was from. Warily, I told him New Hampshire.

'I'm from a small town in Indiana and moved here only a year ago. New York can be so daunting at first, but you'll get used to it.' He offered me a smile. 'If you want to learn more about wines, we have a free tasting every Saturday from four to six. I hope to see you here. My name's Chad.'

I had set my bundles down on the counter in order to pay for the wine, so I felt obliged to take his hand and tell him my name. As I picked up my bundles and left the shop, I felt some confusion over one of *them* befriending me the way this one had – and even more so because for a brief moment I saw him as something other than one of *them*. It made me wonder how many of the ones I'd picked up in the past I might've felt similarly toward if given the chance.

SIXTEEN

Jill was delighted by the wine I'd bought to accompany our meal, and even more so by the bouquet of daisies I gave her. She had already spooned our dinner on to plates, so I immediately removed the foil covering the top of the wine – only to reveal a cork stuck so deep in the neck of the bottle that I couldn't grab any piece of it in order to pull it out. I studied it and decided I wouldn't be able to dig the cork out with a knife. With the right tools, I could saw off the top of the glass bottle without making too much of a mess, but I didn't have access to those tools. I was trying to decide whether I needed to smash the top of the bottle with a hammer when Jill offered me a small tool consisting of a handle and a spiral of metal. After a quick study, I realized that if I were to screw the tool into the cork it would grip the cork and allow me to pull it out. Ingenious! I removed the cork from the bottle quickly enough for it to appear as if I knew what I was doing from the start. If Jill noticed my earlier confusion, she didn't comment about it.

The wine was very different than the type Brittany had given me. The color was a light yellow, as opposed to the darker purple, and the flavor was lighter, less earthy, but still very enjoyable. It also let me forget entirely about the cravings for a short few minutes. Even though the cravings were still little more than a nuisance, it was a relief to have them lessened for any length of time.

Jill and I were still drinking our first glasses of wine and had only had a few bites of our meal, when she grinned at me as if she had a secret she couldn't contain any longer.

'It's about time I tell you the good news,' she said. 'I was calling around today hunting for an apartment for you, and one of the professors in the psychology department needs to sublet a studio apartment for three months. From what he told me it's only four hundred square feet, but it's furnished, and it's under rent control so he can let you have it for five hundred and twenty a month – which is ridiculously cheap for Queens, especially since every month Queens is turning more and more into the next Brooklyn. And best of all, it's only three blocks from here!' Jill's grin grew mischievous as she added, 'The only downside is it won't be available for three weeks, so you'd have to rough it here until then.'

The thought that I'd be staying three more weeks in Jill's apartment was highly pleasing, and the knowledge that I would be able to start courting her afterwards even more so. I remarked that she was right, this was very good news. Jill beamed as she told me that after our meal we would be meeting with this professor at the apartment, and she was positive everything would work out.

Her news and what it would mean for our future raised both our spirits. And just as I enjoyed the wine, I also enjoyed the meal that Jill had prepared. While none of the vegetables she'd used were new to me, I found the sauce and the spices different and very tasty. With the wine loosening my tongue and making me temporarily forget about the cravings, I was more exuberant in my praise for the meal than I might otherwise have been. Jill seemed pleased by this, and I was finding the evening extraordinarily pleasant – maybe the most pleasant I'd ever experienced, especially given how buoyant Jill appeared.

All of this changed when a heavy pounding sounded on Jill's door. Immediately she tensed, her high spirits obliterated. When the pounding continued and a man's voice yelled for her to open the door, the color in her face dropped several shades.

'Just go away, Ethan, I don't want to see you,' she yelled back, although not nearly as loudly as the man had yelled. It was obvious that his presence outside the door had sapped her of much of her strength.

'I'm not going away, Jill. This is fucking ridiculous. For fuck's sake, open the door. Let me apologize so we can move past this bullshit.'

'If you don't go away I'm calling the police!'

'Really?' He let out an ugly, barking type of laugh. 'Go ahead and call them. I don't fucking care. I'm not leaving until we work this out and you quit your goddamn'd martyr act!'

Jill looked like she wanted to cry, which made me want to go out there and rip the windpipe out of her former boyfriend. During the last two days some of *them* had annoyed me to the point where I might have enjoyed the idea of stuffing them into burlap sacks and taking them back for the clan. Even though I'd grown to strongly dislike Patience before she did me the favor of dying from a tooth abscess, I don't think I ever truly experienced hate until that moment. More than anything, I wanted to bolt from my seat and end his life, but the pleading look Jill gave me kept me seated where I was.

'Please,' she whispered to me. 'Don't get into any trouble because of him. He's not worth it. I'll take care of him, but please stay calm and don't let him egg you into doing something we'll both regret.'

I forced myself to nod. I had to. The way she implored me struck deep within, and I knew my future with Jill depended on me not doing what I badly wanted to do.

As slender and slight as Jill was, she seemed to grow even smaller as she left the table to answer the door. It took all my control to stay where I was, but I knew that was what Jill wanted me to do.

She was soon out of sight, but I heard Jill open the door and then say, 'Ethan, there's nothing more for us to talk about. It's over. Please, just leave me alone.'

He laughed at her. 'Overly dramatic, much? Because of you, we had a thing. That's what we do, we have stupid things now and then, almost always because of you. And we work our way past them.'

'Listen to me, Ethan. There's no longer anything for us to work past. Please, just leave.'

From the way he laughed again at Jill, and her pleading with him to stop, I knew he had pushed his way past her and was heading further into the apartment. It took all my strength to stay seated as Jill had asked, especially after hearing the unhappiness in her voice. A smug, mocking tone had entered his voice as he said, 'Sweetheart, what we have is too good to toss away because of something stupid that never would've happened if you hadn't done such a superb job of pressing my buttons—'

I watched as he stepped out of the hallway and into my view. The instant he caught sight of me, he clamped his mouth shut and stared at me, contempt quickly filling his face. He had an even crueler look in his eyes and mouth than when I had seen him at that rest stop in Massachusetts. As I watched him, I became aware once again of the cravings gnawing at me. Jill hurried past him and continued on until she was an arm's length away from me.

'Who's this clown?' he demanded, his eyes dark and beady as he glared his hatred at me.

'He's my guest,' Jill said.

Both puzzled and incensed, his glare seemed to intensify. 'Who the fuck are you?' he demanded of me.

If I hadn't had two glasses of wine, I probably wouldn't have said what I did, but the wine had loosened my tongue. I told him, 'I'm the one who rescued Jill after you so chivalrously abandoned her on the Massachusetts Turnpike. And I'm the one who's going to do whatever I can to win her heart.'

His jaw dropped open. Uncertainty clouded his eyes as he goggled at me, not quite sure at first what to make of what I'd said. Then his eyes hardened again, and he turned his glare back to Jill.

'Are you out of your fucking mind?' he said, his voice strained and angry. 'You take a ride from some dumb goober? How do you know he's not a serial killer, for fuck's sake? And what do you mean, this goober's your guest? He's staying here? Is that what you're saying?'

Jill looked too stricken to say anything, and her discomfort only acted to incite him. The muscles surrounding his mouth tightened into something mean and spiteful. It looked as if he was going to spit a mouthful of saliva on to the floor, but the words he spat out instead were much fouler.

'So this goober is staying here and you're fucking him, aren't you? You stupid, stupid whore, you're already spreading your legs for this ugly goober.'

It had been a struggle to keep my true self hidden while watching him, and even more so while listening to him, but I knew I had to. Not because I cared what he saw, but because I couldn't afford to let Jill see me like that. But at that moment my pure hate for this person boiled through me so quickly that a redness glazed my vision. I was barely aware of leaving my chair and striding toward him. From the look that came over his face, I must've shown my true self, though fortunately I did this only after passing Jill and facing away from her, so she didn't see that aspect of me. The realization of what I had almost shown her gave me just enough self-control to stop myself from doing to him what my instincts were driving me to do, and instead I came to a halt one foot from him.

'We've had enough of you,' I forced out, my voice sounding very odd and foreign to my ears. 'Apologize to Jill and leave now.'

It was likely that I had shown only a flash of my true self to him, and maybe he'd convinced himself he didn't actually see what he thought he saw. That could've been why he stood his ground instead of stumbling backwards, like he clearly wanted to.

'Do you think I'm going to let some dumb hick tell me what to do?' he said with a manufactured bravado that was betrayed by the glimpse of fear I caught in his eyes. What he did next was just plain dumb. He tried poking me in the chest with his right forefinger. I had little trouble grabbing it before it touched me, and if I hadn't regained my self-control I might've ripped his finger from his hand or at the very least broken it into pieces. Instead, I simply twisted it enough to send him to his knees, aware that I didn't want Jill to think me a savage from my actions.

'You can leave now in one piece or in several pieces,' I told him, my voice low and as icy as death. 'Do you understand me?'

I twisted his finger until tears flooded his eyes and he nodded his assent. I let go of him, and he grabbed at his barely injured finger. He stumbled to his feet and skulked away to the door. Before he reached it, he promised Jill that he was through with her and she could fuck all the dumb imbeciles she wanted to, for all he cared. Once the door closed behind him, I turned to Jill dreading what I might see because I knew she had wanted me to stay seated throughout the whole sorry episode and, although I didn't realize it while it was happening, I also knew she had tried to hold me back from approaching her former boyfriend. What I saw left my heart heavy. She looked so utterly crestfallen, almost as if she might crumble apart in front of my eyes.

'I'm so sorry,' she said.

This confused me. I shook my head slowly. 'You have nothing to be sorry about,' I said.

Jill bit her lip, struggling to keep her tears at bay. Her voice was a fragile thing as she told me how awful she felt for having subjected me to Ethan's behavior. 'You must think so little of me for having ever been involved with someone like that,' she said. 'I ignored telltale signs of his abusive personality, but he kept himself better in check, at least early on. This evening he reached a whole new level, probably out of frustration for not being able to control me anymore. I am so sorry you had to see that.'

I was shaking my head more as I stepped toward her. 'You did nothing wrong. I can't blame someone for being sprayed by a bad-tempered skunk. I also meant what I said about doing whatever I can to win your heart, at least as long as you allow me to. And I promise you, if I'm ever fortunate enough to succeed, I will do whatever I need to until my last breath so that I may keep your heart.'

As I stepped toward Jill she stepped toward me, and we met in an embrace. For a long moment we stood like that, her head burrowed against my chest, her body warm and small against mine. Then she was looking up at me and pulling me down so her lips could press against mine. As we kissed, my head became dizzy and my heart pounded wildly in my chest. I understood fully then the romantic passion that I had read about. The feelings I experienced were completely unknown to me, and utterly unlike anything I'd ever felt toward Patience, even when we were engaged in marital relations. When we separated from the kiss, Jill's eyes were half-lidded and filled with the same desire that was overwhelming me. I badly wanted to continue kissing her, but even though I didn't understand why it was important we stop after that one kiss, I told her we needed to wait before we kissed again. Much later that night when I was alone, I realized why it was so important. Her former boyfriend's visit had wrecked her emotionally, so if we had done anything further I'd always have felt I took advantage. Even more important, I had promised her I wouldn't be courting her until I moved into my own home. So far we had held hands and sat close to each other on her couch, and we had allowed ourselves that one kiss. For me to prove to her that I could be trusted to honor my word, that was all I could allow for now.

But it was damned difficult willing myself to end our embrace. Up until that point in my life it was the most difficult thing I'd ever done, even more so than deciding to betray my clan.

SEVENTEEN

'Would you be throwing parties here?'

The question asked by Dr Harris (which was how Jill addressed the psychology professor) made me smile. When Jill and I arrived at the one-room apartment, he had us sit on something he called a love seat – a smallish couch that had been upholstered with a tanned and softened cow hide dyed the color of milk – while he sat on a similarly upholstered armchair, with his right leg crossed casually over his left knee. He explained that he was renting the apartment for his son, who had plans to spend three months in another part of the world (at the time he told us the country, but I have since forgotten it, which is understandable given everything that followed), and he was looking for a conscientious person to rent the apartment to during his son's absence. After that, he proceeded to ask me a slew of questions in order to gauge whether I could be that conscientious person. While he asked these questions, he smiled pleasantly, but his eyes were nearly unblinking and he gazed at me similarly to how someone might study an insect under a piece of glass. Fortunately, by omitting certain facts, I was able to answer all of them truthfully, because I had little doubt that he would've sniffed out any lie I told him.

'No, sir,' I said. (I was familiar enough with their world to know it would best for me to address him as 'Sir'.) 'I will be working as hard as I can and for as many hours as I can during those three months while your son is away. I will have little time, and even less inclination, to host any social events. The only guest that I can foresee having is Jill, and that would only be for a quiet dinner. If you allow me stay in your son's apartment, I can pledge to you that there will be no parties here, and I will keep his home clean, and you will find it in better shape when your son returns than it is now.'

He raised an eyebrow at my last claim.

'For starters, several of the kitchen-cabinet doors have gotten off-kilter and need to be adjusted,' I said, answering his unasked question. 'I will also fix the leaky faucet in the bathroom and the slow drain in the kitchen sink, the loose closet door in the entry hall, and any other problem that I discover.'

He was satisfied with my answer, and the thin smile that now twisted his lips looked more genuine than the pleasant one he'd been displaying earlier.

'You have a certain old-world way about you,' he remarked. 'Are you a first generation American?'

I shook my head. 'My kin's been here for a long time.'

He made a 'Hmm . . .' noise, then commented that Husk was an unusual name. 'Is it Anglo-Saxon in origin? Are your people from Britain originally?'

'I couldn't say. I've never been able to get a direct answer about that.'

He nodded in such a way as to indicate that these last questions were only to satisfy his curiosity. 'In any case, Jill has certainly vouched for you,' he said. His lips twisted into a more amused smile and he added, 'And I certainly pride myself on being a good judge of character. Mr Husk, I believe I have found my subletter. If you can pay me the first month's rent now, we can consider our deal sealed.' He raised a questioning eyebrow at Jill. 'You did tell Mr Husk what the rent would be?'

'Yes, sir, she did,' I answered for her. I counted out $520 from my wallet, leaving it much thinner, and handed the money to the psychology professor.

'Cash,' he said, winking. 'My favorite kind of payment. Yes, I do believe I found the right subletter. Jill, thank you for introducing me to such a responsible young man.'

We talked a bit more, to arrange the time and date for when I would move into the apartment, and when I would pay the subsequent months' rents. After that we exchanged handshakes, and Jill and I departed. As we walked back to her apartment, her hand found mine and soon her slender fingers were interlaced between my thick ones, and her body stayed close to mine. Excitedly, she extolled the virtues of the apartment where I'd be living. It was on a quiet street with a vegan restaurant only a block away; the building was well maintained; and the apartment, while small, was nicely furnished and had been kept up, even if some of the kitchen cabinets were askew, the faucet in the bathroom leaked, and there were the other small problems I'd mentioned. She had other points to make too, and I was pleased that her high spirits seemed to have been restored. Whatever chaos and disagreeableness her 'jerk' (to quote Jill) of an ex-boyfriend had brought, they were gone and seemingly forgotten, and there was once again only a comfortable feeling between us. Starting tomorrow, I might have to work washing dishes, but that was something I'd gladly do as long as I could court Jill in only three weeks' time.

My mood, though, dampened (although not enough for Jill to notice) as I drifted into worrying about the cravings, because if I didn't find a way to hold them at bay none of this would matter. But I gritted my teeth and decided I couldn't let myself be burdened by these thoughts now. I would search the East Flatbush area of Brooklyn until I found the thick-jawed man who I was convinced had to be one of my kind.

When we returned to Jill's apartment, she suggested we watch another of her favorite movies, which she wanted to share with me, and I told her, truthfully, that anything she wanted to do was fine with me. This movie was called *Don't Look Now*, and it was a very different type of movie from the other one we had watched. First, it was in color – not black, white, and shades of gray – and secondly, it wasn't a romantic story but a sad and tragic one. Instead of lying curled up on the sofa with her head resting on my leg, this time Jill sat next to me while we held hands, our fingers interlaced.

Early on, the movie showed something that surprised and, in a way, shocked me. The actor and actress who played the husband and wife were naked together on the bed, engaged in marital relations. It wasn't their nakedness that shocked me. The slaughtering rituals require *them* to be stripped of their clothes, so I'd seen many of *them* naked. What shocked me was the manner in which they engaged in relations. It was completely different and foreign to the way Patience and I had performed our marital responsibilities. Given that Jill reacted to that scene in the movie as if what the husband and wife were doing was completely normal, I realized that even in this respect the ways of *their* world were very different from those of my kind.

A shiver ran through me as I realized how disastrous it could've been if I hadn't stopped after our kiss. Jill probably would've thought me a freakish thing if I had tried to engage with her the way I had with Prudence, which was the only way I had known or imagined before this movie played out in front of me.

Jill noticed that I'd shivered, and pressed a button that caused the movie to stop playing. She smiled at me apologetically. 'Wow, that was stupid of me picking this movie. I mean I love it, and it's one of my favorites, but I know you're not used to TV or movies and I should've warned you about the content. Charlie, I'm so sorry if the movie made you uncomfortable.'

'That's not why I shivered,' I said. 'It was the thought of losing a child, as this couple did, that caused me to react that way. If anything, I find the story gripping. I'd like to watch more of it.'

I'd lied to her again. But as much as I hated piling any more lies on top of the ones I'd already told her, I had little choice. I certainly couldn't tell her the reason I reacted the way I did. Moreover, I badly wanted her to continue playing the movie so I could understand how in their world a man and woman engage in relations.

Jill gave me a funny look, as if she wasn't sure she believed me. Perhaps she thought I was humoring her. But she restarted the movie, though after that scene ended there weren't any more of that kind, so there wasn't any risk that I'd shiver further, if I was so inclined to do so. At the end of the movie, we talked about it for several minutes and I was able to tell Jill, without lying, that I'd found the story gripping and affecting. Jill told me that the movie always left her too emotionally distraught to sleep, and asked if I'd mind if we watched the news. I told her that that would be fine, although secretly I dreaded what they might show.

The first story they mentioned was the murder of the well-fed orange-haired man. I concentrated, so I would appear relaxed and not reveal to Jill any of the worry I felt in case they showed a photograph with me in it. My worry turned out to be unnecessary as they only showed the photograph and drawing of the round-faced bearded man that I'd seen in the newspaper. The woman on the television who talked about the story made it sound as if there wasn't any question that this man committed the murder, and asked for anyone who could identify him to call the police.

As luck would have it, the very next item on the news program was regarding the police officer I throttled. The woman who presented it made a point of talking about the extreme savagery of the murder, and how the police officer's throat had been crushed almost as if by a wild animal rather than a man. The part I was most anxious to hear was the statement that there were no witnesses and the police were imploring anyone with knowledge of the crime to come forward. As the story unfolded, Jill quit holding my hand and her body seemed to shrink inward as if she were trying to avoid any physical contact with me. I don't think this was because she suspected me of being the one to murder the officer, but because the story genuinely upset her. At its conclusion, Jill murmured about how awful it was.

'That poor man,' she said. 'Kissena Lake is only two miles from here.'

I didn't comment about the 'poor man'. If he hadn't felt obliged to bully a sleeping man who was minding his own business, he'd be alive now. What was that saying I'd read in one of my books? *Let sleeping dogs lie . . .* There's a good amount of truth to that. And you should definitely let a sleeping wolf lie, as that police officer discovered. Besides, what choice did I have, with him trying to aim his gun at me so he could shoot me dead? Of course, I couldn't fault him for reacting the way he did once he saw me fully unmasked. Even though *they* always had us greatly outnumbered, it wasn't until a thousand years ago that the imbalance became so massive that we had little choice but to disappear into the wilderness. Before then we used to live out in the open and hunt them with impunity, and it must be that ancestral memories of that time still lurk in their brains and cause the fight or flight panic I saw in that officer and others who'd caught a glimpse of my true self.

Jill seemed shaken by the story. She knew I had been out roaming the streets last night and I wanted to make sure she didn't have any suspicions that I could've been the police officer's killer, so I removed the map of New York from the back pocket of my pants, unfolded it, and asked Jill where Kissena Lake was. Her brow furrowed as she studied the map before pointing out the small lake.

'So it's north of here,' I said, frowning. 'Last night I walked west to a different lake and fell asleep by it.'

I pointed out a body of water on the map called Lake Meadow. I took no satisfaction in lying to Jill about this, but felt it necessary to dispel any thoughts she might've had that I could've been the one who savagely killed the police officer. At least I refrained from commenting about how fortunate it was that I'd walked to the lake I did, or otherwise might've been the one murdered.

Jill pressed a button to turn off the television. She looked worn out as she said, 'Whoever killed that officer is a pure psychopath. That's obvious given the extreme brutality of this killing. Until they catch him, please don't go walking late at night. It's not safe to. Will you promise me that, Charlie?'

I had little choice but to do as asked, so I promised I wouldn't walk around late at night. At least it made her smile, even if it was only a bleak one. She got off the couch, leaned forward, and kissed me on the cheek.

'I've gotten really tired all of a sudden,' she said, her slight smile still present. 'It must be the wine. I'm going to bed. Your job starts at six? So I probably won't see you until tomorrow evening. Goodnight, Charlie.' She hesitated before adding, 'And please, if you have trouble sleeping, tell me and I'll give you one of my pills. Don't go outside walking around. Whoever this psychopath is, he's not done killing yet.'

I watched as Jill disappeared into her bedroom, amazed at how perceptive she was. Because I had been planning on going out later that night. Yesterday I had looked through the small address book she kept by her phone, and found an address for her ex-boyfriend, Ethan. He lived in a neighborhood of Queens called Fresh Meadow, and earlier I had located his address on my map. After the way he brutalized Jill this evening, I'd planned to go to his home later on and end his miserable life. Now I could no longer do that. Even if Jill didn't realize that I'd left her apartment, she would wonder whether I was the one who killed him – and maybe she'd even start wondering whether I had killed the police officer at that small lake. I decided that I couldn't kill any more of *them*, especially people Jill knew, and leave their bodies around for the police to find. I'd read enough books to know that if I did, the police might stumble upon me as the killer.

I was going to keep my promise to Jill that night. She had closed her bedroom door, but I didn't want light from this room to seep in and disturb her, so I turned off the lights, which left the room in a murky grayness. I picked up *Frankenstein* from where I'd left it, as I still had a few pages to read. The grayness wasn't dark enough to keep me from reading, and I soon finished the novel, disappointed that the monster didn't have a happier outcome. I then picked out another of Jill's books to read.

EIGHTEEN

After an hour of reading, I started to feel drowsy, and I put the book down to rest my eyes. Surprisingly, I fell asleep. Possibly I was getting more used to my new conditions than I'd realized, such as the city noises, the hazy grayness of their nights, and the softness of Jill's couch. But I was sure other factors had come into play, including all the walking I'd done among *them* the past two days and the wine I'd drunk that evening with Jill.

From what I'd been able to gather over the years, nightmares were unusual for the members of my clan. At least, whenever I'd asked my siblings or cousins if they'd ever experienced disturbing dreams they'd look at me as if they couldn't understand what I was asking. Once, I even worked up the courage to ask an elder the same question, and he looked at me as if I were an imbecile and told me such things were impossible. Of course, I knew that wasn't true. Even if I decided that the books I'd read in which characters suffered from nightmares were fanciful tales with no basis in real life, I would've known that what the elder told me wasn't true, since I'd been having nightmares from a young age, maybe even starting when I was ten. I didn't have these every night. Most nights I didn't remember my dreams, and even when I had a nightmare it would only leave a vague impression on me and I'd never be able to remember much about it, though I'd wake up perspiring heavily, with my heart pounding and a dread filling me, so I was left with no doubt that I'd had one.

Not only did I have a nightmare last night. I could remember every detail about it. And I was sure I'd never had one before that left me so sickened and horrified.

In this nightmare, I was in my parent's shack back at the clan's homestead. I was groveling on my knees in front of my pa, sobbing uncontrollably as I pleaded with him. In my misery, my words didn't make any sense and sounded more like the

noises a wounded animal might make. During all this my pa
didn't say a single word, and instead just gave me a look as
if I was absolutely worthless. When I reached for his hand so
I could further implore him, he stepped forward and struck
me a hard blow above my ear, in the same way that I had
struck some of *them* I'd picked up so I could knock them
unconscious. His blow didn't knock me out, but instead drove
me to the dirt floor, so that I was lying on my face.

'You're either one of us or one of *them*,' my pa said to me,
his voice filled with disgust.

Dreams don't always move in ways that make sense, and
that's what happened with this one, because the next thing I
knew I was with the rest of the clan in the sacred hall for the
slaughtering rituals. At first I couldn't see which one of *them*
was being prepared for slaughter, as several of the clan
members were in front of this person, tying a rope around his
wrists and hoisting him up so that his feet dangled just enough
to leave his toes barely touching the floor. But as these clan
members moved away, they revealed that it wasn't a *him* that
they had tied up, but a slight girl with muddy brown hair
and an awful gray pallor. As my eyes focused better, I realized
that her hair wasn't really brown; it was dirt that had colored
her hair that shade. To my horror, I was able to see through
the extreme terror disguising her and realized it was Jill who
had been hung up for slaughtering. In my cowardice, I stood
there both unable and unwilling to rescue her.

The slaughtering ritual demands that one of the elders strike
the silencing blow, but when the elder called me forward and
handed me the truncheon, I took it from him and struck Jill
across the jaw with it as the ritual required. The elder then
took the truncheon from me and handed me the slicing knife,
and I pulled open her shattered jaw, took hold of her tongue,
and sliced it off as the ritual demanded.

I woke up then, my skin ice cold, a nausea twisting my
stomach. At first I was confused as to where I was, thinking
that I was still at the slaughtering ritual and that I had actually
done what I'd dreamed about. I don't think it's possible to
feel worse than I did during those moments before I collected
my wits and realized that I was only dreaming. Before that

happened, all I wanted to do was use the slicing knife to cut my own throat and end my agony. Then I recognized Jill's apartment and understood that it had only been a nightmare.

I know that dreams aren't prophecies, and long ago realized that the purpose of a nightmare was to make me confront a fear I'd been ignoring. As the thudding inside my chest slowed and I was able to think more clearly, I understood the fear that I'd been hiding from. This awful nightmare literally made no sense. It would be impossible for my clan to find me. They weren't about to kidnap Jill and me, and I certainly wasn't ever going to take her back to them. They posed no risk to us. But what this nightmare was trying to warn me about was that if my cravings got bad enough, I might harm Jill without being able to control myself. I resolved that that would not happen. If I was unable to find a way to keep the cravings at bay, I would flee far enough away from Jill for her to be safe from me, no matter what murderous madness the cravings drove me to. I was not ever going to let any harm come to her.

Even after I understood all that, ghostly images from the dream continued to haunt me. I made my way over to Jill's kitchen so I could read the clock embedded in the oven's display. Three thirty-eight. I wasn't about to close my eyes again to try for more sleep and risk seeing those terrible images. I wanted to go outside and roam the neighborhood, feel the night's air on my face even if it were only the stale city air. But I was determined to keep my promise to Jill, so I went back to the couch and tried to read more of the book I had chosen, though I found it exceedingly difficult to concentrate on the words.

In my clan, and I suppose all the other clans, our women cook our food. The most I'd ever used a kitchen for was to reheat one of their stews, or for slathering honey or jelly, or both, on a biscuit they'd baked. But I figured if I could teach myself how to fix the vans and use the power tools I'd brought to the clan to build homes with indoor plumbing, I could also figure out how to cook something. One of the items that I had selected from the market was a package containing the wherewithal for making vegan pancakes, and after reading the instructions I decided that this morning I would make breakfast for Jill and myself.

The cooking went easily. I found the bowl and skillet that I needed, and all that was required was to empty the pancake mix into the bowl, add some of the almond milk that I had bought, stir the mixture, and then spoon lumps of it on to the skillet. On my own initiative, I added blueberries to the mix, which seemed to work out nicely, and before long I had a plate piled thick with pancakes.

I was going to keep Jill's pancakes warm in the oven and leave her a note saying that they were waiting for her, since I didn't expect her to be up early enough to eat with me and certainly wasn't going to wake her, but she wandered out of her bedroom wrapped in her flannel robe. Her face looked as craggy as the other time I'd seen her after waking, and more than beautiful enough to bring a small lump to my throat. I said I was sorry if I'd made any noise that woke her, and explained how I hadn't expected her to be up at this hour. I asked if she'd like to join me, or if I should leave her plate warming in the oven.

'This is so unbelievably sweet of you,' she said, her eyes moistening with tears as she realized that I had cooked food for both of us. 'Sometimes I have to keep reminding myself how completely different you are from Ethan and others I've dated. And no, you didn't make any noise. I'm not sure why I woke up this early. And yes, Charlie, I would love to have breakfast with you.'

I retrieved her plate from the oven and placed it on the table opposite my own plate. Between us in a glass jar were the daisies I'd bought Jill the night before. Also on the table was a bottle of maple syrup that I'd bought. We didn't have any maple trees near the area of wilderness where my clan lived, but we did have pine trees and we tapped them for their sap and made a syrup out of it. I figured the maple syrup would be similar, but it was very much different. At first I was put off by it, but as I tasted more of it I grew to appreciate it almost as much as the pine syrup.

After her first bite, Jill commented on how good she thought the pancakes were. 'I never would've imagined that vegan pancakes could be this tasty and fluffy. And adding blueberries was a really nice touch.'

I wasn't sure whether it was her words or the way she smiled at me that made me blush, but I felt my cheeks heating up. I grunted something about being glad she was enjoying them, while in my embarrassment I tried to hide my blushing from her. This made her smile in a way that made me blush even more. I could even feel a burning in my ears.

I finished my pancakes first, and waited for Jill to finish hers so I could wash the dishes before leaving. I had already scrubbed and dried the skillet, bowl, and other utensils that I'd used in preparing the pancakes. Once Jill was done, I got up and took our plates and forks to the sink. She told me I could leave them there and she'd wash them later. I shook my head, and commenced to clean them.

'Charlie, I lied before,' she said. 'I know why I woke up so early. I felt awful about how weird I acted last night, and I wanted to see you before you left this morning.'

She had gotten up from the table, and I could feel that she was standing close by. I turned to face her, and could see that her eyes had again moistened with tears.

'I don't know. I think I was just creeped out after Ethan's bizarre performance and then hearing about that awful murder only two miles away. But I'm sorry if I acted weird.'

'You didn't act in any way that was wrong,' I said.

She reached up and took hold of me by my neck and lowered my head so that she could kiss me passionately on the mouth. After she broke off, I said, with my voice little more than a pant, 'We shouldn't do that again until I start courting you. It is too difficult after a kiss. I don't know if I'm strong enough to stop if you kiss me like that again.'

She smiled at me in a wicked way. 'Too late, Charlie. That boat has sailed. We're going to keep kissing, maybe several times a day – though it's not easy for me to stop either. But OK, we will keep it at just kissing, at least until you move into your sublet apartment.'

NINETEEN

I left Jill's apartment early enough to have time to stop at a nearby market for a cup of coffee before starting my job as a dishwasher. I was also curious to read the day's newspaper and see if it was reporting anything new about the two of *them* I'd killed, but that would have to wait until later.

When I arrived at the restaurant I was surprised to see how crowded it was. All of the counter space was taken and most of the tables were occupied. While six o'clock wasn't early for me, I thought it would be for *them*, but I guess they're out at all hours in this city.

Since there was no one standing behind the cash register and I couldn't see the short, stocky man with a big head named Chris who'd hired me, I stopped one of the two waitresses as she hurried from a table and told her I was supposed to start working there that day.

'Yeah, OK,' she said, giving me a quick impatient look. 'Eddie's waiting for you in the kitchen. Be a hon, and drop this off on the way.'

She tore a slip of paper out of a pad and handed it to me, and pointed with her eyes to where she wanted me to leave it. Before I could tell her I'd gladly do her the favor, she hurried off to grab a coffee pot. I ignored her rudeness and, having left the paper on the counter, where she'd indicated, continued on into the kitchen.

The smell of grease and burnt animal flesh was far more pungent inside the kitchen than it had been in the front part of the restaurant, so much so that I found myself breathing in through my mouth to avoid it. A heavy man with a rag wrapped around his bald head was standing by a large grill cooking food, while a much smaller man stood by a sink spraying water on a plate. I decided he had to be the Eddie who was waiting for me. When I approached him, he barely looked at me before telling me I was late.

That wasn't true. When I walked into the restaurant, a clock on the wall showed that I was five minutes early, and I told him that.

'You going to fucken' argue with me? It's going to take me fifteen minutes to train you, so you should've been here fifteen minutes ago. So don't mouth off to me.'

I felt my eyes glaze as I looked at him. He was short and scrawny, and another of *them* I would've liked to stuff in a burlap sack, even if there might not have been enough meat on him to justify the effort. Nobody there knew my name or where I was staying. As his insult burned like acid inside me, I considered killing him, but if I did that the police would be after me and they'd probably find me, given that Chris and the waitress I spoke with would be able to describe me fully. If I only beat him into a bloody mess instead, nobody would probably care. Though if I did that, I'd lose my lowly dishwasher work, which I needed so I could pay for the apartment – and given the way I felt after Jill kissed me this morning, I desperately wanted to move into that apartment so I could start courting her. As galling as it was having one of *them* treat me with disdain, I decided that retribution for their insults wasn't nearly as important as being able to court Jill.

'I'll arrive twenty minutes early tomorrow to make up for it,' I said.

He turned off the water in the sink and gave me another look, this one not as sour. 'You're OK,' he said, nodding. 'What's your name?'

'Charlie Husk.'

'Eduardo.' He edged closer to me and, with his voice lowered, said, 'The dumb fucks here think it's a joke to call me Eddie.' He walked past me and signaled me to follow him.

'This is where you hang your apron when you leave,' he said pointing to a hook that had an apron dangling from it. 'If you wear a coat, you hang it on that hook while you're working. Put the apron on.'

I did as he asked, and he walked me over to where there were two plastic trays on a stand. One of them was half filled with dirty plates, glasses, and eating utensils. The other was empty.

'The waitresses leave the plates and shit in these trays,' Eduardo said. 'They fill one up before throwing the shit in the other. Whenever you run out of dishes to clean, you come here and pick up the tray that's got shit in it, and bring it over to the sink. No good if you let both trays fill up. One of the girls will bitch to Chris if you let that happen, and you'll be out on your ass. Always rinse the tray out before you return it. Now pick up the one that's full.'

I picked it up and brought it over to the sink, with Eddie tagging behind me. 'We got two machines. One on the right needs to be emptied, one on the left needs filling up,' he said. 'Dishwashing ain't no rocket science All you do is rinse everything off before you put it in the machine. The scraps that can go down the disposal, you put down the disposal. Bones and shit that's too big, you throw into one of those trash cans. And when the trash cans get filled, you take them out back and empty them into the dumpster. Always close the dumpster afterwards, or cops can give us a fine. And if that happens, Chris will fire your ass. You go empty that machine. I'll tell you where to put the shit.'

I did as he asked, and he pointed out where I needed to store the plates, glasses, coffee mugs, and utensils. Once I'd done that, he watched with his arms crossed as I rinsed off the dirty dishes from the tray and finished loading the other machine. After that, he told me how to load soap into the machine and how to start it.

'I saved those pots and pans over there for you to scrub,' he said, nodding to a large pile of dirty pots. 'When things slow down, you get to them. Cook will add more to the pile. Before your shift ends, empty the garbage cans and scrub them clean using the hose out back. If they ask you to clean a restroom or some other mess, don't argue, just do it. Cleaning supplies are in that closet. That's it.' He smirked and added, 'Congratulations. You're ready to be a dishwasher here.'

While I was loading one of the machines, both waitresses had dumped dirty dishes into the other tray. The redheaded one who had sent me to talk to Eddie, entered the kitchen again to dump off more dishes. Eduardo watched her as she left. He winked at me.

'You see that nasty look she gave us? That's because the tray over there is getting filled. You better return this empty one, and grab that one for emptying. It won't be slowing down till nine thirty, maybe ten, so you'll be kept hopping till then.' He gave me a reflective look. 'You serious about coming in twenty minutes early tomorrow?'

'I said I would.'

'You're OK then.' He smiled at me, showing off several missing teeth. (My clan has strong teeth and my kin seldom lose any, which made the tooth abscess Patience suffered a surprise, although I figured later that the Webley clan isn't blessed in that way like my clan is.) 'Let me give you a tip. Get rubber shoes like I'm wearing. Those work boots you have on are going to be soaked by ten this morning, and in a week they'll be ruined. I'll get you a couple of plastic bags from up front, so you can put them over your boots till you get better footwear.' He wiggled a finger for me to lean closer to him. 'Those girls might look sweet, but they're fucken' piranhas. If they see you doing anything wrong, they'll bitch about it to Chris. Mr Cook over there is OK. He keeps to himself. But the one who takes over from him you got to be careful with. I don't trust him one bit.'

'The cook's name is Mr Cook?'

'No. I don't know what his fucken' name is. But don't worry about him. It's the other one you got to worry about. That one's a sneaky bastard.'

As promised, Eduardo brought the back plastic bags for my boots. Then he left me to my dishwashing. He was right about me being kept busy. My morning became a steady stream of rinsing plates, loading the machines, unloading them, and scrubbing the pots and pans waiting for me whenever I could fit them in. At times the cook would add more pots and pans to my pile, but he never said a word to me.

I didn't mind the constant work, even though it was washing dishes. It kept my mind focused on simple tasks, and kept me from thinking too much about the cravings. By this time the cravings had worked deeper into my jaw and into my skull and sinuses, making me feel like I was suffering from a dull, constant headache. At times, when I forgot to breathe in only through my mouth, the smell of the grease and cooked animal flesh that assaulted my nose made the cravings worse, and several times I winced because of it.

Around ten o'clock the work slowed, as Eduardo said it would. Also around then, the cook left and the one Eduardo warned me about took his place. This new cook was black-skinned, and he was as heavy and bald as the other one. He too wore a rag tied around his head.

With the work slowing down, it gave me a chance to finish scrubbing the pots and pans that had piled up and also to empty the garbage cans, which by this time were close to overflowing. At times, while I was working at the sink and had my back turned to him, I'd feel the new cook staring at me, and a quick glance over my shoulder showed that I was right. Whenever I caught him like that, he immediately looked away and acted as if he hadn't been doing anything, though he was. And all those times I caught him, he was wearing a thick scowl on his face. I didn't like the idea of one of *them* sneaking angry looks at me that way, but after thinking about it I decided it would be best not to say anything to him. As I've already mentioned, I wasn't going to do anything that would risk delaying me being able to court Jill. If this cook's behavior bothered me enough, I could always follow him later, after he left the restaurant, and make sure he understood where he was on the food chain.

It wasn't until nearly eleven o'clock that I saw Chris for the first time that day. He stood with his hands on his hips, glaring at me as if he resented the fact that I was working for him. Otherwise, he didn't acknowledge me, which I preferred, since it gave me an excuse not to acknowledge him in return.

'Both restroom floors need mopping,' he said after a minute of his silent glaring. 'Scrub the toilets also. If you haven't had your first fifteen-minute break yet, take it before eleven thirty or you'll lose it. And don't go out there with those bags on your feet.'

Just as I didn't like the way that cook looked at me, I also didn't like being bossed around in such a condescending manner by one of *them*. But what I discovered that morning was that I much preferred work – any kind, even washing dishes and scrubbing pots – to not having work. Without uttering a complaint, I removed the plastic bags from my boots (Eduardo had been right about them, I needed them to keep my boots from getting drenched) and got the mop and other cleaning supplies from the closet and cleaned the bathrooms as directed.

The rest of the day went pretty much the same. I stopped glancing back every time I felt that cook glaring angrily at me, but I knew he was doing it. I also decided it didn't matter, and mostly ignored it. Around eleven thirty, work picked up again and didn't slow down until two thirty. This gave me a chance to finish the pots and pans that had piled up, and empty and clean the trash cans. At four o'clock I untied my apron and left it on the hook where I'd found it. As I left the restaurant, Chris glanced at his watch and then gave me a look I knew all too well from the elders – the type of look that meant he was trying to think of something to complain about but couldn't. I left the restaurant before he was able to come up with something.

The smell of grease and cooked animal flesh stayed with me once I was outside. It must've gotten on my skin and into my hair. I bunched up my shirt and sniffed it. Even though I'd worn an apron, the smell had saturated my shirt, and probably my pants too. Jill had mentioned yesterday that I needed to buy more clothing, and I could fully see the need for it now. Given how important it was for me to find the thick-jawed man I spotted in Brooklyn, I was going to have to live with that smell on me for now, and just keep breathing in through my mouth to avoid it.

I stopped off at a market and bought a newspaper and several pieces of fruit and a Vidalia onion, which the clerk told me was sweeter and tastier than other types of onion. I sat for a spell on the sidewalk so I could peel the onion, then I ate it and the fruit as I walked to the nearest subway station.

Given how long it had taken to travel to East Flatbush, I wasn't going to have much time for my searching since I had arranged to meet Jill at seven that evening, but whatever I could fit in I would. Knowing how much more intensely I was feeling the cravings, I had to find that thick-jawed man soon.

I read through the newspaper as I waited for the subway car and while I rode on it, and found stories about both men I had killed, although they added nothing new to what I had seen on the television news last night. There appeared to be a lot of outrage over the killing of the police officer, but from what I could gather no witnesses had yet come forward and the police were unable to offer any reason for the killing. As far as the well-fed orange-haired man was concerned, the police were still trying to identify the round-faced bearded man in the photograph, and it sounded as if they were convinced this wrongly accused man was the killer. They didn't show any other photographs, and I felt a momentary anxiety that a photo might still surface with me in it. Not that I was worried anymore about the possibility that that girl might have witnessed me striking the well-fed man, or that the police might start believing I was the killer. But I was worried that Jill might see the photograph and I would have to explain why I was in it.

It took me longer than it did yesterday to get to the Kingston Avenue subway station, which left me only an hour for my searching if I was going to get back to Jill on time. I visited more streets and marked them off on my map, but had no better luck than I previously had. However, I did find a store that sold rubber shoes and bought a pair. And I also found something called a thrift shop that offered used clothing. I bought three more shirts, two more pairs of pants, and three pairs of wool socks, and for once the cost was less than I expected.

TWENTY

For the next two days I fell into a routine, which began with preparing a meal for myself and Jill before leaving for work. Other than a short exchange of greetings with Eduardo, who'd seemed genuinely surprised when I showed up twenty minutes early as promised, I'd do my work quietly until four o'clock without speaking to anyone other than Chris, who barked orders at me a few times each day, and afterwards I'd search the East Flatbush neighborhood without any luck.

When I made the early morning meal for Jill and myself, I didn't expect her to join me. I knew it was early for her and planned to simply have her meal waiting for her. But she insisted on joining me, saying that it gave her a chance to see me since she now had less available time due to getting busier with school and work. Each morning she kissed me passionately before we parted, which made me even more determined to find the thick-jawed man who I was convinced could tell me the secret of keeping the cravings at bay.

Wednesday night Jill had school and work commitments until nine-thirty, which gave me more time to search, fruitlessly, for my quarry. When Jill and I met that night, we walked around her neighborhood together, her hand quickly slipping into mine. Later, when we returned to her apartment, she played more of her favorite Mozart music, and leaned against me on the couch while she read one of her psychology books and I engaged myself with one of her novels. It was soothing feeling her body next to mine, and feeling her soft, rhythmic breathing. The cravings were getting worse each day, but when I was with Jill I noticed them less.

Later, when Jill went to bed, I turned the television set on low so I could watch the news. I learned that they had found the round-faced bearded man, in Vermont. The police were convinced that he had murdered the well-fed man, but his lawyer stated that they would fight having him brought to

New York. The district attorney spoke to the news reporters, saying their case against this man was a strong one and they expected to have him indicted in a New York court soon. No other photographs were shown, and I was beginning to believe no others existed. That night the news report gave only a short mention of the police officer I'd killed, and that was only regarding his funeral.

Thursday night I met Jill back at her apartment at nine o'clock, as we had arranged, and her friend Brittany was there also. The two of them were planning to go to a bar for drinks, and Jill wanted me to join them.

'It will give you two a chance to sort of start over and get to know each other better.'

'Hey, we were fine before,' Brittany insisted, as she gave me the kind of look a bobcat might give a slow-moving bird. 'Best buds already. Right, Charlie?'

I felt the cravings gnawing deeper into my skull as I nodded in false agreement.

Jill gave her friend a wary look, but didn't argue the matter. 'Some of us have to get up at the crack of dawn tomorrow. We won't stay out past eleven. Right, Brit?'

Brittany rolled her eyes. 'Right, mom.'

I joined them only because Jill had asked me to. I certainly didn't want to spend any time with her friend Brittany, especially given how much worse the cravings had gotten. Although it had been less than a week since I'd last had one of my clan's meat stews, I was surprised by how much deeper the cravings had worked their way into me. In my mind's eye, I imagined the cravings like little worms burrowing into my bones and muscles, and trying to eat their way toward my brain. I had hoped work would calm these thoughts, but it did little to help. All day I had been looking forward to spending time alone with Jill, hoping that her presence would allow me to forget about the cravings, if only for a few minutes. But as Brittany drove us to the bar she wanted to go to, I knew that her aggressive personality would cancel out whatever benefit Jill's presence might have provided in helping me to temporarily forget the cravings.

The bar Brittany took us to was a dark, cavernous place,

located in a basement and aptly named *A Hole in the Wall*.
Instead of sitting at a table, as Jill and I had done at the
restaurants we'd gone to, Jill and I sat together on a small
sagging couch while Brittany sat in an armchair opposite us,
close enough that her knees nearly touched mine. Wine was
the only fermented beverage I'd had, but I'd read about scotch
and knew it was more potent, so I ordered myself one hoping
its effects would lessen the cravings. When the waitress asked
me what kind I wanted, I told her something that didn't cost
too much, and Brittany let out a short burst of her braying
laugher.

'Give the man a twelve year-old Macallan.' She winked at
me. 'My treat.'

I didn't argue about her paying for me. With the way the
cravings were weighing on me, I didn't feel up to matching
wits with anyone, especially this Brittany girl.

'How would you like it?' the waitress asked me.

I wasn't quite sure what she was asking. I was about to say
that I'd like the scotch in a glass, but Brittany answered for
me, telling the waitress, 'Neat.' I had no idea what that meant,
but it seemed to satisfy the waitress, who moved on to talk to
a group of *them* sitting nearby on two sofas that kitty-cornered
each other.

While we waited for the waitress to return with our beverages, Brittany said, 'Jill told me you're working already. So
where are you building houses?'

'I'm not doing that yet. For now I'm doing other work.'

'Oh?' She opened her eyes wide as if this was a surprise
to her, but I was sure it wasn't. 'What job did you take?'

Jill said, 'Brit, it's not important. What's important is the
initiative Charlie showed in getting a job while he's waiting
for a home-building position.'

'Jill, darling, I'm just asking your friend an innocent
question. Why so defensive? Charlie's not doing something
incredibly embarrassing like scrubbing toilets or washing
dishes, is he?'

She smiled in an innocent sort of manner that convinced
me her comment was anything but innocent. Earlier, when I
returned to Jill's apartment I had still been wearing the rubber

shoes that I now wore for work and clothes that smelled heavily of grease and cooked meat, and hadn't yet switched to my work boots or changed into the cleaner clothing I now had on. I remembered the way she smirked when she glanced at my rubber shoes. Maybe she reasoned from them that I was working as a dishwasher. Or she could've figured it out from smelling the stench from my work clothes, or she may have been spying on me. Whichever it was, I had little doubt that she knew the type of work I was doing, and her comment was meant to belittle me.

'I'm working as a dishwasher,' I said. 'And I'm not ashamed of it. It's honest work. It's not as if I'm studying a profession that will allow me to rob people blind, such as being a lawyer.'

I had only a vague notion of what lawyers did from my readings, but in one of the novels I had read a line about lawyers robbing people blind, and I thought my comment might strike to the heart of the matter. And it did, given the way Jill laughed for the briefest of moments and then squeezed my arm. Brittany reacted by her smile dulling a bit while her eyes sparkled with malice.

'*Touché*, Charlie. Though I'm planning to be a prosecutor, not a defense or corporate lawyer, so I won't be quite the bloodsucker. But I can have a big mouth at times and, as Jill has told me on numerous occasions, I do sometimes suffer from verbal diarrhea. Still, it was a completely innocent, although obviously dumb, comment on my part. I'm sorry for insulting you.'

'You didn't insult me. The person you insulted in this bar is right now standing in the back of the kitchen, performing diligent work for little money so you can drink out of a clean glass.'

'*Touché* again,' she said, her smile tightening even further. She turned to address Jill. 'I like your Charlie. He can give as good as he takes.'

The waitress returned with our drinks. Jill and Brittany had ordered concoctions that were a mystery to me, their names having never appeared in any of my readings. I sipped my scotch in the same manner I saw Brittany and Jill sip their drinks, and felt the heat of it on my lips and throat. I took several more sips and decided I liked its sweet and at the same time smoky flavor. As we sat there sipping our drinks, Brittany started peppering me with questions which seemed harmless regarding how I liked New York, though I had an idea she was really laying a trap for me. After six of these questions, Jill steered the conversation in other directions, mostly regarding common friends of theirs and how Brittany was finding her third year of law school. Somehow the conversation ended up with the police officer I had killed (although, of course, that's not how they referred to him) and how it had happened at a lake which Jill and her friend had been to a dozen times in the past to walk. Out of the blue, Brittany asked me if I had been to the lake the night the killing happened.

'What?' Jill demanded, her voice strained by either anger or surprise, her body suddenly tensing.

'What do you mean by "what"? I asked Charlie an innocent question. After all, you told me he likes to go hiking around Queens late at night. Maybe he was out that night and ended up near Lake Kissena. And maybe he even saw something that could help the police. That's all I was asking.'

'Yeah, right. You know, Brit, you're being a world-class jerk right now.' Jill was quickly on her feet and fumbling blindly through the small leather bag she carried. She pulled out a $20 bill and flung it on to the small table next to the couch. 'Come on, Charlie,' she said, her face bright with emotion. 'Let's get out of here.'

I gulped down the rest of my scotch, because I liked the way it was dulling the cravings, and stood to join her. Brittany was imploring Jill to sit down again. 'Jesus, Jill, lighten up! I was only joking around and giving Charlie a little bit of a hard time. He was fine with it. You're the one acting like you got a stick way up your butt.'

Her words had little impact on Jill other than making her move even faster as she determinedly strode out of the bar. She's a little thing with legs far shorter than my own, but I had to walk at a fast clip to keep pace with her. She led me a block away from the bar before she started slowing down.

'Sometimes she just goes too far,' Jill muttered angrily, her face flushed. 'But she had no right joking around about something like that.'

'Your friend was only curious about whether I might've seen something. After all, I did roam about your neighborhood that night. It was just luck on my part that I didn't go in the direction of that lake.'

Jill shook her head as she seethed. 'That's not at all what she was implying. But never mind. She owes both of us apologies. You more than me.' She breathed air deeply into her lungs, and then let it out slowly in an effort to calm herself. When she was done emptying her lungs, she breathed in deeply again and then offered me a brittle smile.

'If Brittany wants to act like that, screw her, I don't care. So Charlie, we're about five miles from my apartment. Since I'm not about to go back there and ask Brittany for a ride, we can either walk it or I can call for an Uber. It's not a bad night for walking. Which would you prefer?'

It wasn't hard to tell that not only did Jill prefer the idea of walking, but that she needed to so she could release some of the pent-up anger she was feeling toward her friend. I therefore told her I'd prefer to walk. It was an usually warm night, the warmest since I'd been in New York, but the heat didn't slow her down, at least not for the next ten blocks as she raced ahead. Not only was it uncomfortably warm, but also more humid than the other nights, and since I was used to the drier, cooler nights offered by the New Hampshire wilderness, I soon found myself perspiring as I tried to match Jill's stride. After those ten blocks, she slowed down to a more reasonable pace and her hand once again searched out mine. For the rest of our walk, she was quieter than she usually was, and even though we held hands it was almost as if she were alone. When we returned to her apartment, she informed me that she was tired and was going to bed. She kissed me before she did so, but it was different from our other kisses. It was as if she was preoccupied and wasn't really thinking of me. After she disappeared into her bedroom, I turned on the television set so that I could watch the news, and afterwards settled down to read one of Jill's novels in the murky grayness of the room.

Given the way the cravings were once again gnawing at me (whatever reprieve the scotch had provided was short-lived) and that I'd picked up an overall uneasiness from Jill, I didn't expect to be able to sleep that night, at least not cooped up inside the apartment. I was tempted to do more roaming outside and maybe head west to Lake Meadow, the lake that I'd lied to Jill about going to the night I killed the police officer. The prospect of lying on grass by water was appealing, and I thought I might be able to sleep if I did that. But I knew that if Jill found her living room empty she might be suspicious about it, and possibly even give more credence to her friend Brittany's suspicions. It was also possible the police had reasoned that the person who killed their fellow officer was someone who'd been sleeping beside the lake when the officer encountered him, and they could be searching for others sleeping beside lakes as possible suspects. For these reasons, I resolved to ignore the temptation to head outside, as strong as it was, and instead keep myself occupied by reading, in the hope that I might find myself a few moments of respite from the cravings.

Friday morning I prepared an early meal as had become my habit, although I wasn't sure Jill would join me given that her friend's behavior had left her in such an unhappy mood. She did, though, and her demeanor was back to what I had grown accustomed to. When she kissed me before we separated for the day, it was as passionate as any of her other kisses, possibly even more so considering how dizzy it left me.

For several minutes her kiss mostly took my mind off the cravings, which had been gnawing deeper inside me, making it difficult for me to be still. The cravings had become far more than a nuisance. They left me feeling twitchy and jumpy, and at some point during the twilight hours I started thinking about drinking more scotch, reckoning this might dull them. But deep inside I knew that whatever relief a drink of scotch might provide it would be fleeting at best, and I knew Chris would take away my job if he smelled scotch on my breath. As I walked to the restaurant, I gave up that thought, and became more resolved that this would be the day I'd finally find the thick-jawed man and learn his secret for dealing with the cravings.

Work that morning progressed as it had every other morning. This changed, though, shortly before eleven o'clock. The stream of dirty dishes had slowed to a trickle, and the heavy black-skinned cook who Eduardo had warned me to be careful around spoke to me for the first time. Up till then I'd been aware of him glaring at my back numerous times each day as he stood at his position by the grill and I rinsed dishes or scrubbed pots at the sink – but no words were spoken between us and, save for the hostile looks he gave me, neither of us had bothered acknowledging the other.

He wore shoes that allowed him to move about noiselessly, but I knew he had crept up behind me before asking me something in words so thickly mumbled I couldn't make out what he was saying. I was going to ignore him but the cravings made it hard for me to do that, so without bothering to look at him I told him I didn't understand what he'd said.

His words were thick and seemed to get stuck in his mouth, but he spoke in less of a mumble and I understood him this time as he said, 'Have a smoke with me.'

I put down the pot I was scrubbing and turned to him. He was smiling in a friendly way, but none of that friendliness reached his eyes. 'Why should I do that?' I said.

He shrugged. 'You never take breaks. You like a robot. Work, work, work. What's the harm in taking a break? You entitled to one. So why not step outside with me and have a smoke? It's good. It will get the smell of grease out of your nose. Besides, I'd like to ask you something.'

The thought of not smelling grease for a few minutes appealed to me, so I followed him out of the back door, which led to the dumpster and the back alley. He stopped about twenty feet past the dumpster and took a small package from his back pants pocket, and from this he pulled out two cigarettes. I'd read about cigarettes, and during my past forays into their world I'd seen some of *them* smoking them and had caught occasional whiffs of their acrid odor. Since coming to New York, I'd seen many more of *them* smoking them and had little choice but to breathe in the smoke they exhaled. To me, the smoke had smelled dirty, worse than the foulest air that this city had, but I was curious whether it was different if you breathed it in directly. I also wanted to know whether it would get the smell of grease out of my nose, as the cook had promised. And so when the cook offered me a cigarette and a book of matches, I took both, lit the cigarette the same as he had done with his, and inhaled deeply on the cigarette as I saw him do.

The taste and feel of the smoke in my lungs was worse than anything I'd previously smelled from others smoking, and I dropped the cigarette to the pavement after that one inhalation. I couldn't fathom why this had become a custom among some of *them*. The cook had watched me while I tried his cigarette, and he smiled at my discomfort when I started coughing as a result of inhaling the smoke.

'This your first cigarette? Too bad you threw it out. You smoke more, and you learn to like it.'

'What did you want to ask me?'

He inhaled deeply on his cigarette, then let the smoke out of the side of his mouth so only a small amount of it drifted to me.

'You an impatient man,' he said, nodding at me, his eyes narrowing. 'You also a puzzle to me. You not a junkie, I know that. You also no college student. Also no illegal. So I keep asking myself why a strong, able man like you take this shit job? You don't got no prison tats that I can see, but I'm thinking that must be it. Are you out of prison? Is that why you doing this shit work? Because if that's it, I can help you.'

'How can you help me?'

'Easy.' He grinned widely, showing teeth that had yellowed. 'I can get you papers and new name. After that, you don't got to tell no one you been to prison. They check on you and everything is clean.'

'I haven't been to prison.'

That surprised him. 'You got arrests on your record, is that it?'

I shook my head and tried to hide my excitement as I said, 'I need a social security number. Can you get me one of those?'

'Why can't you get one yourself?' he asked suspiciously. 'You illegal?'

'No. I was born in New Hampshire, but I don't have a birth certificate and I can't get one.'

'This is same as I was saying before. I can get you papers so you legal. A guy I know can do this. Two thousand dollars and you be legal and don't have to do this shit work.'

'I don't have that much money.'

'Then get it. It ain't hard if you motivated. And don't wait too long. No telling how long I'll be here working for that shit Chris. And don't think I get rich from your two thousand. My taste will be small, most of the money will go to the guy I know. I'm doing this for you as a favor.' He showed that scowl I'd often seen on him and said, 'I don't like how Chris treats us like dirt.'

His cigarette had burned down to a stub, and he flicked it away. He used his forefinger to tap on the side of his head, and said, 'Be smart.' And after that, he went back inside. I stood in the alley and thought about how long it would take me to get $2,000 so I could pay him. After paying one month's rent on the apartment I was going to be subletting, I had less than $600 remaining. I still had to pay two additional months' rent, but if I was frugal with the money I spent on food, and if I stopped buying newspapers and coffee, I might be able to save enough from the $250 I made each week to have that $2,000 in three months. That seemed like a long time to have to be spending my days cleaning dishes, but none of that'd matter if I didn't find a way soon to deal with the cravings. If I found a way to make the cravings go away, those three months would go by fast.

Eduardo had warned me not to trust him, and I wouldn't. When I gave him the $2,000, I'd make sure he gave me what I was paying for. As I stood there, I thought of other ways I could more quickly get $2,000. But I also thought of how angry Jill had become when her friend hinted that I might've been a murderer, and I knew how much it would hurt her if I tried one of those other ways and got caught. I grimly accepted that I couldn't take the chance of Jill suffering that kind of hurt.

After work ended, I traveled again to East Flatbush and continued my searching. Even though I had resolved that today would be the day I found the thick-jawed man, my search turned out to be as fruitless as all my previous searches.

TWENTY-ONE

I'd agreed to meet Jill at eight o'clock that evening since she was planning to be done with work by then. I had considered going earlier to her apartment and preparing a dinner of rice, beans, and avocado, so it would be waiting for her, but before I left for work Jill had mentioned that she wanted us to try a vegan restaurant near her college. I felt uneasy about this now, knowing I needed to save $2,000 and aware how expensive these restaurants were, but I decided that if it took me a week or two longer before I was going to be able to give the cook his money I'd survive the extra time. Besides, more pressing on my mind was figuring out how I was going to survive the cravings.

Jill's spirits were running high that evening, and on seeing me enter her apartment she made a running jump into my arms, making me rock back half a step, and wrapped her arms around my neck. As I recovered my balance, she kissed me hard enough that my head was soon swimming. In the passion of our kiss, I hadn't even realized that I had wrapped my arms tightly around her and was pressing her body against mine. Once our kiss ended and I realized what I'd done, I lowered her back to the floor, my face reddening in my embarrassment.

'That was really nice.' Jill showed me maybe the most beautiful smile I'd yet seen from her. 'I'd been waiting hours to do that to you.' Her smile became one of mischief. 'Are you sure we have to wait any longer before we officially start dating?'

'We do,' I said, my voice rough and raspy as it rumbled out of my throat. 'I gave you my word before, and it wouldn't be right not to wait.'

Jill laughed in a soft, gentle manner that warmed me as much as her kiss. 'OK, OK. I don't want to corrupt you with my wicked city ways.' She took hold of my hand and led me further into her apartment. Before we went more than a few steps, she picked up an envelope from the table that her television set sat on and handed it to me.

'This is from Brittany,' she said.

I opened the envelope and took a card from it that showed a drawing of a plump young girl with overly rosy cheeks and yellow hair tied in pigtails. This girl was drawn so that she looked both contrite and guilt-ridden as she stood next to a vase that lay shattered on the floor. Inside the card were printed the words 'I am so, so sorry!', and underneath that an indecipherable scribble which I guessed was Brittany's signature.

'It appears that she's sorry,' I said, not convinced.

'Yes it does.' Jill's own beaming smile turned apologetic. 'She came by the college and dropped that off. She also talked me into having a girl's night tomorrow night. Me, Brit, and three friends of ours. I'll be out late, and depending how much Brit coaxes me into drinking, I might not be back until Sunday morning.' She hesitated, her smile weakening. 'Given how hard both of us have been working this week, I was looking forward to us having fun tomorrow night. But Ethan was so damned possessive I think it would be good for me to reconnect with friends I lost touch with over the last two years. I'm sorry that I'll be abandoning you tomorrow.'

'There's nothing for you to apologize about.' I forced a smile (what I learned after almost a week of living among them is that smiling doesn't come naturally to me or my kind, at least not as it does with *them*, and I have to keep reminding myself to smile when it's expected) and joked, 'First, we're not dating yet.' Then more seriously, 'And second, I will never hold any claim over you. Even if I am lucky enough for us to one day marry, I will never expect or wish for you to do anything other than what you want to do, and I will consider myself fortunate for any moments that you are willing to share with me.'

Jill took hold of my neck so that she could lower my head and kiss me again. This one lasted longer and was even more passionate than her earlier kiss.

'That's one of the reasons I think you're so great,' she said. 'I know you're not bullshitting me and really mean that.'

I nodded, because I did. I might've lied to her dozens of times since we met, but in this I was talking truthfully.

We stood for a long moment with my hands lightly touching her hips and hers reaching up to my shoulders. If she had asked me again about us not waiting any longer to date, I might've weakened. But she didn't ask me that, and instead suggested we head out for dinner.

Later, as Jill led me down streets where I hadn't been before, we passed a restaurant named *The Cultured Cannibal*. Somehow I didn't stop in my tracks, or even noticeably slow down, though every instinct I had was screaming at me to investigate this restaurant right away. I knew restaurants and bars like to use clever names, and most likely the owner of this one thought the name funny, but I still couldn't help wondering whether the restaurant actually lived up to its name. Was such a thing possible? Perhaps they'd named it as such so ordinary passersby would think it a joke, but wayward people of my kind would be drawn to it to find the food they desperately need. Maybe the restaurant even had two different menus – one for *them* and one for us. After all, didn't Jill once tell me you could get anything in this city? I started thinking that maybe this was how the thick-jawed man was surviving in New York – that he ate there just often enough to keep his cravings satisfied. The thought that this restaurant might actually serve meat that came from the slaughtering ritual, and had been prepared according to custom, caused saliva to leak from my mouth. I quickly wiped it away with my sleeve before Jill could notice.

Even though the cravings were keeping me from thinking straight, I kept these thoughts to myself and didn't mention them to Jill. Nor did I comment to her about the odd name of the restaurant.

TWENTY-TWO

had two of *them* speak to me Saturday morning while I was washing dishes. First, Chris came over to tell me I would be paid at the end of the day and should find him before leaving work at four o'clock. Then, a short time later the cook again asked me to join him for a smoke. I wasn't going to answer him, but the cravings made it hard for me to simply ignore him, so I told him I didn't much care for the cigarette I had tried and would rather smell of grease than cigarette smoke.

'You smoke a few more, you grow to like it. But that's not why I want you to join me. My reason is so we can talk more about what we spoke about yesterday.'

Work had slowed at this point, so I followed him out the back door and into the alley. The cravings had made me edgier and jumpier, and as he watched me he must've noticed.

'What you craving?' he asked. 'H? Meth? Oxy? 'Cause I can hook you up, brother.'

I didn't know what he was talking about, so I didn't answer him.

He shrugged. 'Whatever, bro. You change your mind, you tell me.' He took his pack of cigarettes from his back pants pocket and tapped one out and stuck it between his lips, then offered the pack to me. 'You should smoke one,' he said. 'It will help calm that wild look in your eyes.'

'What did you want to ask me? I said.

He shook his head over my not accepting one of his offered cigarettes, put the pack away, and then lit the one he had in his lips. After sucking on it deeply and blowing out twin streams of smoke from his nostrils, he said, 'What we were talking about yesterday. You going to take me up on my help so you can get a decent job and tell Chris to kiss your ass?'

'Will I get a birth certificate and a social security number?'

He looked annoyed by my question and snorted out more

smoke from his nostrils. 'You get whatever you need so you can work legal,' he replied, his words thickening with annoyance.

'Find out what I'll get,' I said. 'If your friend can get me a birth certificate and a social security number, I'll give you two thousand dollars after I've saved it up.'

He muttered what sounded like profanities under his breath, then tossed his half-smoked cigarette away. It looked as if he was going to walk back into the restaurant without saying another word. But instead he shifted his stare back to me, his thick scowl once again folding his face.

'I will ask him,' he said. 'When you going to have the money ready?'

'Soon.'

'What do you mean by "soon"?'

'As soon as I can.'

He shook a finger at me. 'Don't wait too long. No telling how long I stay at this shit job working for a fucker like Chris. If you wait too long you might find yourself stuck here without me around to help you.'

Then he went back inside. I stood for a long moment thinking about how he'd seen the cravings in me. He'd have thought it was something else, but he still saw what he called a 'wild look' in my eyes. And if he saw it, then Jill must've seen it this morning, too. Or maybe not. Early on, I'd tried to breathe in only through my mouth, but recently I'd been getting careless. It was possible that a morning of smelling the nauseating odors from the grease and burnt animal flesh had made the cravings worse. I couldn't help thinking that if I was spending my days building houses and doing carpentry, the cravings wouldn't be progressing in me so quickly. That kind of hard labor in the open air – even if it was this dirty city air – would still the cravings somewhat and give me more time to find the thick-jawed man who I knew could help me. But as things were, I wasn't going to be able to survive three weeks, as my clan did during that dark time. If I wasn't doing so already, soon I'd be showing Jill glimpses of the madness that the cravings brought on, just as I had to the cook, and I couldn't let that happen.

My thoughts turned to the restaurant I spotted last night while walking with Jill: *The Cultured Cannibal*. In the light of day, the idea that they might serve the kind of meat I needed seemed fantastical. But then again, so much in this city and in their world at times seemed fantastical to me. In any case, I couldn't shake the thought that it just might be so, and that the restaurant's name wasn't meant to be a joke but a beacon for my kind. I decided that after I was done working today I would investigate *The Cultured Cannibal*, and if the name turned out to merely be something the owner thought was clever, I would head back to East Flatbush and continue my search. Since Jill was planning to be out late with her friends, I'd have all night to finally find the thick-jawed man, if I still needed to.

I glanced up at the position of the sun and saw that I'd been on break for almost fifteen minutes, so I headed back inside.

When I found Chris at four o'clock, he counted out $140 and thirty-three cents and handed it to me. I stared confused at the money he'd placed in my open hand. When I could find my voice, I pointed out that we'd agreed $250 a week.

'You didn't work Monday,' he said. 'That's forty-one dollars and sixty-seven cents I took out. Twenty dollars more for the weekly rental fee for the apron, and forty-eight dollars for broken dishes.'

'You didn't tell me you'd charge me for wearing one of your aprons. And I didn't break any dishes.'

'Aprons ain't cheap, and you dishwashers are always wearing 'em out. Twenty bucks is a standard charge.' He clamped his mouth shut as if he were losing patience with me, but then added, 'And dishes were broken.'

He turned away as if we were done and nothing else I had to say mattered. As I stared at him, a redness glazed my vision. Maybe if it weren't for the cravings my vision wouldn't have reddened like that, but still it was galling to have one of *them* so brazenly cheat me. A murderous rage filled me so completely that I was choking with it, and my vision dissolved into redness. I could hear my breath echoing inside me, sounding like the heavy panting that might come out of a wild beast. I fought to keep my true self from being revealed and, just as import-antly, to stay anchored where I stood and not allow myself to move even an inch. Because if I moved, I'd have killed him. Much later I understood it would've been much worse than simply killing him – the cravings would have driven me to savagery. But my thoughts were all jumbled at that time, and all I knew was that I needed to keep myself frozen in place because I couldn't allow myself to kill him there and then. If I did, I'd lose Jill for certain. I was already worrying that my battle against the cravings was turning out to be utterly futile – that time was quickly running out and, no matter what, I was going to lose her because of the cravings. But even though I had little hope left, I wasn't ready to give up yet.

Fortunately, Chris walked away without saying another word to me. If I'd heard his voice again, I don't think I would've been able to stop myself. Eventually, the redness faded and the roaring in my head quietened, and I was able to leave the restaurant without killing anyone.

At first, I wandered aimlessly, and even though I was fairly certain I was keeping my real self masked, the people walking about were perceptive enough to give me a wide berth. Once my thinking'd become clearer (at least, as clear as the cravings would allow), I sat down on a doorstep, buried my face in my hands, and tried to decide what to do next. I'd promised myself that I would leave Jill before there was a danger of my letting the cravings hurt her – and I knew I was getting perilously close to not being able to trust myself with any of *them*, not even Jill.

I fell into a deeper despair then. It didn't seem possible any longer that I'd ever find that thick-jawed man. Or if I somehow did, I would discover that he wasn't one of my kind and had no secret to reveal to me. It seemed the only option I had left was to give up and accept that living with *them* was madness. I'd seen vans on the streets that I could steal and had enough money to buy burlap sacks and rope. I started planning which of *them* I'd bring back with me to my clan. Jill's ex-boyfriend would fill up the first sack, Chris would fill up the next one, and I'd make sure to save a sack for that surly market clerk I encountered. As I sat there in my misery, I contrived a story

I could tell the elders and decided there was a chance they'd believe it. But as I settled on all this, I felt as if my heart was being shredded. The thought of never seeing Jill again became something too painful to bear, and I started weeping.

The weeping lasted for several minutes before I was able to shake myself out of my despair. I came to a decision then. It wasn't time yet to give up. The cravings hadn't yet taken full control. I still had *The Cultured Cannibal* to investigate and, if needed, a whole night to search for the thick-jawed man who I had to hope was of my kind. If I had no cure for the cravings by Sunday, I'd still be left with one full day with Jill before having to leave her. Or maybe I'd even be able to stay a couple of additional days before the cravings made things too dangerous.

I dried my eyes with my sleeve and got to my feet. I had a restaurant to visit.

The Cultured Cannibal didn't open until six o'clock, but they had a menu posted outside that showed the food they offered, such as tripe, bone marrow, pig's head, lamb belly, and different steaks (both raw and cooked). One item on the menu caught my eye: CANNIBAL STEW. Was it possible that when people of my kind ordered this dish, they would be given the meat they sorely needed? At $95 it was the most expensive food they offered. Considering how Chris was cheating me, after paying for the meal I'd have little left over from what I made each week, so I'd be condemned to work as a dishwasher for the rest of my life. But that wouldn't matter. As long as I had a way to keep the cravings from driving me mad, I'd gladly scrub pots each day if that enabled me to be with Jill.

I knocked loudly and after a short while a very thin woman answered the door. There was a grotesque gauntness to her face that was exaggerated by the blood-red color her lips were painted. The black dress she wore reached only halfway to her knees, revealing how thin her legs were – like the tooth-picks I took each day from Chris's restaurant. She gave me an inquisitive look, but didn't say anything.

'I'd like to work here as a dishwasher,' I said.

She showed no immediate reaction to my request, and for

several seconds stared at me with such an utterly blank expression that I wondered whether she'd heard me. I was trying to decide whether I needed to repeat myself when she told me to wait where I was and closed the door on me.

It didn't matter that she wasn't one of my kind. If the fantastical thought that I had turned out to be true, although most of the people working there could be *them*, the cook would have to be one of my kind . . . unless he was kept ignorant of what type of meat was used in their cannibal stew. That was possible. But I reckoned there would have to be at least one of my kind working at *The Cultured Cannibal*, so he could spot others of my kind who ate there and know which stew to serve – unless, of course, they didn't care and served the stew to anyone, figuring that those who weren't my kind would never know what they were eating.

I was still sorting these thoughts out in my mind (and because of the cravings, they were far more jumbled than how I'm writing them now) when the thin woman in the black dress opened the door again. She told me they didn't need a dishwasher right now, but I could fill out an application form if I cared to. I told her I would do that and followed her into the restaurant, where she had me sit near the entrance.

'I'll be right back,' she said in the same monotone that she'd used earlier.

I wanted to explore the kitchen and see if the cook or anyone else was one of my kind – or better still, sneak a taste of the stew if it was simmering in a pot. But for now I decided it would be best to stay seated and continue my charade. That way I wouldn't attract undue attention or the police, and I might spot other of the restaurant's workers. It took several minutes before the woman reappeared with an application form, but all this time she remained the only person I'd seen in the restaurant.

'Your cannibal stew is very expensive,' I said. 'What's in it?'

'Rare and exotic meats.'

'What kind?'

'A secret.'

She said this with such an enigmatic expression that I wasn't sure whether she knew the answer. It was possible – even likely, if the stew was what I hoped it was – that she didn't know what kind of meat was used. I glanced quickly at the application form. I wasn't going to fill it out. There were too many questions I didn't have an answer for, such as a phone number to contact me. Even if I'd known Jill's phone number and had answers for the other questions, and even if they paid far more than my current dishwashing job, I wouldn't have filled it out, for the simple reason I wouldn't want Jill questioning why I was trying to get work at (for her) such an odd-sounding restaurant.

'Can I try a small taste of your cannibal stew?' I asked.

She didn't bother to answer me, not even to shake her head.

'I'd like to eat here tonight,' I said.

'Reservations are required. We're currently booked through the end of the year.'

I rubbed the back of my neck, trying to think, though the cravings were making it difficult to do so.

'I'd like to order the cannibal stew to take with me,' I said, remembering that restaurants sometimes offer that service.

Her expression turned more enigmatic as she stared at me for a long moment before telling me they didn't do that. 'Our chef requires the food to be eaten only at the table, so that it is enjoyed at the correct cooking temperature and properly presented. We don't do takeout, nor do we let diners leave with food. Are you planning to fill out that application?'

I debated in my mind whether to take some of the stew by force. But even though the cravings were clouding my judgment, I knew that would be a bad idea, possibly even a disastrous one.

'I'll fill it out at home and return with it soon,' I said. 'Who's the owner of this restaurant?'

She smiled, if you could call the way her lips barely turned upwards a smile. 'We keep that a mystery.'

TWENTY-THREE

At a subconscious level I knew it was after one in the morning when I pounded on the door. I knew that because I must've passed a clock, and for whatever reason that piece of information had stuck in my mind. At the time, I don't think I was aware of this or much else. I was being blindly driven by the cravings, just as a wild beast might be driven by bloodlust, and it wasn't until later, after the cravings became dormant, that I was able to piece together the events of that night and make sense of what happened.

As I walked aimlessly for hours through Brooklyn, my night of wandering and searching had become a blur, with long stretches of time skipping by. If I'd passed the thick-jawed man, I don't think I'd even have noticed. Early on that evening, I had stopped marking off streets on my map, and my walking had become haphazard, or at least it seemed so. I must've left East Flatbush hours ago, as I suddenly found myself at the back door of the restaurant where I sold Sergei my van and was pounding on it. If anyone had asked me what I was doing there, I wouldn't have been able to articulate an answer, assuming I was able to understand the question.

Coming from the other side of the door was some cursing in a language I didn't recognize, or perhaps the person was yelling something at me. This was another fact I wasn't consciously aware of at the time; it was something I only understood later, once I'd pieced together what had happened. When the door began to open inward, I jerked it toward me then pushed into it with all my brute strength. A dull thud sounded as it hit the skull of the same blond man who had answered the door the other time. He collapsed backwards on to the floor, and as I rushed into the room I stomped on his face.

There was more shouting from inside the restaurant, and I moved toward it. Later, when I tried to reconstruct in my mind what had happened, because of the mad frenzy brought on by the cravings I couldn't tell whether the shouting had been in English or in another language. Either way, whatever was shouted I couldn't say. As I moved into the kitchen from the back room, Sergei was entering the kitchen from an opposite hallway. As our eyes locked, his face became a swirl of violence and he moved swiftly toward me. He held a gun, and as he swung it up to aim at me, I jumped at him with all the ferocity of a kill-crazy catamount. The speed and power of my jump surprised him. The look that flooded his eyes was one of the few things I was easily able to remember afterwards.

I knocked him to the floor and grabbed his gun hand while, with my other hand, I groped for his throat. He was trying to wrench his gun hand free so he could shoot me. I pulled it toward me and sank my teeth into his wrist. He would've howled if my other hand hadn't been squeezing his windpipe. When he dropped the gun, I sank my teeth in deeper, severing a vein. Even though I nearly had him choked to death, he somehow bellowed out his anguish. Soon after that he went limp, but I didn't release my teeth from his wrist until I noticed a shadow moving toward me. Or maybe I only sensed it. Whichever it was, I ducked in time for the meat cleaver to miss my head.

I rolled over, and spun around as I came to my feet. When the meat cleaver was pulled back to deliver another blow, I sprang forward and blocked the arm, swinging it while driving my shoulder hard into the man's chest. A dull 'Oomph . . .' sound came out of him, and he stumbled backwards and tripped over Sergei's body. The back of his head bounced off the floor, the blow dazing him so he put up little fight as I grabbed the cleaver from him. Before he could do much of anything else, I sank the cleaver deep into his throat.

Again, all of this I was able to reconstruct in my mind once I was able to think clearly, though while it was happening it was only a mad red-hazed blur. I know I resorted to savagery then, because once the cravings began to subside and I was able to think clearly, I realized that I'd been lapping up, like a dog, the blood pooling from the deep wound I had carved out of his throat.

I stumbled to my feet. The fever that had been burning up my brain was gone. In its place a coolness filled my head, and my thinking once again became clear, no longer the jumbled mess it had been only minutes earlier. The cravings had let go of me. In my mind's eye, I again pictured them as hundreds of little worms. But no longer hungry and agitated ones. Now, they were fat and satiated as they crawled drunkenly out of my brain and bones and muscles so that they could disappear to wherever they went when they slept.

I looked around at the carnage I was responsible for, and slowly understood where I was and what I had done. A weak groan came from the back room. When I investigated it, I found the blond man still alive, and struggling to get to his feet even though his forehead was dented from where the door had struck him and his mouth and nose had caved in from my stomping on him. He tried pleading with me, but his words came out as gurgling sounds because of the damage done to him. As he feebly tried to fight me off, I took hold of his jaw and the top of his head, and with a twist of my shoulder broke his neck.

I went back to the kitchen and surveyed the scene. For the first time in almost a week the cravings were completely gone, replaced by a most welcome stillness. I realized that the blood I'd drunk had satisfied the cravings every bit as much as *their* meat ever had, maybe even more so, although that might've only been because of the large amount of blood I'd lapped up, compared to the small amount of meat that's in a serving of one of my clan's stews. I knew that the cravings had brought me to this place and driven me to my savagery. I also accepted that I had little control over it. Still, the thought of what I'd done sickened me.

I have little doubt that if any of *them* ever witnessed our slaughtering ritual, they would see it as the height of barbarism and savagery. For us, however, the ritual is critically important for two reasons. First, it reinforces the idea that they serve only one purpose. And second, since the ritual must be performed precisely according to tradition before we can make use of *their* flesh, it keeps us from resorting to the kind of savagery I had committed that night. If any of my kind had witnessed what I did, they would have been ashamed.

I held my breath for a long moment so I could listen for any others of *them* that might've been hiding in the restaurant, but I didn't hear anything. After washing the blood off my hands and taking off my shoes, I crept through the restaurant and searched each room before looking into the dining area. Normally, if any others of *them* had been there, I would've smelled them, but with the taste of blood so thick in my throat I didn't trust that ability now. I looked through each room thoroughly, checking closets and other hiding places. When I opened any of the doors or needed to touch anything, I used a rag I'd taken from the kitchen. I did this for the same reason I took off my bloody shoes: I knew from the forensics article I'd read that they'd be able to identify me from my fingerprints and match my shoes to any bloody shoe prints I left. If the police later arrested me, I didn't want them to be able to tie me to these murders, for the simple reason that I would never want Jill to know that I'd committed such savagery.

Once I'd satisfied myself there was no one else in the restaurant, I went back to the kitchen and used the meat cleaver to cut pieces from Sergei and the other man where I might've left teeth marks or saliva, and I fed this into the sink's waste-disposal unit, which was powerful enough to grind a chunk of wrist bone to nothing. I did this for the same reason I didn't want to leave fingerprints or footprints – so the police wouldn't be able to identify me from teeth marks and saliva. With that taken care of, I stripped off my bloody clothes and washed the blood from my face, arms, and legs, then rinsed it off my rubber shoes. Before heading off to Brooklyn earlier, I'd almost gone back to Jill's apartment so I could switch to my work boots. It was fortunate I hadn't. Because if I had, my work boots would now have been stained red with blood and would have had to've been thrown out.

I found a plastic bag and, after emptying my pockets, put my bloody clothes in it. As with the restaurant where I worked, this kitchen had a closet holding cleaning supplies, so I was able to mop away the bloody shoe prints I'd left in the kitchen before taking off my shoes. Then, for good measure, I mopped up the rest of the blood (there was a lot of it) in an attempt to hide any evidence indicating that I had drunk any of it. After I was done, I rolled Sergei on to his side so I could take his wallet from his back pocket. It was as thick as the other time I'd seen it. I counted more than $6,000 and added the money to my own wallet. I now had more than enough money to pay the cook for a birth certificate and social security number, and grimly noted that I'd also found a way to keep the cravings satisfied.

When searching the restaurant, I'd found some spare clothing, which had most likely belonged to Sergei, in an office. I first stopped in the bathroom so I could check myself in the mirror and wash off any of the blood I might've missed. It turned out I had a good amount of it in my hair. After that, I went back to the office so I could put on the clothes. The pants were short on me and loose around my middle, and the shirt likewise ill-fitting, but I decided they would make do until I could return to Jill's apartment. I went back to the kitchen so I could retrieve my wallet, and after consulting my map I put that in my back pocket too. I next wiped my finger-prints off anything I might've touched, then picked up the plastic bag containing my soiled clothing and left through the back door.

I was careful as I emerged from the alley, making sure there were no cars driving by or people walking on the sidewalk. I moved as swiftly as I could in the shadows and crossed a number of streets, looking for the darkest ones to travel down. It wasn't until I had gone six blocks that I spotted anyone outside, and it seemed likely no one even noticed me. I waited until I had put several miles between myself and the restaurant before hiding the bag of bloody clothes in a dumpster behind another restaurant, making sure the bag was buried in food scraps.

Using the pale light of a street lamp, I consulted my map to find a subway station connecting Brooklyn with Queens, as I didn't want to use one anywhere near the restaurant where my savagery'd occurred. As I walked, I pieced together what I could about what had happened and realized why the cravings had gripped me so thoroughly after only one week, while my clan had gone three weeks before being driven to the same blind madness. It was because I'd been living among *them*, and that had proved too much of a temptation for the cravings. In my mind I could picture those worms being worked up to a wild frenzy, with the scent of so many of *them* close by and at the same time being starved. As disgusted as I was over the savagery I'd resorted to, I kept thinking about how much easier it would be to live among *them* knowing that their blood satisfied the cravings. I knew that if I needed to abduct some of *them* and perform the slaughtering ritual, more likely than not I'd be discovered by the police, even if I was able to find a private place in their city for the slaughtering ritual and meat preparation. The savagery I committed earlier was something very different. That could be done quickly and in countless number of places. And I might not have to kill them. I might not even have to break any of their laws.

The book I read after *Frankenstein* was *Dracula*. When I saw that book buried among the others on Jill's shelves, I felt my heart race and quickly grabbed it. During my first year of picking *them* up for the clan, I found a paperback copy of that book among the possessions of those I had collected. When one of the elders learned that I had added *Dracula* to the clan's library, he was furious with me and had the book burned. He also warned me that if I ever brought a copy of *Dracula* back to the clan again, all the books in our library would be burned and reading made taboo. This surprised me, as I didn't think the elders or anyone else in the clan had any interest in or knowledge of the books in our library, since I was the only one reading them. But he knew enough about *Dracula* to make it a forbidden book, which was why I had to read it once I spotted it. And this was why I knew about vampires.

Of course, I knew they were make-believe, but I had made it a habit when riding the subway between Queens and Brooklyn to read the free newspaper distributed at Chris's restaurant, and in the back pages I'd recently seen an advertisement announcing that a woman was looking for someone to be her vampire and drink her blood. At the time I considered it an absurd joke, like many of the advertisements in those back pages, but perhaps it wasn't. Maybe she really was looking for someone to pretend to be a vampire and drink some of her blood. And maybe there were others like her in New York. As repellent as I found such an act of savagery, if I could make a deal with those people so I could keep the cravings satisfied and be able to live safely with Jill, I wouldn't hesitate to do so.

TWENTY-FOUR

I t was after four in the morning when I got back to Jill's apartment. Her bedroom door was closed, and I listened with my ear pressed against it for the sound of her breathing but couldn't hear anything other than the hum of something electric. Even though her pleasant scent permeated her apartment, I reckoned it would've been stronger if she was home. I didn't open her door so I could be sure, but I was fairly certain she hadn't returned yet.

I changed out of Sergei's clothing and into my own, then slipped back outside so that I could dispose of his clothing someplace miles away. It was an hour later before I came back to Jill's apartment. Once again I sensed that it was empty.

Maybe it was because of how quiet and content the cravings had become, but I fell into a deep sleep seconds after lying down on the couch even though early morning light was brightening the room, and I stayed in that same deep sleep until the sound of her apartment door opening woke me.

I lifted my head, blinking groggily, and watched as Jill and her friend Brittany stepped out of the hallway and into the living room. My blood chilled when I saw that Jill's shoulder and arm were bandaged.

I was quickly off the couch, and my voice was barely a croak as I asked, 'Are you hurt?'

Jill showed me a tired smile. 'I have a shoulder strain, that's all.'

'Bullshit!' said Brittany. 'You've got torn ligaments!'

'I have one slight tear. And that's basically what a strained muscle is.'

Brittany looked like she wanted to argue the matter, but before she could do so I asked what'd happened.

'Once again Ethan is what happened,' Brittany said, her mouth twisting into a spiteful, angry smirk.

I must've looked as perplexed as I felt. Jill explained that

Ethan was at the after-hours club they went to last night, and when Jill tried to walk past him he grabbed her by the arm and yanked her to him.

Brittany interrupted, saying, 'I've been trying to talk sense into her about filing charges against that asshole!'

'I'm not going to do that.'

'What he did was assault and battery!'

Jill was shaking her head. 'I refuse to believe he meant to hurt me,' she said. 'He was drunk, and he overreacted badly when I ignored him.'

'He didn't mean to hurt you?' Brittany stated incredulously. She fixed bloodshot eyes on me and said, 'You should see how badly bruised Jill's arm is under those bandages. Quite an ugly shade of black and purple, believe me. You don't grab someone that violently unless you're trying to hurt them. Charlie, can you talk sense into your girlfriend and tell her she needs to go to the police?'

'No.'

She reacted as if I had slapped her. 'What do you mean by "no"?'

I smiled at Jill with as much gentleness as I could muster, even though my blood was boiling over because of how her ex-boyfriend had hurt her.

'I'm never going to tell you what to do,' I promised her. 'If there is anything I can ever do to help or comfort you, I will do so gladly. But it's not my place to tell you what you should be doing.'

Brittany let out a snort of derision, but Jill's reaction was very different. Her eyes moistened with tears, and when one of them ran down her cheek I stepped toward her so I could wipe it away with my thumb. She took hold of my hand with her unbandaged one and pressed it against her lips. When Brittany tried to enlist my help in involving the police, the reason I gave for declining to help was not the one that first occurred to me. But, although I had a very different reason for not wanting her ex-boyfriend to be locked away in jail, I had still ended up speaking truthfully.

'This is just great!' said Brittany, her eyes angry dots as they fixed on Jill. 'You're just going to let that asshole Ethan get away with this. Incredible! You don't think you're empowering him so next time he's in the mood he'll hurt you even worse?'

'There's not going to be a next time,' Jill said quietly and confidently. 'I understand all too well how his mind works. He's a classic narcissistic personality. Everything is somebody else's fault. If I have him arrested, he'll blame me for losing his job – and then he'll spend months planning some sort of bizarre revenge against me. But I won't just ignore this. I'll file for a restraining order against him. Deep down inside he's also a coward, and once I file for a restraining order he'll keep his distance.'

Brittany was shaking her head, her lips once again pressed into a tight, angry smirk. 'Forget it,' she said. 'I'm too tired to argue about this anymore. Five hours in an emergency room is far more exhausting than spending the same number of hours jumping around in an after-hours club. Toodles, darling. I still love you, but I need to get home and collapse.'

She gave Jill a careful embrace, making sure not to touch her injured shoulder. Before leaving, she pointed an index finger at me and warned me to take good care of her girl. 'And if you get a chance to knock that asshole Ethan's teeth out, I'll owe you one.'

According to the clock embedded in the electric stove it was now ten minutes after eleven, so I asked Jill if I should make her brunch (I'd learned that that was the name of a meal that combined breakfast and lunch).

'Charlie, I'd be eternally grateful if you could make a pot of coffee and pour it into me.'

Jill made her way over to the couch and gingerly lowered herself on to it. A familiar lump formed in my throat as I saw how worn out and frail she looked, in no small part because of her damaged shoulder. I told her that of course I would do that for her. A few minutes later as I waited for the water in the coffeemaker to percolate, I heard a light snoring coming from the couch and, sure enough, Jill had fallen asleep.

I picked her up, being careful not to wake her or touch her injured shoulder, and carried her to her room. She didn't wake as I lowered her on to her bed, nor when I removed her shoes or fitted a blanket over her so that it rested just under her chin.

I hadn't been in Jill's room before, nor had I seen it. Most of the time Jill kept her bedroom door closed, but those times her door was left open I avoided looking inside so I wouldn't encroach upon her privacy. Now that I was in her bedroom, I allowed myself several moments to soak in how pleasing it all was. Of course it was filled with Jill's wonderful scent, but everything else in it seemed to fit Jill so well. The way the walls were painted the same bright gold as her hair. The bed that was so soft and frilly, covered with inviting pastel-colored blankets and pillows. The delicate but finely crafted desk and other furniture. The small paintings of nature that decorated the walls. The stuffed bear (perhaps meant to resemble a cub without claws or teeth, as the adult ones I'd encountered in the wilderness didn't look so gentle) that sat on a corner of her desk, and the colorful glass figurines and other knick-knacks that lay scattered about the room. I'd read about such rooms, but my imagination must be lacking because I'd never imagined a room being such an oasis. As I gave the room one last look before leaving Jill to sleep, I realized that not only had that lump in my throat returned, but that my chest was aching with both longing and happiness. The reason for the pain of longing was obvious, but I also knew why I felt such intense happiness. Because I understood that having found a way (as distasteful as it might be) to keep the cravings from forcing me to leave Jill, there was now a real chance that I might court her and someday be invited into this wonderful room.

I quietly closed the door behind me so as not to disturb her sleep, and let the coffee finish brewing. I was going to need it myself, as I had some thinking to do.

I didn't want to leave Jill alone in case she needed me, so I ignored the temptation to turn on her television set (I didn't want the noise to wake her) in order to learn whether anyone had spotted me leaving Sergei's restaurant. Instead I finished the book I'd been reading, which was titled *The New York Trilogy*, written by an author named Paul Auster. I chose the book because Jill had talked about it as being one of her favorites, and also because I thought I could learn more about

New York from it. At first I thought it would consist of mysteries like the Sherlock Holmes stories I'd read many years ago, but it turned out to be very different. Although it was puzzling to me, it seemed to be more about the nature of mysteries and of people losing their identities. After drinking more coffee and mulling over what I'd read, I returned the book to its shelf and picked out a new book to read – this time choosing one by the author whom I'd picked up on the Boston streets, the one who had written a fable about a man who believed he was saving the world each day by weeding a field. This book was very different from that other one. It turned out to be about a disgraced police officer who is let out of jail, and all the damage he causes through denying his true nature. After finishing it, I found myself for the first time regretting taking the life of one of *them* that I'd picked up for the slaughtering ritual. I found myself wishing I'd left him on that Boston sidewalk so he could now be writing more books. That thought stunned me. It wasn't just Jill I was seeing differently, not merely as one of *them*, but that writer too. And if I was being honest about it, Eduardo as well. I hadn't allowed myself to realize this (or accept it) until now, but I had to admit that I'd appreciated the jokes and kind words he greeted me with each morning when I arrived at work.

It wasn't until after five o'clock that Jill emerged from her bedroom. Her color was better than it had been earlier, but it was obvious that the pain from her injured shoulder was weighing on her more heavily. When I asked her about this, she explained that she had been medicated earlier, but she was trying to limit the amount of painkillers she took.

I had a pot of coffee and a meal of pancakes waiting for her, and she was grateful for both. I didn't have any blueberries left and resisted the urge to go to the market to buy more in case she woke up and needed me, but Jill told me the pancakes were perfect and exactly what she wanted after last night.

After we ate, Jill needed to do more reading for college, so we read together on her couch while more Mozart music played. I picked *Wise Blood* by Flannery O'Connor from her bookshelves, another novel that Jill had spoken highly of. As the night wore on, I grew more anxious to learn what the police knew about my killings, both recent and otherwise, but I kept myself from asking Jill whether we could watch the news. Shortly before eleven o'clock, she bid me goodnight, telling me she needed to start grading some papers before going to bed. The kiss she gave me was more tender than passionate, but from the look in her eyes I knew nothing had changed between us, and that she was simply tired and in some pain from her shoulder.

After Jill disappeared into her bedroom, I turned on the television set and kept the sound low. The very first story on the news was about my killings. An ashen-faced police spokesman talked about how they were the most brutal and gruesome murders he'd ever encountered, but other than saying that the bodies had been mutilated he didn't reveal much else. Certainly nothing about whether anyone had seen me leaving that alley or fleeing the area. I did learn that Sergei and the others I'd killed were criminals who were involved in sex trafficking, bank robberies and extortion, and that the police believed the murders were committed by rival criminals. One thing that stunned me was that the police didn't believe robbery was a motive – both because of the extreme brutality of the murders and because a very large sum of money was found in one of the offices. When I searched the restaurant, I was looking only for more of *them* who might've been hiding, and wasn't opening desk drawers to look for money. I speculated about what a very large sum of money might be, but decided it didn't matter. My wallet was thick enough with the $6,000 I'd gotten from Sergei.

TWENTY-FIVE

This time when the work slowed I was the one to ask the cook to join me in the back alley behind the restaurant. He looked surprised by my invitation.

'You got the money?'

'Yes.'

'OK then. After I get these on a plate.'

He nodded to a couple of pieces of cow meat that he was grilling. I left him to wait out in the alley so I could get away from the grease and the smell of burnt animal flesh. After several minutes he joined me. He was too excited to bother shaking a cigarette loose and lighting it. Instead, he stood in front of me grinning widely.

'I told you, if you tried hard enough you'd find the money,' he said. 'You got the money with you?'

'I'll get a birth certificate and a social security number?'

'Yes, brother, you get both.'

'You don't even know my name or where I was born.'

He made a face as if he was disappointed in me. 'I was going to ask you to write both those down. You gotta have trust, brother. I'm not trying to cheat you. I'm trying to help you out.' He winked at me. 'I'll be making a small piece of cash for myself out of this, but that's only fair, right?'

'How is your friend going to get me those papers?'

He made another face, this time as if he was losing patience with me. 'He knows people who work in those government offices. The birth certificate will be fake, but the social security card will be real. When you get that, you'll be able to tell Chris to go fuck himself, and get yourself a real job. Maybe you even kick Chris's fat ass on your way out.'

I'd already taken $2,000 out of my wallet. I knew if he watched me taking the money out of my wallet and saw how fat it was, he'd be scheming to get the rest from me. I handed him the money, which quickly disappeared into one of his pockets.

'You don't want to count it?' I asked.

'Trust, brother,' he said. 'I trust you, and you need to trust me. World don't work without trust.'

I nodded as if he had said something profound and that I actually trusted him, which I didn't.

'When will I get my papers?'

He looked past me, as if he was anxious to be done with me. 'I'll see my guy tonight, and tell you tomorrow,' he said, his words more thick and mumbled than earlier. 'I gotta get back inside before that fucker Chris is on my ass. Tomorrow, brother.'

We both went back to work. I didn't feel him staring at me, not even once, during the rest of the day. Instead, it was as if he was intentionally trying not to look in my direction. I wasn't as stupid as the cook believed I was. I knew Eduardo had told me the truth earlier, that the cook would cheat me if given the chance, and I knew he'd been planning to do so from the moment he offered to help me.

When my work finished at four, I found a spot a block away from which I'd be able to watch for the cook leaving the restaurant. I knew that with $2,000 in his pocket, he'd be going straight home once he left work – that he'd be too afraid of somebody taking the money from him to do anything else. As long as he didn't have a car, I'd be able to follow him wherever he went. If he had a car, I'd be out of luck, and I'd have to hope he'd been telling me the truth. I knew there was probably some truth in what he'd told me. His story about knowing someone who could get people like me the legal papers we needed was most likely true, since he was too dull-minded a cheater to come up with such a story himself out of the blue. So while I had little doubt he knew someone like that, I also had little doubt that he was planning to keep my money for his own purposes.

A few minutes before five, a heavy, bald man entered the restaurant, and from his demeanor I guessed he was going there to work and not eat. I further guessed he was there to take over the cooking chores. My guess turned out to be correct, as a few minutes later the cook I was waiting for came out of the restaurant. He looked guarded and secretive as he turned and walked in the opposite direction from where I was standing. He didn't notice me as I followed him to the subway station, nor as we rode on three different subway lines.

When he got off the last train and exited a subway station in the Bronx, I continued to follow him. I made sure to keep nearly a full block's distance behind, and he continued to appear oblivious to my presence. He stopped once to enter a liquor store, and when he left five minutes later he carried what must've been a celebratory bottle. After another three blocks, he appeared to arrive home as he trudged up the steps of a tenement building. I raced to catch the entrance door before it closed and locked, which I was able to do with half a second to spare.

The building had four floors, and it had both an elevator and a staircase. I guessed the cook had taken the elevator, so I took the stairs, and I caught a glimpse of him as he came out of the elevator on the third floor. He walked in my direction but didn't see me during the brief moment when I poked my head out of the stairwell, nor when I hid in it and listened for a door being unlocked and then opened. Once I heard that sound I waited a second, and was able to see him as he closed his apartment door behind him.

I walked over to it, and noted the apartment number. After I left the building, I checked the list of residents by the security buzzer, which provided me with the name of the cook.

Now that I possessed my own secret for satisfying the cravings, it seemed pointless to continue searching East Flatbush for the thick-jawed man, who had probably also discovered this very same secret, so instead of traveling to Brooklyn I took the subway back to Queens. It was almost seven by the time I got there. Jill and I had arranged to meet back at her apartment at eight o'clock. Originally, I had planned to cook her dinner, but I still didn't know how to do much more than make pancakes, oatmeal, and rice and beans, so I decided to use some of the $4,000 I still had from Sergei's money to treat her to a nice meal at a nearby vegan restaurant. Instead of waiting for Jill at her apartment, I headed back to *The*

Cultured Cannibal so I could satisfy my curiosity about what exactly they served.

The same skinny woman was working again as a hostess. She had painted her lips even redder, and now also wore black eye paint on her eyelids and rouge on her cheeks, which made her face look even more gaunt. As I approached her, she gave me another enigmatic look but didn't say anything.

I counted $200 from my wallet and placed it on the platform next to where she stood.

'That's more than twice what you charge for your cannibal stew. I'd like a serving to take with me. I'm fine if when I eat it it's not heated to the proper temperature or served the way your chef wants it.'

She didn't bother to do so much as glance at the money, or even look down her nose at it. 'If you pester us any further, I will call the police,' she stated in a flat, emotionless voice. 'Now leave and do not come back.'

I was flabbergasted. I was sure she was going to take the money. That's what *they* do in their world. Even though I now had a way to keep the cravings satisfied, I'd hoped the cannibal stew was what I thought it was, so I wouldn't have to do anything as demeaning and repugnant as act as a strange woman's private vampire the next time the cravings demanded feeding.

I picked up the $200 I'd placed on the platform, and as I returned this woman's blank stare I promised myself that if I ever needed to commit an act of savagery to satisfy the cravings, I'd find her. Though I doubted that I'd be able to wring much blood out of her skinny body.

After leaving *The Cultured Cannibal*, I found a spot on the other side of the street from which I could discreetly watch the restaurant's entrance. But I wasn't being as discreet as I thought I was, because after no more than fifteen minutes (at which point I'd seen four people enter the restaurant, none of them my kind) a police car pulled over to the curb and the officer behind the wheel leaned toward me and yelled through the open window, demanding to know what I was doing there.

At first I was simply perplexed and wasn't sure that he had meant to yell at me, except that he was staring straight at me and there wasn't anyone else for him to be yelling at. Was it really against the law in *their* world to simply stand on a sidewalk, minding your own business? But then I'd had that other police officer disturbing me simply for sleeping peacefully by a small lake.

'Hey you, what's your problem? You don't speak English? Or are you just stupid?'

There was no doubt any longer that he was speaking to me. There also wasn't any doubt from the way his eyes had slitted and his nostrils flared that he was getting furious at me for not answering him right away.

'What law am I breaking?' I asked.

When I said that, his face reddened and he all but blew steam out of his nose.

'You're going to try me?' he demanded. He turned off the engine of his car, and nearly fell out the driver's side door in his haste to approach me. 'How about being a public nuisance?' he said when he was less than two feet from me, his breath strong and smelling like sour milk, his hand resting on his nightstick. He nodded toward *The Cultured Cannibal*. 'The people at that restaurant think you're planning to rob one of their customers. How about I bring you in for suspicion of robbery, and see what we find?'

I couldn't let him do that. They'd find all the money I had in my wallet, and when I couldn't come up with a satisfactory answer for why a dishwasher making $140 and thirty-three cents a week (after being cheated by Chris) had that much money, they'd accuse me of committing a crime. They probably wouldn't accuse me of killing and robbing Sergei, or the other killings I'd committed, but they'd find a crime for which they could get a conviction. This police officer was thicker in the middle and more burly than the other officer I'd killed, but I'd be able to kill him just as easily if needed.

'I didn't know I was causing any trouble standing here, but I'll leave now, officer. Besides, I have a friend waiting for me elsewhere.'

Fortunately for both of us, he didn't make any effort to stop me. If he had, he'd have been another one of *them* who ended up dead and I'd have had little choice but to go into

The Cultured Cannibal and kill that skinny woman with the grotesquely painted face. The one who for whatever reason had decided to cause me trouble simply for wanting to taste their stew. And how in the world did she know I'd been standing out here?

If I'd killed them, then I'd have had to hope that nobody else witnessed either of these killings, because if they did and they got a good enough look at me to help the police come up with a drawing (or worse, took a photograph of me), I'd be losing Jill just when I'd discovered a way I could stay with her.

TWENTY-SIX

I t didn't surprise me when ten o'clock in the morning rolled around and the cook hadn't shown up for work. That fact did seem to agitate Chris, who ten minutes later all but accused me of being in some sort of conspiracy with the cook.

'Don't think I haven't seen you two sneaking outside by the dumpster. What have you two been talking about?'

At first I was going to ignore him and continue scrubbing the pots that had piled up, but after some consideration I decided there was no point in doing that.

Without bothering to turn to look at the one of *them* who was cheating me so blatantly, I said, 'He wanted money from me.' After another moment of consideration, I added the lie, 'As a loan.'

'Did you give him any?'

'Yes.'

Even though my back was turned to him, I could feel the heat rising off of him as he fumed.

'That rotten sonofabitch,' he swore. 'He hit me for an advance on his pay, and like an idiot I gave it to him out of the goodness of my heart. He ripped both of us off.' He shut up to gnash his teeth. Then, his voice even more bitter, he said, 'I'd bet anything he gave me a phony address. And a phony name. We're never going to be seeing that bastard again.'

The idea of this cheater loaning anyone money out of the goodness of his heart was laughable. I was sure he'd planned to get something out of it. I didn't bother telling him that he was wrong about neither of us ever seeing the cook again.

Chris tried to bully the other cook into staying longer, but this one insisted that he had to leave by ten thirty as he had family commitments he couldn't break. At ten thirty, Chris tried bullying him further, but the cook took off his apron and handed it to Chris, then left without saying another word.

Chris vented out a number of angry profanities aimed at

both cooks – the one who'd left at ten thirty, as he said he would, and the other one whom I was better acquainted with. After several minutes of this, one of the waitresses deposited a food order on the counter and Chris had no choice but to tie the apron around his middle and take over as cook. I had the sense that he did a poor job, because only a short time after he took over at the grill one of the waitresses brought back a plate, telling him that the customer had complained that both the eggs and the bacon were overcooked. Even though my back was turned to him, he must've sensed me grinning over his humiliation, because he barked at my back, first accusing me of loafing (which I hadn't been doing, as I was still scrubbing the last of the pots that had piled up from the morning rush) and then ordering me to clean the toilets since I obviously didn't have enough work to do. I enjoyed a moment of imagining him being trussed and gagged, then stuffed into a burlap sack. But I held my tongue over his pettiness, and did as he ordered.

At four o'clock Chris was still behind the grill, and sweating heavily. Throughout the day I felt him glaring my way whenever one of the waitresses returned a plate of food that a customer had complained about, usually because it was overcooked. When I took off my apron after the completion of my workday, I once more felt him glaring at me. But whatever he thought of saying, he held his tongue.

I took the subway to the station in the Bronx where the cook had gotten off the other time, and walked to the address I'd followed him to previously. I waited near the entrance until an elderly woman lugging a two-wheel cart filled with groceries approached the door. After inserting a key to unlock it, she struggled with both the door and the cart. I rushed forward and held the door so she could drag the cart into the building more easily. She smiled at me and thanked me, and I kept the door from locking as she trudged to the elevator. I waited until she disappeared inside the elevator, then entered the building and used the stairs to make my way to the cook's apartment.

He must've been waiting for someone else, because he had

a big grin on his face when he answered the door after I
knocked, and his grin quickly turned sickly as he blinked his
eyes several times, not quite making sense of why I was
standing there. As it dawned on him that I must've followed
him from the restaurant to his home, he manufactured a
display of outrage.

'You spied on me,' he spat out, his words thicker than any
other time I'd heard him speak. He wasn't simply glowering
angrily at me as I'd caught him doing in the past, but he had
both hands clenched into fists and his face was contorted the
same as a wild beast might do when trying to scare off a more
dangerous predator. 'Go to hell, and fuck you and your two
thousand dollars. You lose that for spying on me.'

He was a large man and must've outweighed me by eighty
pounds and, although a lot of his weight was fat, he still had
thick, beefy arms and even beefier hindquarters. But, as
mentioned earlier, I have a lot of strength in my chest, arms
and hands, and I'd put bigger and stronger ones of *them* into
my sacks. So when he tried pushing the door closed on me,
I pushed the door hard into him, sending him stumbling backwards into his apartment. I followed him in and his eyes opened
wide with surprise. This time, his outrage was fully genuine.

'I'm going to bust your head open,' he swore. 'You piece
of shit, thinking you can push your way into my home. I was
going to help you, but now I'm going to bust your stupid,
ignorant head open.'

He didn't move, though, and as he stayed rooted to the spot
where he stood, a cautiousness crept into his eyes as he tried
to make sense of how I was able to overpower him with as
little apparent effort as I had done with the door. Since I knew
all along that he had been planning to cheat me, I felt no anger
over this, not even over his insolence. But I was beginning to
feel wearied by his behavior, the same as one of *them* might feel
after being confronted by a small, yapping dog. I unmasked
myself and let him see me for what I truly am, making sure
he knew the singular purpose that he and his kind serve. A
deep primordial fear woke within him, and as his horror grew
he shrunk backwards.

'What are you?' he whispered.

'I am the one who will hunt you down if you don't deliver me what you promised,' I said, my true self completely unmasked, my voice as cold as death. 'If you think you can cheat me, you're wrong. Same if you think you can run from me. I'm better at tracking down ones like you than you could ever imagine.'

This last part was a lie. I'd probably have been no better than any of *them* would have been at tracking him down, but I was certain that in his panicky, horror-stricken state he'd be too frightened to test me.

At first, when I unmasked myself he stared at me as one of my kind might've stared at some terrible raging wildfire threatening to consume our homestead, but I'd become too awful to gaze at for long. Instead, he looked away and focused on a spot on his worn-out mottled carpeting.

'You spying on me got my temper up,' he said. 'That's why I said what I did. But I didn't mean it, I wasn't going to cheat you—'

'You're quite a liar. You were never planning to go back to Chris's restaurant. If I hadn't tracked you down, I would never have seen you again.'

'Uh-uh.' He shook his head fiercely, still making sure not to catch so much as a glimpse of me. 'That's not true. I swear that's not true.'

He was lying, and he realized that he was doing a poor job of it so he stopped talking. I'd read in newspapers and magazines about severance packages in their world. Chris would never have given him one, so I guess he decided to cheat one out of me and Chris. As he waited for me to say something, his face grew more sickly by the second, and it wasn't just out of fear but the realization that he wasn't going to be able to keep the money he'd stolen from us.

'I want what I paid for. My birth certificate and social security number. And I want them by tomorrow.'

He looked like he was about to start bawling. 'I can't do that,' he said. 'I need time.'

'How much time?'

He shook his head. He didn't know, because he hadn't talked to his friend yet, as he'd never planned to give me anything.

'Does a friend who can get you these documents actually exist? Or was all of it a lie?'

'I promise I have a friend who can do this, my brother. I swear it.'

He tried calling me his brother to put us on friendlier terms, but he knew that, whatever I was, I wasn't close to being his brother, and the words cracked and nearly crumbled as he tried to say them.

'Call him now.'

He did as I asked, probably grateful to do anything to get his mind off what he'd seen when I unmasked myself.

'Al, I need the same you did for my cousin,' he said, once the other phone picked up. Over his phone, I heard a man with a deep, heavy voice ask who was calling. 'Yeah, it's me, Garfield.'

There was more talking on the other end, most of which I could hear. It seemed to be along the lines of asking what was wrong – why was the cook sounding like he was about to piss in his pants? If Al had been in the room with us and had seen the carpet growing wet by the cook's feet and smelled the stench of urine, he'd have known that his question wasn't as funny as he might've thought.

'Nothing wrong, brother', the cook lied. 'I just need a favor.'

'Birth certificate and social security number,' I said.

'Yeah,' the cook said. 'You hear that? Birth certificate and social security. How much?' He lowered his voice, hoping I wouldn't hear him. 'Five hundred?'

They dickered back and forth before reaching a price of $900. Along with looking terrified, the cook seemed relieved he was still going to make eleven hundred dollars from the transaction, but also nervous that I might demand some of my money back. I didn't care that the cook was charging me more than twice the amount the birth certificate and social security number were going to cost him. I had agreed the price and, besides, it was Sergei's money I'd be using. Before he ended his conversation, I said, 'When?'

He wiped a hand across his brow. He'd been sweating quite a bit since seeing my true self. Even more than Chris had sweated standing by a hot grill.

'When the stuff be ready?' he asked.

I heard his friend's answer. 'In two weeks.'

'Not good enough,' I said. 'I want it by Thursday.'

The cook showed a pained grimace, but told his friend he needed it by Thursday.

'Not possible', I heard his friend Al say over the phone. 'I'm no magician. Earliest possible's Friday. But it will cost more . . . Five hundred more.'

'Friday's acceptable,' I said. 'But no later.'

They dickered back and forth, or at least the cook tried to, but his friend wouldn't budge on the additional $500. The cook risked a peek at me, to see if I'd be willing to accept a two-week delivery date. Dejection joined the other emotions battling on his face as he saw that I was standing firm on a Friday deadline. After he'd reluctantly agreed to the price and got off the phone, he told me he'd get my papers to me as soon as he got them, just as he had promised.

'You need to trust more, my brother,' he said, still making sure not to look at me. 'I was never going to cheat you. You just too untrusting.'

I didn't bother arguing the obvious. 'You're going to show up for work every day at Chris's restaurant until you get me my documents. I don't trust you having time on your hands to scheme or run.'

He looked more surprised by this than by anything else that had transpired since I knocked on his door.

'That fucker won't let me work there any longer. Not after today.'

'Call him. Tell him you were ill and will work the rest of the week for free to make up for today. Or tell him something else, I don't care. But if you're not there tomorrow, I will hunt you down and it won't be as pleasant for you then as it has been today.'

He wanted to argue with me, but couldn't work up the nerve to do so. I had him get me a piece of paper and a pen so I could once again write down the information needed for the documents he was going to get me, since he claimed to have misplaced the details I'd given him.

I wasn't worried about him not showing up at the

restaurant the next day. Nor about him telling anyone what he'd seen when I revealed my true self. Because how could he possibly explain it to anyone who hadn't witnessed it for themselves?

I made sure to mask myself before leaving his apartment.

TWENTY-SEVEN

When I got back to Queens (I had plans to meet Jill that night at seven thirty), I took a detour and walked to *The Cultured Cannibal*, this time choosing a spot further up the street from which I could watch the entrance. During the time I was there, I saw several of *them* enter the restaurant, but not one of my kind. After no more than ten minutes of my standing guard, the same gaunt woman with the toothpick-thin legs emerged from the restaurant. Even from a distance of over two hundred feet I could see her face was as heavily painted as the other times I'd seen her. She must've known I was there, because her eyes locked on me the moment she exited the restaurant, and as she stood staring at me like some strange-looking bird she lifted the cellphone she was holding and started dialing. I didn't feel like having another confrontation with the police, especially with my wallet still stuffed with money that I couldn't explain, so I left.

When Jill arrived back at her apartment, I could see the pain from her shoulder injury etched on her face, even though she tried to hide it from me. She kissed me in the same tender sort of way she'd been doing since getting injured, her discomfort robbing her of her passion.

'I'm sick of feeling like an invalid,' she told me, her lips forming an unhappy smile. 'Maybe tomorrow morning I'll take all this stuff off.'

She had told me earlier that the doctor wanted her to keep her shoulder bandaged for two weeks. I once again felt a lump filling my throat. I also thought more about her ex-boyfriend, Ethan, and why I didn't want the police to put him in jail. But hard as it was, I told myself to be patient. I needed to think things through. From what I read in the newspapers, the police were still baffled over the killings I'd done, but I knew I couldn't keep leaving dead bodies behind, especially not someone who could be connected to Jill. When the time came for me to deal with her ex-boyfriend, he would have to disappear. There couldn't be any crime scene left for the police to investigate.

Since Jill couldn't carry grocery packages due to her injury, she needed me to accompany her to the market, which I was more than happy to do. On the way back, I insisted we stop off at the shop where I had bought wine earlier, and I treated us to a bottle of a type of wine called Pinot Noir which Jill picked out. Back at her apartment, Jill taught me how to sauté broccoli (a new vegetable for me) in garlic and olive oil, and how to cook the vegan pasta she'd bought at the market. I also heated up the tomato sauce she'd bought, and once everything was ready we had an enjoyable meal that was complemented nicely by the wine and the music she'd selected from her collection. This time the music wasn't by Mozart, but something called the Brandenburg concertos. Jill explained that the musician who composed them was named Johann Sebastian Bach and that he had preceded Mozart, his death occurring six years before Mozart was born. I wouldn't say I enjoyed the music more than the piano concertos Jill had previously played, but I did find it livelier and soon found that I was glad this man was never picked up by one of my kind. From the way Jill's face lit up, I could tell that at times she forgot about her shoulder pain. But this never seemed to last more than a minute or two, and then I'd catch her fighting to keep me from seeing her grimacing.

After dinner, we spent a quiet evening reading together on the couch (Jill reading one of her college psychology books while I read *Something Happened* by Joseph Heller, another book she'd recommended), with Jill resting her back against me, her knees pulled up almost to her chest. At some point early on, she commented how much calmer I'd seemed the last couple of days. 'Less on edge' was the way she put it.

'Charlie, just sitting up against you like this, I can feel how much more relaxed you are. I guess you're getting more used to New York.'

I agreed with her, telling her that I had every reason to be more relaxed since in a short time I had hopes of dating the most beautiful girl I'd ever met. Of course, the real reason was that the cravings were mostly still sleeping contentedly after the blood feast I'd provided for them. Earlier that evening I'd started to feel some slight stirrings, but this was nothing compared with how I had felt after my first day away from the clan. It was barely even an itch. In any case, Jill appreciated my answer. She twisted herself around enough for me to kiss her, and this time it was more of the passionate variety.

'By my count, only two more weeks,' she said, her eyes half-lidded. She showed a wicked smile and added, 'Unless you've found someone else I don't know about.'

I shook my head. 'Not a chance.'

As I said, it was a nice evening, though at times I found myself drifting into thoughts about her ex-boyfriend and what I'd have to do to make his body disappear.

Shortly before eleven o'clock, Jill got up to go to bed. A few minutes later I turned on the news with the volume set low. The first story was about the 'Slaughter at the Caspian' (this was how the news had dubbed the killings at Sergei's restaurant, which was named the Caspian Café). The police still appeared to be stumped and were asking the public for information. There was nothing further reported about my other two killings.

Once the news program ended, I turned off the television and read until one thirty, then left Jill's apartment. I knew she was avoiding taking her pain medication during the day, but took it before going to bed so she'd be able to sleep. I also knew that the medication would keep her sleeping deeply enough, so I wouldn't have to worry about her waking up and finding the apartment empty.

I walked back to *The Cultured Cannibal*. They were closed at that hour and I didn't have to worry about that gaunt heavily painted woman calling the police on me. I inspected the alley behind the restaurant. As with Chris's restaurant, that was where they kept their dumpsters. There were two of them, both secured by thick padlocks. I examined the locks and determined that I wouldn't be able to break them open with a brick (I'd have little trouble finding one if I searched enough alleys), but instead would need a bolt cutter. I also perused the back door. I'd be able to break in with a crowbar easily enough but there was the possibility that, like Chris's restaurant, they might have a security alarm. There was nothing further I could do at that time to investigate further, or to discover the ingredients they used for their cannibal stew, so I returned to Jill's apartment.

Next morning, I prepared an early meal of oatmeal, stirring in chopped-up strawberries and maple syrup. When Jill emerged from her bedroom to join me, she did so without her arm and shoulder bandaged up.

'I feel so much freer without that on me,' she said. A flash of guilt showed in her smile, probably because of how willfully she was disobeying her doctor's orders. I told her I was glad she had removed the bandages, and I was. She looked more like her old self. Happier. Less fragile. Although I still caught her at times wincing with pain.

As with every morning I'd worked as a dishwasher, Chris wasn't there when I showed up. It wasn't until a quarter to ten that he made an appearance in the kitchen, which was still the earliest I'd seen him there since I'd been working at the restaurant. He didn't say anything, either to me or the cook who was working, and within a minute he left again. At ten o'clock, the other cook – the one I had business with – took over at the grill. He did this so quietly that I almost didn't notice him come in. Under different circumstances I would've been able to smell him if he entered the same room as me, but not in this kitchen with the smell of grease and burnt animal flesh so thick in the air. I turned to watch him. His usual angry glower was gone, replaced by something meek and fearful. He made sure not to look in my direction, not even a quick glance. He'd seen something worse than death yesterday, and he didn't want to see it ever again.

A few minutes after the cook arrived, Chris reappeared in the kitchen, arms folded across his chest, his face set smugly. He looked triumphant, as if he had won a battle of some sort. As if he were actually concerned, he asked the cook how he was feeling. The cook mumbled out, in thick words, that he was better.

'Good, good,' Chris said, loud enough so I'd be able to hear him. 'Good also that we made our arrangement.'

Of course, I knew he had said this for my benefit. So I'd know he had gotten the last laugh. Whatever deal he had made and however he was cheating the cook, I didn't care. As long as the cook showed up each day until I got from him what I'd paid for, I didn't care.

TWENTY-EIGHT

I no longer had any reason to search for the thick-jawed man. Even if I found him and even if he turned out to be one of my kind, like I believed, what secret could he tell me regarding the cravings that I hadn't already figured out? Still, I was back in East Flatbush Thursday evening searching for him. Maybe it was curiosity that sent me back there, or maybe a sense of not having finished what I'd started. Or possibly I just needed to kill some time until I saw Jill, which wasn't going to be until much later that night since she had commitments at her college.

The cravings were still sluggish thanks to my night of savagery and were stirring only slightly more than yesterday, so I could've spent the evening alone in her apartment reading, but for some reason the thought of doing that made me uncomfortable. Instead, I felt as if I needed to keep moving and breathe in as much outside air as I could, even if it was only this foul city air. (Which, I have to admit, I was now getting used to. In fact at times I even found it hard to imagine what the unpolluted wilderness air smelled like.)

As I walked, I realized what it was that was making me feel so restless. Earlier I had scrutinized the back-page advertisements in the free newspaper given away at Chris's restaurant, and again found the one where a woman was searching for someone to pretend to be her private vampire. In order for me to contact her, I would have to send her something called a text message and a photograph of myself, neither of which I knew how to do, although I assumed a cellphone was needed, which I knew most of *them* used. But that was only a small part of why that advertisement made me feel restless. Or to be more accurate, troubled.

While my kin and kind would have been ashamed of me for resorting to savagery, they'd be disgusted enough to disown me if I entered into an agreement with one of *them* just so that I could satisfy the cravings in such an unnatural way and they discovered I had done so. Of course, they would also renounce me and blacken my name among all of my kind if they ever learned that I had chosen to live with Jill, as they would only be able to look at her as one of *them* and not as how I saw her. That part I was OK with. Whatever my kin might think about that didn't matter, because when I was with Jill I felt more normal than I had at any other time in my life. But the thought of acting as some strange woman's private vampire made my skin crawl. Even though the advertisement didn't spell it out, I understood that I'd be helping this woman engage in a sexual fantasy and that I might even have to be intimate with her to fulfill my end of the bargain, the idea of which was utterly repugnant. I was sure Jill would also find it so if she ever discovered that I was doing this. But it would be far worse if she discovered I was engaging in acts of savagery instead. If that happened, she'd look at me as some-thing monstrous, which I don't think I'd be able to bear. And it would be even worse if she ever learned about my clan and what we did to survive.

This was why I felt so conflicted. And troubled. And perhaps this was the real reason why I continued my search for what was quickly becoming an almost mythical thick-jawed man. I needed an excuse to spend hours walking the streets so I could release the pent-up anxious energy that had built up inside me. That had to be why I was doing this, since I no longer expected to see the thick-jawed man I was purportedly searching for. And why I didn't believe my eyes when I spotted him working in a salvage yard.

Except I soon realized it wasn't the same man I'd seen earlier. This man seemed younger, maybe by as much as twenty years younger, and while he was stocky and short like the other man he wasn't as broad in the shoulders. But he *was* one of my kind. Even though he was too far from me to catch his scent, there was no question about it.

I don't know how long I stood transfixed, not quite believing what I was seeing. Maybe twenty seconds, maybe longer. Long enough for him to notice me, and for me to notice that there were others like him working in the salvage yard. All of them with thick, heavy jaws and short, stocky bodies. All with the same coarse black hair and eyes dark as night, like my own, and all of them unquestionably of my kind.

I came out of my stupor as more of them started to notice me, and more of them came out of the salvage yard's main building. I counted eighteen of them, all different ages. Some looked as young as thirteen, others as old as seventy. Only boys and men, though. None of the clan's women were within sight. I knew why that was. They must've been occupied with other chores, and were probably in other parts of the salvage yard.

The salvage yard's main building was large enough to house a dozen families as well as whatever work was done there, but there were other shack-like structures scattered about the salvage yard, enough for a clan roughly twice the size of my own. As I scanned the salvage yard and saw more of my kind emerging, I was amazed at how large the yard was. Where I was now was a hidden part of Brooklyn. It was only by chance that I'd stumbled on the maze of streets leading to it, as none of them were on my map.

For as much as a minute, I stood silently looking at them and they stared back at me. And all the while more of them emerged from different structures, until there were at least fifty of them in view. When several of them started moving toward the gate in the chain-link fence that enclosed the salvage yard, I turned and ran as fast as I could, my heart pounding so ferociously that I felt it pulsating violently in my temples like a beating drum.

It made no sense for me to be running away from them like this. These were my kind. They would've assumed that I had gotten stranded in New York and would've treated me kindly, at least as kindly as any of my type are capable of. I couldn't explain the blind panic that filled me. I'd never felt fear like this before. It was almost as if I were one of *them*. But however irrational my fear was, I couldn't help it and I ran the same as if I were being hunted down.

Without turning to look, I knew they'd opened the gate and that some of them were running after me, and I knew they'd be chasing me with one or more of the trucks that I'd seen in their yard. Knowing this made me run faster.

I escaped from the maze of desolate streets that kept their salvage yard hidden, and found myself on a busy Brooklyn street alive with traffic and thriving businesses. As I dodged pedestrians strolling aimlessly on the sidewalk, I didn't slow down. Even though they were silent, I could feel the clan members were gaining on me. This made no sense. Like the other men in my clan, I was taller and rangier than the men I'd seen in this Brooklyn clan, all of whom, because of their short, stumpy legs, I should've been able to outrace. But that wasn't happening.

I didn't risk looking over my shoulder. I knew that would slow me down. But I could hear them, and knew they were now no less than twenty yards behind me and were gaining every second. But even if I could outrace them, I wouldn't be able to outrace their trucks, which would be upon me at any moment.

I darted into the traffic, narrowly missing a motorcycle while another car slammed on its breaks and blasted its horn at me. The ones chasing me didn't follow me into the street. Once I'd made it on to the opposite sidewalk, I gave them a quick look and saw three of them staring at me across the street. A chill ran up my spine as I realized they were looking at me as if I might be one of *them*. But I couldn't give that much thought, as I saw one of their trucks fast approaching.

The reason I crossed the street when I did was that I'd seen a diner-style restaurant on the other side. I entered it just as the truck pulled up to the curb and two of the clan members spilled out of it. They must've been undecided whether to risk a public commotion, because none of them followed me into the restaurant, at least not right away. So I kept going, ignoring the protestations of a waitress as I continued into the kitchen. The cook yelled at me, but I kept going until I was out the back door, emerging in the alley where their dumpsters were kept. Diagonally across from where I was standing were more dumpsters, and the back door of what had to be another restaurant.

This door was unlocked, and I found myself in another restaurant's kitchen. Someone yelled, 'Hey, what the hell?' I didn't so much as glance in this person's direction, but rushed through the kitchen and out into the main dining room. Two of the waitresses gave me funny looks, but before they could say anything I was out the front door.

Cutting through both restaurants and the alley left me one block away, and it didn't look as if the clan members had any idea that that's where I was. Maybe they were waiting outside the first restaurant for me to leave, or maybe they had eventually followed me in and decided I was hiding in the bathroom.

For now, I had lost them.

TWENTY-NINE

I was distracted later that night when I met up with Jill, and felt the same the next morning when we had breakfast together and also while I washed dishes. How could I not be, knowing that a clan of my kind lived in Brooklyn? The idea of it was staggering. I knew about many of the clans of my kind, but certainly not about all of them. Still, the ones I knew about all lived hidden deep in the wilderness, as my clan did. I would never have imagined a clan situated in the middle of a large city like this. The more I thought about it, the more envious I became of this clan. They didn't have to live in the backward manner that my kin did. And they never had to risk the cravings' wrath because of a snowbound winter lasting longer than expected, nor did they have to go on the long perilous pickups that I had done and my great-uncle Jedidiah and others before us had had to do. This city had so many stragglers and other such loners and lost people who could be picked up from the street as easily as I could pick up apples from a market. They didn't have to plan ahead or bother rationing their meat. And their salvage yard was more than private enough for them to perform slaughtering rituals and meat preparation without risk of discovery, and more than large enough for them to hide several thousand years' worth of crushed bones. I couldn't help wondering if the elders knew about this clan's existence and had kept us in the dark, or if they were as ignorant about it as I had been.

That Friday morning, at times I found myself lost in thought as I wondered about this clan and whether there were other clans like them hiding in other large cities. Consequently, I was surprised when I looked over my shoulder and saw the cook I was doing business with taking his position behind the grill. I hadn't seen him enter the kitchen, nor would I have guessed that four hours had passed since I arrived at work. As with the other day, he looked timid without even a hint of his earlier angry countenance showing. Also as with the other day, he was making sure to not so much as glance in my direction as he cooked meats and eggs and other foods on the grill.

I left the sink and approached him. Even though I did this silently and his eyes were fixed on the food he was cooking, he sensed that I was standing near him, and his eyes became fearful and his body shrank into itself, almost as if he were trying to hide from me.

'Do you have the documents I paid for?'

He looked as if he was surprised by my question, and shook his head in a panicky sort of way. At that moment he seemed incapable of speech.

This infuriated me, and I was aware of some of my true nature slipping back into my voice as I snarled at him, 'We had a deal that you'd deliver my documents to me today.'

He winced the same as if I'd struck him, but found his voice, claiming, 'My brother, I swear, I'm getting them today. It's too early now. But I'll be getting them tonight, and we can arrange to meet after and I'll give them to you. I swear it.'

I felt my anger fading as I studied him, and decided he was telling me the truth. I took a deep breath and tried to calm myself. I knew the cravings were making me quick to anger. Although they were moving more sluggishly within me than when I first arrived in New York, they were working their way into my joints and skull and were now noticeably worse than yesterday. Still, if they continued to move lethargically, I might have as much as another week before needing to feed them again.

'Bring them tomorrow morning when you come to work, and then we're done.'

He nodded, his eyes remaining stubbornly focused on a single spot on the grill, as if he were afraid he'd die if he so much as caught a glimpse of me. I would've liked to have met him later that night so I could collect my documents from him, but I had plans to meet Jill as soon as I finished work.

I left him and went back to washing dishes.

THIRTY

'What will you tell them about me?'

Jill grinned at my question. At times I'd still catch her wincing from pain, but overall her color was better and she was moving more freely.

'That you were the one who rescued me after that jerk Ethan stranded me on the Mass Pike, and that we've since become good friends.' A playfulness entered her voice as she added, 'Don't worry, Charlie, I won't tell them you're my boyfriend, since we're not officially dating yet.'

We had walked from Jill's apartment to the Parsons Boulevard subway station, where we were going to take the subway to the White Hall Terminal in Manhattan, and then from there a ferry to Staten Island and finally an Uber ride to her parents' house. Ostensibly, I was helping Jill by carrying a duffel bag filled with the clothing and school books that she was going to need that weekend, but her real reason for having me accompany her was so I could meet her parents. Once we were seated in the subway car, Jill scooted along the bench, so that her uninjured side was up against me, and took hold of my closest arm with both her hands.

'Don't be nervous,' she said, grinning. 'My parents will love you. After all, you're the one who rescued me.'

My uneasiness wasn't caused by the thought of meeting her parents, but rather was the work of the cravings. I had thought earlier that I'd have another week before I'd need to feed them again, but now I was beginning to believe it would have to be earlier than that. I tried to ignore the discomfort the cravings were causing and focus only on the feel of Jill's body against mine, and for the most part this was successful.

Later, when we were on the ferry, as we approached the Statue of Liberty Jill pointed it out. I'd long known about this structure as there was an illustration of it in one of the clan's books. Jill and I were holding hands at this point, and standing by the railing so we could get a good view of the statue. Her body leaned against mine, and she told me how she and her pa used to take the ferry to Manhattan when she was a child.

'I used to love doing that as a kid. We'd always end up in Central Park and he'd buy me a hot pretzel or sometimes roasted chestnuts, and always a cherry ice.'

I didn't want to imagine Jill as a child. I was afraid if I did I might see her at that age as one of *them*, and I didn't want that to ever happen.

'I'll take you to Central Park soon,' I said. 'And I'll buy you a pretzel, or roasted chestnuts if you'd prefer, and a cherry ice, whatever that is.'

'You don't know what ices are?'

Obviously, I knew what ice was, but I was sure that wasn't exactly the same thing as what Jill was talking about. I shook my head.

'We'll have to rectify that soon.'

We moved from the side of the boat to the back so that we could watch Manhattan as we floated away from it. 'This is the first time I've been on a boat,' I said.

'Over here, bub.'

I looked at Jill. Her eyes were half-lidded and face tilted upward, and she was using the index finger of her right hand to wave me to her. When we kissed, it was so deeply passionate that it ached when it ended. I don't think I'll ever forget the way her eyes glistened, and the little smile she showed when she realized the effect her kiss had had on me. I certainly hoped I'd never forget it.

Jill's parents' house was bigger than the houses I built for my clan, but that was mostly because they only had a single level, while her parents' house had two. The street her parents lived on was filled with similar houses, each separated by a small strip of land, and – except for the maze of streets that led to the salvage yard where the Brooklyn clan resided – it was far quieter than any of the other streets I'd roamed since coming to New York.

They met us at the door. They were both on the small side, like Jill. Her ma was about the same height, her pa five or six inches taller. Neither of them would've provided my clan with much meat if they were ever picked up. It was hard for me to guess their ages since they both looked so much younger than my parents. Since they were important to Jill, I tried hard to see them as I did her and not as *them*, and after a minute or so I was mostly able to succeed at this.

Her pa smiled at me, although his smile seemed strained somewhat by nervousness. 'You're the young man who rescued our daughter,' he said, his voice also betraying nervousness. 'I'd like to thank you for that.'

He extended his hand, which I took. He might've been small, but his hand was hardened enough by calluses to let me know that he worked with his hands.

'Jill's also told us that you've been the perfect gentleman since she's gotten to know you.'

'Dad!' Jill interjected, her cheeks peppering nicely with red. 'Cut it out. Please.'

'Well, you did tell us that,' he stubbornly insisted. 'And your mom and I appreciate it. But never mind.' He turned to me, and said, 'Charlie, how about joining us inside for some coffee and pie? Or some beers if you'd like.'

'I don't think so, dad,' Jill said. 'You're not giving Charlie the third degree today. Besides, he has plans and has to head back. He came along only to help me with my duffel bag.'

None of this was true. I didn't have any imminent plans, at least none that Jill knew about. But as I'd already mentioned, Jill had her ulterior motives for bringing me, so I didn't correct her.

'Your friend doesn't have fifteen minutes to spare?'

'No, he doesn't.'

Her pa didn't seem to want to accept that answer, but before he could say anything further, her ma stepped forward. 'Well, at least let me kiss you,' she said.

This was awkward for me, though I was no longer seeing her as one of *them*, at least not completely. Still, my own ma had never kissed me, at least not that I could remember, nor had any of my other women kin. With Jill it was different, but with any others it was a custom I'd rather not have participated in. Still, I lowered my knees and leaned forward, and

submitted to Jill's ma kissing me on my cheek. Almost immediately after that, Jill took me by the hand and informed her
parents that she needed to have a word with me in private
before I left. Her parents stayed where they were while Jill
led me down the short walkway in front of their house, and
then further down the sidewalk until she felt we were far
enough away for them not to be able to overhear us if we
talked softly.

'I love both my parents dearly, but fifteen minutes would've
turned into three hours,' she whispered to me. 'By the time
they were done interrogating you, you'd have been ready to
dump me for the first girl whose parents aren't so damn nosy.'

'Not possible.'

'Don't be so sure. Anyway, this was meant to be just a
quick meet and for you to help me with my bag . . . I'll bring
you back another time when we're both better prepared.'

Her eyes melted a bit as she smiled at me. 'It really was
sweet of you to come here like this. So, any plans now that
you're going to have a weekend free of me?'

'Nothing more than spending some quiet time alone
reading,' I lied.

THIRTY-ONE

For a reason I couldn't explain, I looked over my shoulder at the precise moment when the cook entered the kitchen on Saturday morning. He didn't stop at the grill, but instead continued toward me as I rinsed off dishes in the sink. I wiped my hands on the apron and took the large envelope he held out to me.

'That has what you want,' he said, his voice barely a croak, his stare frozen at a spot on the floor. It had been almost five days since I showed him my true self, and he was still afraid to catch so much as a glimpse of me. 'You'll keep away from me now?'

I took out the birth certificate and social security card from inside the envelope. The birth certificate claimed I was born at the Catholic Memorial Hospital on February 20, 1987, which was the date I'd written down for the cook. I knew I was twenty-eight, but I didn't know what day I was born since it isn't our custom to celebrate the day of our birth, as *their* world does. My ma, though, once told me that I was born during a harsh February snowstorm, almost as if she were accusing me of picking that time to make things more difficult for her. Anyway, I needed a date of birth for the certificate and the one I gave the cook seemed like it would be close enough. The other document in the envelope was much smaller, only a few inches long, but it had printed on it the number that would allow me to work in *their* world and do jobs such as carpentry and building houses. I examined both documents carefully.

'You'll never see me again,' I promised.

I took off my apron and carried it with me as I walked out of the kitchen. Chris was standing by the cash register, and when he saw me coming toward him his jaw set and his eyes slitted as he gave me a shrewd look. He waited until I reached him before telling me to get back to work.

'I'm counting this as your fifteen minute break,' he added.

'Do whatever you want with your breaks. I'm no longer working here,' I said.

'Yeah? Well guess what, you want to get paid, then you work till your shift's finished. You're not leaving me high and dry like this, at least not if you want any money for this week.'

I grabbed him by the throat, moving too fast for him even to blink, let alone back away. This surprised him, to say the least, and he tried to struggle against me, his eyes bulging with both outrage and shock. All I had to do was squeeze my hand, and I'd crush his windpipe. He couldn't yell for help. He could barely make a gurgling noise. As he clawed at my hand that was gripping his throat, he looked into my face and that was when I showed him a glimpse of my true self. When he began trembling in fear over what he saw, I let go of him. He stumbled backwards a step, gasping for air, his hands clutching his throat.

This all happened in a matter of seconds. What I'd noticed during my short time as a dishwasher was that fewer of *them* came in on Saturday mornings than during the week. At that time there was only a scattering of them sitting in the booths and at the counter, and none of them noticed what happened. Also on Saturday mornings only one waitress worked, and she didn't notice either, although she turned our way after I let go of Chris's throat.

'You'll pay me what you owe me,' I said, keeping my voice low.

'You son of a bitch,' he forced between his gasps. He backed several more steps away from me. 'I should call the police on you.'

He knew I would kill him if he did so. Maybe not right then, but he knew I'd come back another time for him. He saw that in the glimpse I had shown him, and the knowledge of it made him tremble more.

'Pay me what you owe me and you'll never have to worry about me again.'

He was torn between fear and greed. Reluctantly he came to a decision. 'I'm not paying for today,' he said. 'Not with you leaving me without a dishwasher.'

'You're paying me for all the hours I've worked. You can put on the apron and wash dishes yourself if need be.'

Most of the people in the restaurant were beginning to look at us. All three of them at the counter had turned to watch us, and I was sure several of them in the booths were also watching. Chris was aware also that he had gained an audience, and this seemed to embolden him. But then he remembered the glimpse of my true self he had caught, and lost his nerve.

'Good riddance to bad rubbish,' he muttered. 'I knew you were a mistake, but I tried being a nice guy and helping you out. This is what I get. Fine, I'll pay you. It will be worth it to never see your face again.'

I told him what he owed me for five days and four hours of dishwashing. He didn't argue the amount, but when he counted out the money it was $68 short.

'Rental for the apron and cost for broken dishes,' he grunted out with a straight face.

'No. You're not cheating me any longer. You're paying me the full amount. Also for what you cheated me of last week. Otherwise it will be as bad for you as if you didn't pay me anything.'

His first impulse was to fight me on it. I saw that in his eyes. If he hadn't caught that glimpse, he would've tried it. But he did catch it, and the fight quickly bled out of him. Grudgingly he counted out $136 and laid it on the counter.

'You lowlife ingrate,' he said. 'Take it and get out of here. You're never welcome back here.'

I took the money and left. I was done with him, and done with dishwashing.

When we met, at a coffee shop in Brooklyn, the girl introduced herself as Annabelle, but from the way she smiled with her small and darkly painted lips I had the idea that she had made the name up. Yesterday after I left Jill, I found a store in Manhattan where a clerk sold me a smartphone capable of sending text messages and taking photographs. As mentioned earlier, I can have a friendly face when I want to, and that evening I showed my friendliest face (even though the cravings were gnawing deeper into me and had become worse than a nuisance) and the sales clerk not only patiently taught me how to use the phone but treated me to doe-eyed looks and insisted on giving me her own phone number; and when the opportunity arrived she let her hand linger on top of my own. Once I left the store, I sent a message to the girl advertising for a private vampire, who turned out to be Annabelle. After an exchange of several more messages and photographs, we agreed to meet at this coffee shop, where we were now sitting across from each other at a table in the back.

'I like what I see,' she said.

I took a sip of my coffee and told her that I did too, which was the truth. Despite the fact that she was extraordinarily pale (although she might have looked more pale than she actually was because of the way her mouth was painted and the thick, ropy dark-brown hair that framed her face), she looked like she'd be full of blood and wouldn't miss a pint or two. She wasn't fat, but she had this round, overflowing shape. I remember once reading about a girl described as having an 'hourglass' figure, which I later understood when I found an illustration of an hourglass. This girl Annabelle could've been similarly described, and with the short, sleeveless dress she was wearing plenty of her flesh was on display. In spite of her paleness there was nothing anemic about her, and I reckoned her blood would satisfy the cravings as effectively as that of any of *them*.

She lowered her voice and gave me what could only be described as a coquettish smile. 'You understand that I don't want you to just break my skin with your teeth. I want you to draw blood. And when I'm close to climaxing, you have to drink my blood. Actually drink it. I have a way to make my nose bleed when I want it to, and you have to lick up all the blood that comes out. I need that.'

'I will do that,' I said.

She took a nibble of the chocolate pastry she'd bought. Her eyes darkened with intensity. 'It can't just be something you're willing to do,' she said. 'You have to want to do it as badly as I do.'

'I can promise you that that will be the case.'

'I need you to hunger for my blood.'

'I will.'

Her smile became more of the excited, nervous kind. She held out her arm with her wrist upwards. Like the rest of her, the appendage wasn't fat or sagging but round, and the flesh was firm. My clan would've done very well from her.

'I've got goosebumps,' she said. 'Feel them.'

I had little choice but to do as she asked, if I wanted her blood. I felt the small bumps on her skin.

'So when do we do this?' she asked eagerly. 'Now? Tonight?'

'I can't today. I have plans. Perhaps later next week? Wednesday or Thursday?'

I did have plans, though only for much later that night. And I wanted to postpone this sordid act until it was absolutely necessary. The last two days the cravings had been waking up, but I thought I might have until Thursday before I'd have to feed them again or risk being driven to savagery. Possibly Friday.

She pouted. 'You're being such a tease. You get me all worked up, and now you're telling me I have to wait.'

'I'm sorry. But that's how it has to be.'

Her pout faded, and she gave me a slow, calculating look. She leaned forward and in a harsher voice said, 'You're not getting cold feet, are you? Because if you are, for Christ's sake just tell me now and don't waste my time.' She let out an angry exhale and confided, 'The guy I was talking to before dragged things out for three weeks before chickening out. The coward.'

Although I was repulsed by the thought of it, I said, 'You have nothing to worry about. I'll be looking forward to our time alone together. Hopefully it will be just the first of many such encounters.'

Somewhat mollified, she said, 'OK, then. Anticipation will make it sweeter. How about Wednesday after I finish work. Eight o'clock? My apartment in Manhattan?'

'Let's make it the midnight hour. That seems more appropriate for what we'll be doing.'

I'd have to hope Jill would be asleep by then, so I'd be able to sneak out and perform this sickening act without her ever realizing it. It seemed likely that she would be, since she'd been retiring to her bedroom by eleven o'clock every night. Of course, this was so she'd be able to get up early enough to join me for breakfast.

But that wouldn't be the case much longer. Five hours previously, having retired as a dishwasher, I'd contacted one of the builders who gave me a business card, and since I now had my precious social security number and they still needed more builders I was hired to start on Monday at eight in the morning. I figured I'd continue waking at five since that was the most natural time for me, but after Wednesday I'd start preparing breakfast later in the morning, which would suit Jill better.

Given the way her eyes lit up, this girl who called herself Annabelle seemed to like my suggestion.

'That's an excellent idea,' she said. 'The only thing better would be the witching hour, but I'd be dragging all day if we connected then. Midnight it will be. Until then.'

She got up from her seat and came over to me, her mouth open as she pressed her lips against mine, her ropy hair shrouding us. I tried (rather unsuccessfully) to imagine she was Jill as I allowed this to happen, since I knew if I pulled away that would be the end of our deal. While I'd rather have resorted to more savagery to satisfy the cravings, I'd already decided that after tonight I needed to follow their laws so as not to jeopardize my life with Jill.

She moved her mouth to my ear and, in a throaty whisper, said, 'When I kiss you again, you can bite my lip.'

I shook my head. I was afraid of how several drops of blood might stir the cravings. 'The first blood I taste from you will be on Wednesday at midnight.'

She seemed to appreciate that answer. 'Anticipation. Wonderful! Until then.'

She kissed me again, this time harder and more violently. It was more like she was mashing her face against mine, and I tried to keep her from knowing how repulsed I was by it.

After she finally (and mercifully) ended it, I watched her as she walked away – and all I could think about was how much meat my clan would've been able to carve from her curvy, firm, overflowing body.

THIRTY-TWO

When Jill's former boyfriend, Ethan, returned home, there wasn't anyone in the car with him. If there had been, I would've taken them also. I glanced up at the moon, and from its position in the night sky guessed it was two in the morning, which meant I'd been waiting for him for over five hours.

When I left earlier, I didn't know that he lived in a house. All I had was his address, and given his age I assumed he lived in an apartment, like Jill. I came prepared, regardless, bringing a crowbar and other tools so I could break into wherever he lived. When I saw the large sculpted bushes by his front door, I realized I wouldn't have to break in, as they provided the necessary cover. I hid behind these bushes and decided to grab him as he walked to his front door. But inside the garage there must've been a door leading into the house, because shortly after he pulled his green-colored sedan into the garage – the very same one I'd seen him in when he abandoned Jill at that Massachusetts rest stop – I heard noises inside the house.

I left my hiding place and knocked on the front door. Very quickly I heard him rushing to the door, yelling before he reached it, 'Fuck you, Goldberg, if you're coming to complain about noise, you need to get your head out of your ass, because it wasn't me. I just got home—'

As Ethan swung the door open, his beefy face contorted into a look of extreme belligerence. When he saw me and realized I wasn't who he was expecting, he blinked dumbly, trying to remember where he'd seen me before. I didn't give him any time to remember and punched him in the chest, hard enough to make him crumple backwards.

I didn't punch him as hard as I'd have liked to. I didn't want to kill him. Nor did I want to leave any forensic evidence behind, which was why I wore gloves, purchased earlier, and why I punched him above the heart instead of in the face, where I'd be leaving blood and broken teeth. I followed him into the house, bringing with me a bag filled with tools I thought I might need, as well as rope and a thick piece of cloth. I dragged him away from the door, so I could close it. In less than a minute I had him trussed and gagged, with him putting up only a feeble fight after the blow he had absorbed. I found his car keys still in his pants pocket, then hoisted him on to my shoulder and carried him through the house and into the attached garage. I laid him on the cement floor (if I'd dropped him on to it, like I was inclined to do, I might've left blood behind), so I could open his car's trunk. It was filled with stuff, and I moved enough of it to the back seat so I could fit him inside the trunk. By this time he had recovered sufficiently from the blow to try to yell for help, but the gag muffled most of the noise and all he accomplished was making his face a darker shade of red. I had to bend him somewhat to get him inside the trunk, but once I had him in there I closed the lid.

When I saw him drive up to the garage, the door had opened without him leaving the car and I figured he had a device of sorts that allowed this to be done. It didn't take me long to find that he kept it clipped to his sun visor. Once I had the garage door open, I drove out and, having used the device to close the garage door behind me, pulled the car on to the street and headed to Brooklyn.

I had to backtrack half a dozen times before I was able to find the hidden maze of streets leading to the salvage yard, but eventually I found it and pulled the car up beside the locked gate. I had bolt cutters with me – though I'd bought them so I could search the dumpsters at *The Cultured Cannibal,* they'd be useful here if needed – but instead of snapping off the padlock securing the gate, I found a rock that weighed about a pound and threw it so it clanged noisily off the metal grate covering the garage bay. I started looking for a larger rock that might make more noise, but that turned out to be unnecessary as the garage bay's door slid open and three of the members of the clan stepped out. I moved over to the gate so they could see me better, and one of them walked toward me. This clan member was much older than my pa, maybe as old as the elders of my clan, and he looked at me as sternly as one of my clan's elders might've under the same circumstances. He didn't say anything to me after unlocking the gate. He didn't need to. It was understood what I was to do, and I got back into the green sedan and drove it into the open garage bay. After the one who must've been an elder followed me into the bay, the door was brought down. I got out of the car and walked to the back of it so I could open the trunk. The three clan members gathered around me while I did this, and I noticed the elder nodding appreciatively as he looked down at Ethan squirming helplessly. Jill's former boyfriend's eyes grew large as he looked from one clan member to the next. A weak, pleading noise escaped from him. That was all he was capable of, given the gag and all the yelling for help he'd tried doing since I took him.

They needed him alive for the slaughtering ritual, which was the only reason they kept their true selves masked. Otherwise, Ethan would've probably expired from a heart attack. That was why we used burlap sacks – to keep *them* from seeing us like that. Still, the fear in Ethan's eyes was something palpable, and seeing it made the cravings dig all that deeper inside me.

'A gift,' I said to the clan members.

Without speaking, one of them who was close to my own age left, only to return a minute later with a large burlap sack. The elder and the other clan member lifted Ethan out of the trunk and dumped him into the sack that the younger one held open. Then he flung the sack over his shoulder and carried Ethan away.

'I need you to make this car disappear,' I said. 'Can you do that?'

The elder grunted to indicate that this would happen. He was studying me carefully. 'You're a Husk,' he said, nodding slowly. 'From the New Hampshire wilderness.'

This surprised me. A clan that I'd never heard of living secretly in the middle of New York not only knew about my clan but was able to recognize me as a member of it.

'The sign out front calls this the Trundull Salvage Yard. Is that your clan's name? Trundull?'

His thick lips compressed into a frown. From the way he looked at me, with such disapproval, I couldn't help thinking of my pa. Or the elders back home.

'How long has your clan lived here in Brooklyn?'

'Longer than yours has been in New Hampshire.'

I tried to absorb that. 'How many do you have in your clan?'

'More than in the Husk clan.'

This made sense, given how large the salvage yard was and how easy it would be for them to get meat. Because they didn't have to go on the long dangerous expeditions I had gone on, and my great-uncle Jedidiah before me, they didn't need to worry about keeping their clan from growing too large. Nor, I imagined, was life as difficult for them as it was for any of the clans hiding in the wilderness.

'Are there other clans like yours living among *them* in large cities?'

He stood stone-faced, not caring to answer that question. I found myself growing increasingly nervous as I watched him, and more to break the silence than for any other reason, I asked, 'Do my elders know about the existence of your clan?'

'Why did you run from us two days ago?' he demanded, ignoring my question.

I shook my head and muttered something about having my reasons. That was all I could muster.

'We thought maybe the cravings made you insane and that's why you ran. But the cravings haven't got that far in you yet. You ain't insane. Boy, why'd you run?'

'I didn't expect to find a clan living here. My elders never told me about you. It surprised me.'

'What do you mean by it "surprised" you? You were searching for us.'

'Not for a whole clan,' I insisted. 'Days ago I saw one of you walking on a sidewalk miles from here. I caught only a glimpse of him, but I thought he might be one of my kind who had gotten stranded in this city. That's who I was searching for.'

'That don't explain why you ran from us.'

My mind was buzzing. I still hadn't figured out the reason, but I needed to tell him something and half heard myself saying, 'It was partly the cravings. I wasn't thinking clearly because of them. Mostly, I thought you wouldn't like me hunting for *them* in your city once I could get myself a new van.'

He grunted. The lies I told him seemed to make sense to him.

'You lose your van? That why you still here?'

'It broke down outside New York,' I said, expanding my lie. 'I hadn't started picking *them* up yet. I was planning to start from New York and work my way back to New Hampshire. When the van died on me, I had to set it on fire so the police wouldn't find any of the dried blood and other material inside of it. But I'll be getting another one soon.'

He grunted again. Apparently, what I said made perfect sense to him. 'You can't hunt here,' he said. 'Your elders should've told you that.'

The younger one who'd carried away the burlap sack returned, and was holding a small package wrapped in white paper. I had no trouble smelling what was wrapped inside the paper. The elder nodded to him, and the younger one held the package out to me.

'A pound of meat,' the elder said. 'It will keep the cravings satisfied until you can return to your home.'

I shook my head. It made no sense that I was turning down his offer, since I came here hoping I'd get properly slaughtered and prepared meat in exchange for Ethan. It was true that, although I wanted Ethan to disappear since I didn't want to leave his body for the police, I also wanted that meat. With Jill gone until Sunday night I'd be able to cook it up in her kitchen, and a pound of meat would keep the cravings content for possibly another two weeks, which would allow me to put off committing that sickening act with that girl named Annabelle. I was confused as to why I was refusing the meat that I so desperately wanted, but no more so than the elder and the other two clan members. At least at first. Then a glimmer showed in the elder's eyes, and his expression became one of scorn.

'You fell in love with one of *them*,' he said, his mouth convulsing as if he had something abhorrent to spit out. 'You think you can live as they do. But you can't. The cravings won't allow it.'

I shook my head, denying what he was saying, even though it was mostly true. But I had found a way to be able to live with Jill while satisfying the cravings. If I told him about how *their* blood fed the cravings as much as their meat did, and how I'd found one of them who was going to willingly let me drink her blood, this elder and the other clan members would've been so outraged that they would've torn me apart and buried me deep in their salvage yard. I didn't dare turn my back on them. I took a step backwards, toward the door, and continued to shake my head.

The elder had taken the package from the younger clan member and shook it angrily at me.

'What you want to do is an abomination,' he spat out. 'It's unnatural to think of *them* as existing for anything other than the one purpose they serve. Don't be a fool any longer. You need this meat. The cravings demand it.'

I kept shaking my head as I took more steps backwards. The two younger clan members were tensing as if they planned to charge me. I prayed they would stay where they were. Up close I could see how powerfully built they were. If they came after me I'd have to fight them, and I didn't like my chances, not against three of them.

'What if you magically found a way to stop the cravings in yourself,' the elder asked, 'but had babies who took after you instead of the mother? How would you explain their appetite? Have you thought of that?'

I had thought about that ever since I realized I was hopelessly in love with Jill. But I continued to shake my head while I stepped backwards toward the door. The younger clan member looked questioningly at the elder, but the elder shook his head.

'When the cravings have wormed their way deep into your brain and bones and you're ready to face the truth instead of this fantasy you've concocted, come back here. We'll feed you and send you back to the New Hampshire wilderness.'

None of them tried to stop me as I opened the door and stepped out of the garage bay into the night air. The elder had left the gate in the chain-link fence unlocked, and I fled through it. My blood was ice cold in my veins as I started running. I knew how fortunate I had been that they'd let me leave. Of course, the elder did so because he was convinced the cravings would send me back to him. Still, if this had been my own clan dealing with a stranger from a different clan who was planning what I was planning, they wouldn't have let him run away.

As I raced through the maze of streets, I began to understand why I'd turned down that meat. Because of how horrified Jill would have been if she ever learned that I'd cooked it in her kitchen. And even if she never learned about it, it would have been an act of betrayal. The money I took from Sergei would've been enough to rent a room with a kitchen and I could've cooked the meat there, but I finally quit lying to myself and accepted that if I did that I'd also be betraying Jill, who would have been equally horrified learning I'd done that. I couldn't change the past, but I could vow to never touch that type of meat again, no matter how much I craved it. That way, I'd be as true to Jill as much as the cravings allowed. Which meant I also had to forget about *The Cultured Cannibal*, even if their stew was what I believed it was and though it was served on a plate in an expensive restaurant.

The cravings were leaving me no good choices. The best I'd be able to do was to commit acts that would disgust Jill rather than horrify her. That was the best option I had.

THIRTY-THREE

I didn't take the subway back to Queens. Instead, I ran a mile or so after I escaped from the secret maze of streets that kept the clan's salvage yard well hidden, and then walked the rest of the way. It was daybreak by the time I got back to Jill's apartment, but the night air and the hours of walking helped me think.

Even though sunlight was brightening the room and the cravings had become more agitated (most likely angry at me for not taking the offered meat), I lay down on the couch and quickly fell asleep, dozing until noon. When I awoke, I sat up and held my head in my hands. The cravings had gotten worse. My muscles throughout my body were achy, and my skull felt as if it was being squeezed in a vise. Even my eyes hurt. Like they were being pricked by pins. The cravings hadn't taken full control yet, but they were punishing me nonetheless. As I sat rubbing circles hard along my temples, I didn't see how I'd be able to wait until Wednesday to feed the cravings.

I took out my cellphone, thinking I'd call Annabelle and see if we could meet that afternoon. When I turned it on, I saw she had sent me a photograph. In it, she must've been sitting in front of a full-length mirror because it appeared to be a photo of her reflection. She was naked, and had made her nose bleed. Blood was leaking from her nose and dripping down her chest and on to her ample belly. Along with the photograph, she included a message: 'Are you sure you want to wait?'

I stared at the photograph for a long minute, both repulsed and desirous. I wanted that blood badly, but that photograph also made me determined to postpone the sordid act as long as I possibly could. I would find a way to wait until Wednesday. I knew I needed to send her a reply and with trembling fingers tapped out 'Anticipation!', figuring she would enjoy that answer.

I sat for a long moment and thought about buying myself a bottle of scotch to help with the cravings, but I knew whatever relief it provided would be temporary. Maybe only minutes. Somehow, I would find a way without scotch or wine to last three more days. I got up and started brewing a pot of coffee, thinking that several cups of coffee loaded with sugar might take the edge off the feeling that my brain was being squeezed.

As soon as the coffee finished brewing I gulped down cup after cup, stirring in a dozen spoonfuls of sugar, then picked out a new book to read. This one wasn't a novel, but one of Jill's psychology books about the power of positive thinking. I'd seen the book on her shelves a week ago, and at the time had thumbed through it and dismissed it as nonsense, but now I decided to read it in the belief that it might have something to offer me.

The book was short. Only two hundred pages. Four hours later I had finished reading it, and sat back and thought about what the book claimed and whether it could be true.

According to the book, the mind is able to make symptoms of illnesses worse and can generate something called 'psychosomatic disorders'. Furthermore, it can create physical illnesses where there are none, and can even cure diseases and be a powerful force for recovery. It also claimed that if you believe strongly enough that you'll become healthy again, or even simply that you'll soon feel better, then the mind could make that happen. What I found most interesting was something that the book called 'mass hysteria' – when a group of people suffer the same delusions, sometimes all of them appearing to show the same symptoms of an illness.

I knew there were physiological differences between my kind and *them*. I knew this from our hair, our eyes, our scent, and our greater strength. I also knew it wasn't anything psychosomatic that made me severely ill when I ate something made with cow's milk or chicken eggs – since whenever that had happened, I'd been ignorant of the fact that what I was eating included any animal material until after I became sick. Our reaction to eating animal flesh or milk or eggs is real. It's not something we've created in our minds. But was that true of the cravings? Could they be a type of mass hysteria that my kind had passed down for thousands of years to each succeeding generation?

I'd always believed the cravings were physiological. That they were simply one of the differences between us and *them*. But what if that was not the case? What if the truth was more like what the psychology book described? That we suffer the cravings only because we believe we're going to suffer them, and they are a form of mass hysteria spawned by the mind.

Even as newborn babies, not only do we suckle milk from our mother's breasts, but a fine paste made from our mother's milk and *their* meat is spread on our gums. Our mothers even dip their fingers into the solution for us to further suckle. As infants, we're eating *their* meat without ever realizing what it is, and this continues until we attend our first slaughtering ritual. Only then do we fully understand what it is we've been eating. Or so it is said. But that's not really true. As small children, we see the burlap sacks carried into the sacred hall where the slaughtering rituals take place. Nobody tells us what's in those sacks, but we still know, even though nobody ever says anything about it. We absorb like sponges what we hear from the elders and others. So even as small children, although nobody tells us what the meat is, we know what it is. That has to be why when we attend our first slaughtering ritual the practice seems normal and natural to us, and why when we see *them* before they're slaughtered we think only of the single purpose they serve.

Of course, the ritual and the words the elders chant during it drive home the message of how necessary it is to eat *their* flesh to stave off our cravings. But what if it isn't purely a physiological need to eat what we do, but more that we're conditioned to doing it? I know our physiological difference has us savoring this particular meat – but because of that, perhaps we have conditioned ourselves to believe we need to eat this type of meat to keep us from suffering from the cravings?

I thought more about the dark time when my clan had gone three weeks without meat and in our madness slaughtered one of our own so we could carve the meat from his bones.

Maybe the simmering stew made us so nauseous because we expected that to happen, and maybe that was why the clan members who ate that stew got as ill as they did as quickly as they did. When I think back of how the clan's small children acted during this time, it didn't seem as if the cravings had affected them anywhere near as severely as they did the rest of us. Maybe that was because the children hadn't yet fully succumbed to the mass hysteria that eventually affects all our kind, if that's what it is. Maybe that is also why the cravings were ravaging me more after only a week than they did after three weeks back then – because I now believe more strongly in the cravings and how they affect us than I did when I was only thirteen.

These thoughts left me stunned. As much as my kind savors the taste of their meat, what if it's possible that we don't actually need to eat it? What if the cravings were simply something we created in our minds?

For the rest of the evening until Jill returned, I tried one of the exercises the psychology book spelled out, telling myself over and over again that the cravings weren't real and that I felt fine. As the book suggested, I tried with all my ability to believe what I was telling myself. But when I stopped several hours later, I felt no better. If anything, I'd only made the cravings angrier.

THIRTY-FOUR

'Y ou look so stressed out. Are you worried about starting
your new job?'

Jill said this while we were eating our early morning
meal together, concern showing in her eyes and lining her
forehead. I'd prepared oatmeal with blackberries, but we
could've been eating mud and I wouldn't have known any
different, given how the cravings were raging inside me. I lied
and told her that that was what was weighing on me.

'You're going to do great today,' Jill insisted. 'I know it.
You should know it too.'

The cravings made it feel as if my brain was on fire. I could
barely think straight. If I was worried about anything, it was
whether I'd be able to keep myself from committing any
savagery before I met up with Annabelle, which was going to
have to be today after I finished work, even if I had to beg
her.

Last night after Jill returned from visiting her parents, I told
her about the new work I'd be starting and we went to a nearby
bar to celebrate. I drank two scotches. The first one dulled the
cravings, but only for about a minute. The second had no
effect. Later, when we returned to Jill's apartment, she played
more Mozart music, this time something called a symphony,
and we sat together on the couch while she read and I tried
to, although I couldn't concentrate on the words because of
how ferociously the cravings were digging into me. After Jill
went to bed, I tried one of the other exercises from her book
on positive thinking, this time imagining the cravings shrinking
and dying within me. Whatever good it was supposed to do,
the exercise failed miserably. Nothing changed. All I could
hope for now was that I'd be kept busy enough with physical
labor to survive the day, at least until I had my chance to meet
up with Annabelle and satisfy these damnable cravings.

When I arrived at the work address in Queens I'd been

given, I could see that a chain-link fence had already been put up around the construction site and that a large hole had been dug out of the ground and lined with cement. I asked around for the man named Carl whom I was supposed to report to, and was taken to the same stumpy man with bulldog-like features who had tested me when I was first looking for home-building work. He looked at me impassively, handed me a hard hat, and told me that he was glad I'd been able to get my situation worked out.

'You can see we've got the foundation ready,' he said. 'Next we're putting up the frame, which means we first need to move the material from the trucks to the site.' He whistled over one of the other workers, a lean and wiry man younger than me who had red hair peeking out from under his hard hat. 'Gerard here will show you what to do.'

I enjoyed the hard labor of building homes for my clan, but that wasn't why I worked so furiously that morning moving materials and supplies to the site. The reason was simple. I was desperately trying to tire myself out, hoping that by doing so I wouldn't notice the cravings so much as they dug deeper into me. It surprised me when Carl interrupted me by clapping my shoulder while I was pulling wood beams from one of the trucks.

'Lunch time,' he said, nodding approvingly. 'So far you're making me look like a genius hiring you. Charlie, you keep this up and we'll be shaving a couple of days off the schedule.'

'I don't care for lunch. I'd like to keep working.'

'You can't. Shop rules. You need to take a full hour. I suggest you join the rest of crew. They like to go to a food truck a block over that's got good steak sandwiches.'

I wanted to argue the matter, but I stopped myself doing so. I knew that *they* are no different about their rules than my clan is about ours. I put my hard hat away where I was told to keep it when I wasn't working, then checked my phone and saw that Annabelle still hadn't responded to the message I had sent her asking if we could meet after I finished my work.

I wasn't going to join the rest of the crew. It would only make the cravings angrier to see *them* eating burnt cow flesh. I walked until I found a market where I could buy an apple and other fruit, and as I ate my meal I squeezed my eyes tight and tried to ignore the way the cravings were screeching at me.

When I returned from my forced lunch break, I tried to work as furiously as during the morning, but we were now putting up the building's frame and at times I found myself having to slow down because of the sluggish pace of the other workers. Later in the afternoon when this happened, I heard the cravings screaming words at me, demanding that I feed them now instead of waiting for Annabelle's blood – that all I had to do was rip out that slow worker's throat and there'd be plenty of blood, so I wouldn't have to keep them waiting. I knew the cravings weren't really screaming anything at me, that it was more that I was being driven to the edge of madness. But it was still a struggle to ignore them. I knew I had to feed them before I returned to Jill's apartment. Either with Annabelle's blood or someone else's.

Work ended at six. I wasn't nearly tired enough and wanted to work more, but Carl told me that was it for the day, that I'd done more than enough already. The cravings were making too much noise in my head for me to argue. I left him to put my hard hat away, and as I turned to leave the construction site, one of *them* was standing in front of me, grinning widely. From his red hair I realized it was Gerard, the one who showed me what to do early that morning.

'The machine!' he said.

I didn't know whether it was because of the cravings muddling my thinking or because what he said made no sense, but I just stared at him without any idea what he meant. He laughed, which almost made me satisfy my cravings then and there.

'You're so damn intense!' he said. 'Damn, you're like a machine, the way you just don't stop out there. But Charlie, man, you got to learn to chill, or you're going to make the rest of us look bad.' He grinned at me again. 'I got something in my car that can help you do some serious chilling. What do you say?'

I didn't know what he could mean by 'chill', other than

that he had something which would make me feel cold, but I nodded anyway. Because I had to satisfy the cravings. It couldn't wait. Annabelle had responded to my message, saying she was going to be stuck at work until late that night.

The cravings had left me with barely enough wits to know that I couldn't feed there. That I had to get him someplace more private. And so I followed him from the construction site to an alley where he kept his car. I didn't attack him, though, once we got to that alley. Something he said while we walked together kept me from doing that. That what he had would help me relax. Would mellow my intensity.

I joined him in his car, and he asked me to hand him a small box that was in his glove compartment. I did so, and he took a cigarette from it.

'I don't smoke cigarettes,' I said.

He winked at me, and he saved his life by what he said next. 'This ain't no cigarette. Swamp kush. Top quality. If this don't relax you, nothing will.'

He lit what looked like a thin, poorly rolled-up cigarette and inhaled deeply on it. The smoke he breathed out was sweeter and more pungent than the cigarette smoke the cook used to exhale. It also didn't smell like poison. He handed me the joint (which was what he later called it), and I breathed in the smoke, feeling its heat in my throat.

He laughed at my effort. 'You should've told me you're smoking weed for the first time. Here's what you do. Breathe the smoke deeper into your lungs and hold it for ten seconds before letting it out. Here, let me show you.'

I handed him back the joint, and he demonstrated for me. When I tried it again, I held the smoke in and tried counting down from ten to zero in my head, but when I reached five I started coughing.

'Next time you'll do better,' he promised, laughing again.

He was right. The next two times I made it to zero. After my sixth drag (which was what he called inhaling on the joint), I noticed something peculiar. The cravings had stopped their screeching. By the time the joint had been reduced to a tiny stub, I didn't even notice them.

THIRTY-FIVE

T he next morning at work I sought out Gerard and asked if he could sell me more of those joints.

He made a signal for me to lower my voice. He looked around to see if anyone else was within listening distance. Then he stepped closer to me and in a guarded voice said, 'Not so loud. Sure, you're a good guy and it will be worth it to chip away some of your intensity so you're not such a madman out there. I'll sell you some at my own cost, and we'll share one of those after work.' He flashed me a grin. 'You liked the way it chilled you, huh?'

'It was a lifesaver,' I said.

What I said was true. I would've resorted to savagery if I hadn't smoked that weed. After smoking with Gerard in his car I found myself free of the cravings for several hours, and when they came back they weren't nearly as voracious as they had been earlier. Even now they weren't as bad as they were the previous day. Although I could still imagine them boring into my skull and eating into my muscles, the pain was tolerable. They weren't driving me to madness anymore. I could live like this if I had to. The problem was I didn't know how long this relief would last or whether smoking another of those joints would help again, which was why I sent Annabelle a message telling her my plans had changed and I'd no longer be able to see her that night, but would like to keep our Wednesday rendezvous as planned. She sent me back a message calling me a tease, but that she'd be counting the minutes to our 'bloody' encounter.

Of course, I sent Annabelle that message before returning to Jill's apartment. I then turned off the cellphone and hid it in her building's laundry room. Also, before Jill got back from her college, I took a hot shower and changed into clean clothes. This wasn't so that I could hide the fact that I had smoked weed, since at the time I didn't realize that their world found

anything wrong with doing so. It was simply that I had
perspired so profusely during my day at work, no doubt aided
by the cravings, that I wanted to be clean for Jill. However,
when we kissed she knew I had smoked, having tasted it on
my breath. Which surprised me, given the apples, potato chips,
and dark chocolate I had found myself gorging on after leaving
Gerard's car.

'I didn't know you liked weed,' Jill said after we separated
from our kiss. Her tone and her expression alarmed me, as
she seemed distressed by that possibility.

'I had it for the first time in my life today,' I said. 'Gerard,
someone at work, invited me to smoke a joint with him. Was
there anything wrong with that?'

She shook her head, although her expression still showed
concern. 'Did you like it?'

'I did. It made me feel more chilled. As Gerard said.'

She laughed. I guess the word 'chilled' did not sound as
natural from my lips as it did from Gerard's.

'A little weed every once in a while is fine, as long as you
don't abuse it like an old boyfriend of mine from high school
did.' She paused, before adding, 'If you're going to smoke,
let's do it together. Or at least, with me around. Promise?'

I told her that I'd do that. I decided I wouldn't keep it secret
if I smoked another joint with Gerard, as the secrets I'd already
had to keep from her were bad enough, and would explain
how that was required in order for me to acquire more joints
from him.

THIRTY-SIX

Tuesday after work I ended up buying six joints from
Gerard and, as he'd requested, we smoked one of them
together in his car. He charged me $5 for each (I
would've gladly paid him far more), and explained that he
bought them from a friend in New Jersey.

'It's legal there for medicinal purposes,' Gerard explained.
'You know, like for glaucoma, cancer, bowel problems,
etcetera. My buddy, he's got his sources, so the weed he gets
me is all medically approved primo stuff.'

At this point he lit up the joint we were sharing and took
his first drag, then handed it to me. His eyes grew distant, and
he said, 'One of these days when things get less fucked up
we'll be able to buy these in New York like they do now in
Colorado. It's complete bullshit that you can buy booze
anywhere but not this.'

He was done talking and turned on his car stereo and played
some music from a group called Pink Floyd, which I found nearly
as soothing as the Mozart music Jill played. We smoked the rest
of the joint, and before we were done with it I found that the
cravings had once again quieted themselves to such an extent
that I didn't notice them. I also found that I was no longer looking
at Gerard as one of *them*.

Later, as I was walking back to Jill's apartment I found that
Annabelle had sent me a message and another photograph.
Her message said she'd been able to escape work and was
waiting for me now if I could make it. As with her last photograph, this one showed her naked, but this time she had painted
her face in a gruesome manner and had used the blood from
her nosebleed to write an obscene message on her stomach. I
dropped the phone on to the cement sidewalk and smashed it
into bits with the heel of my work boot. At least, Annabelle
and the sordid acts she wished us to commit were no longer
going to be another secret I'd need to keep from Jill.

That night when the cravings came back, they did so with even less strength than the previous day. Each night after that, I waited until Jill returned from her college before smoking. When Jill joined me, we'd smoke half a joint together before stubbing it out. On the other nights, I'd only smoke a quarter of a joint before putting it out, which still allowed me to inhale roughly the same amount of smoke as the two times I'd shared a joint with Gerard. Jill seemed impressed by my discipline, and even commented on it. She also noticed how much more relaxed I seemed, which was true. Each time I smoked I'd have hours of relief from the cravings, and each morning when the cravings came back they'd be less. I'd also gotten better at performing the exercise from Jill's positive-thinking book. In my mind's eye, I imagined the cravings withering and dying within me. I'd gotten to the point where I could almost believe that was happening, and by Monday morning they were only an irritant. While we were having our early meal together, Jill remarked how I'd be moving into my sublet apartment in just one day's time.

'We'll be able to start officially dating then,' she said with an impish grin.

'Very true.' I couldn't help grinning back. We'd just had a rainy weekend, which we'd spent together reading, listening to music, sharing wine, kissing passionately, and watching *Casablanca* (another of Jill's favorite movies) with Jill lying curled up on the couch against me. Saturday evening we walked as close together as two people could possibly do as we used a single umbrella in an effort to stay dry on our way to a nearby vegan restaurant. (Later, we had to make a mad dash back to her apartment, as the slanting, driving rain made the umbrella useless.) Now that the cravings had mostly quietened within my head (and more importantly, I no longer worried about them), I was ready to admit that for all practical purposes we'd been dating almost from the start.

Monday morning, the rain had died down to a drizzle. Without the cravings driving me so furiously, I was able to work at a more even pace. I still often had to slow down because of the other workers, but it no longer bothered me to do so. Gerard, as well as some of the others, were still calling me 'the machine', but I could tell they were doing so good-naturedly.

During our compulsory lunch hour, I accompanied Gerard to one of the nearby food trucks (as I had the previous Friday), where I bought a salad and he bought some sort of sandwich made with grilled pig meat. While we ate, we sat together on a bench in a small nearby park and he ranted about subjects that interested him. Although most of what he talked about was unfamiliar to me, I still found it interesting.

Work went quickly the rest of the afternoon. Since Jill didn't plan to be finished at her college until after eight, I would've liked to have gone on working, but Carl told me that, thanks to me, we were already too far ahead of schedule, so he couldn't justify any overtime.

When I got back to the apartment, I was surprised to find Jill waiting for me. I was also surprised by the glum mood she had fallen into. Or maybe not so surprised, because it didn't surprise me when she told me that a police detective had met with her during the day.

'It looks like Ethan disappeared sometime a week ago last Saturday,' she said. 'At least, that's the last night anyone remembers seeing him.'

'What do you think happened to him?'

She shook her head. 'His car's gone. He hasn't used any credit cards or taken out any money from his bank. It doesn't look like he's called anyone, not even anyone at work. The police detective I spoke with thinks he might've driven somewhere and committed suicide. That's what he wanted to ask me about. Whether Ethan ever talked about committing suicide. And if he was going to do something like that, where he would have driven to.'

I sat down next to her, as much to comfort her as to keep her from looking into my eyes. 'Could he have done that?'

'I don't know. People as narcissistic as Ethan don't usually commit suicide. They might threaten to do so to get attention, but they rarely go through with it. But that doesn't explain why the police haven't been able to find his car. His security system allows his car to be located. The police should've been able to find it, unless Ethan purposely had it removed.'

She shook her head as if it was unfathomable that Ethan would've done that. I was relieved that the Brooklyn clan had been so thorough in making the car disappear, especially as his car had a tracking device.

'Why don't I get us some wine?' I said. 'And maybe some takeout food. You look like you could use it.'

She smiled weakly. 'That's an excellent idea.'

THIRTY-SEVEN

The next morning while we were having our early morning meal together, Jill didn't say anything about her former boyfriend, but she still seemed preoccupied (troubled?) by his mysterious disappearance. This continued to confuse me as I would've thought she'd be glad to know he was gone given the disrespectful and brutish way he'd treated her, but I didn't say anything to her about it.

After I left Jill's apartment, I bought a newspaper and in the inside pages found a one-column story about Ethan. According to the police, he was last seen nine days ago at a bar in the Astoria section of Queens. The police were trying to determine whether he had left the bar with anyone, but for the time being they didn't believe his disappearance was due to any suspicious activity. The article further talked about how he worked as an associate at a hedge fund, which it suggested was stressful, with long hours, and had a higher than average suicide rate. It also mentioned a recent breakup with a girlfriend of two years, and one of his coworkers told the newspaper reporter that Ethan had been depressed for days leading up to his disappearance. I breathed a little easier after reading the article. It had been in the back of my mind that a neighbor or someone else might've seen me while I was hiding behind the bushes at Ethan's home, but that didn't seem to be the case.

Later that night, Jill continued to seem preoccupied (saddened?) as we commenced our first official date inside my new home. She didn't say anything about Ethan, but it was obvious he was on her mind, or at least the mystery of his disappearance was. I had cooked a dinner of three-bean chili from a recipe I found in that day's newspaper and had bought a bottle of Merlot wine that the clerk told me was excellent value for its price, but Jill only nibbled on the three-bean chili and barely took more than two sips of her wine.

I asked her if we should go to a restaurant instead.

She gave me a distracted look before shaking her head. 'Charlie, the food's really good and so is the wine. I'm sorry, I'm just in a weird mood.' She showed me a sad smile. 'Maybe we should postpone our first date until tomorrow?'

I nodded, because what else was I going to do? She got up, gave me a quick kiss on the cheek, and headed for the door.

'Should I walk you home?' I asked.

The smile she showed me made my heart hurt a little. 'Not tonight, Charlie. I'd like to be alone right now.'

I watched her leave, and wondered what had happened between us. I'd lost my appetite also. Not just for the food, but for the wine. Fortunately, Gerard had sold me more weed cigarettes that day.

Wednesday morning I spotted another article in the newspaper about Ethan. The police didn't offer any further information, but the newspaper had talked to his parents and a brother, and were convinced that someone had done something to him. Other than that, though, there was no new information. Nor was there anything about the 'Slaughter at the Caspian' or the other two people I'd killed. There hadn't been anything about those killings in over a week.

I had a heavy heart all day, wondering if I had somehow lost Jill. The cravings were only a whisper now – but if I couldn't live my life with Jill, what difference did that make? Even though I was doing work that I enjoyed and had all the books in the world to read, my life here would be pointless if Jill was gone. I worried myself sick over that possibility all day, but when I saw her later that night for our rescheduled first date I realized I had worried myself for nothing. I knew that the moment I answered the door and saw the way she smiled at me. Seconds later we were kissing passionately, and when we finally separated she tried to apologize for the previous night.

'You don't ever have to apologize to me,' I said, my throat once again filled with a lump. I felt my face flushing hot as I looked into her eyes, which had gotten so big. 'I saved the three-bean chili from last night. Also the wine. If you prefer, we could go out—'

She put a finger on my lips to quiet me. 'We'll eat the chili later,' she said. 'And we'll have the wine too. But for now there's something I've been waiting weeks to do.'

She took hold of my hand and led me to the bed. I didn't argue with her.

The next night Jill's friend Brittany interrupted our second official date. This time we were at Jill's apartment when a hard rapping sounded on the door, and then we heard Brittany's voice frantically calling for Jill. At the time, Jill and I were smoking one of the weed cigarettes I'd bought from Gerard, and I was hoping she'd ignore her friend. But she didn't. When Jill answered the door, Brittany breezed in, uninvited.

'Oh my God! I had to come here after reading about Ethan,' Brittany exclaimed. 'This is just so fucking unbelievable.'

As she emerged from the hallway and spotted me, I could tell from the glint in her eyes that she was going to be trouble. I held up the joint and offered it to her.

'Thanks, Charlie, but no thanks. Not my thing. I thought you moved out on Tuesday?'

Jill had rejoined me on the couch and slipped her hand into mine, while Brittany took the chair kitty-corner to us. 'He did,' Jill said, smiling at her friend. 'We're on our second official date.'

'I'm sorry for butting in like this, but I had to see you. Have the police talked to you?'

Jill accepted the joint from me and took a hit. After releasing the smoke, she told her friend, 'A detective came by the college and spoke with me.'

'They don't think you're involved?'

'No, of course not. He just wanted to know about my relationship with Ethan, and I explained that it had been over for weeks. Also whether Ethan ever talked about suicide, or if I had any thoughts about where he might've driven to.' Jill's smile tightened. 'Don't worry, Brit, I'm in the clear. I was able to give the detective an airtight alibi. I was with my parents all weekend.' She laughed, but as with her smile, there was a tightness to it that surprised me, given the weed we'd been smoking. 'Besides, with the way my shoulder was wrecked that weekend, not much chance I would've been able to overpower Ethan.'

'What do you think happened to him?'

Jill shrugged. 'The police think he drove someplace secluded and committed suicide. I think he's driven someplace to hide for a few weeks so he can get attention. Whichever it turns out to be, I don't give a fuck, and I'm not going to waste another second on him. He caused me enough turmoil and pain when we were dating, and he's not going to cause me any more now.'

Brittany nodded, as if she agreed with how Jill was feeling about the matter, but I caught that glint in her eyes again as she looked at me. 'How about you, Charlie? Do you have a guess as to what happened to Ethan?'

I shook my head. 'No idea.'

'Why are you asking Charlie that?' Jill asked.

Brittany pursed her lips. 'I find it an interesting coincidence that a week after Ethan assaults you in that after-hours club, he disappears off the face of the planet the first night you leave Charlie here all by himself. It makes me wonder whether Ethan is buried somewhere in the boondocks of New Hampshire.'

'You're being ridiculous, Brit.' Jill laughed as if what Brittany was saying was a joke. 'Besides, Charlie didn't even know where Ethan lived, or even what his last name was.'

Brittany didn't bother pointing out that Jill had referred to Ethan in the past tense, which seemed to counter her stated belief that Ethan was still alive and hiding somewhere. Instead, she picked up Jill's address book on the small table next to her, and thumbed through it until she found what she wanted. She held the book up, which showed Ethan's name, phone number, and address.

'I'm betting he's the only Ethan in your book,' Brittany said.

'This isn't funny.'

'I'm not trying to be funny. Jill, there's something wrong about him. About Charlie, I mean. I can't say exactly what it is, but there's definitely something off about him.' She turned to me, smiling at me as if this were only a joke. 'Charlie, you want to tell us where Ethan is?'

Jill stood up, her body rigid. From where I was sitting, I could only see her in profile, but the harshness transforming her face was something I never thought I'd see in her.

'If you want us to still be friends, you'd better leave now.'

'Jill, you know I'm right. You're in denial about Charlie, just like you were early on with Ethan. But if you can try being honest with yourself, you'll admit there's something very wrong about him.'

'Get out now. I mean it.'

Brittany made a helpless gesture with her hands. 'Jill, please, just think about what I said. If I didn't love you like my sister, I wouldn't be saying it.'

We both watched silently as Brittany got up and walked out of the apartment. Only after the door closed behind her, did Jill apologize to me for what her friend had said.

'Not your fault,' I said.

'Still, she had no right to do that.'

We had wasted a good amount of the weed cigarette thanks to Brittany. I took a long drag on it and handed what was left to Jill.

'She hasn't liked me from the start.'

'No, she hasn't.'

Brittany had put a damper on the evening. We tried resurrecting the good feelings we had earlier, but it was hard after that. After an hour or so, we decided to reschedule our second date.

THIRTY-EIGHT

The next day I was busy constructing one of the walls for the house we were building when Carl came to me with a perplexed look on his face.

'There's a cop wants to talk to you,' he said.

'Really?'

'Yeah. What's it about?'

I shook my head as if I didn't know. I left Carl and found a large man in an ill-fitting suit waiting for me outside the construction site. He asked me if I was Charlie Husk, and I told him I was.

'I'd like to ask you a few questions about Ethan Kensil, if you don't mind.'

'Sure.'

I followed him to a spot where we'd have a little more privacy.

'You know that Mr Kensil is missing?'

'Yes, Jill told me.'

'Jill Zemler?'

I nodded.

'How well did you know him?'

'I didn't know him at all. I'd only seen him twice.'

He scratched above his ear as he squinted at a small notepad. 'But you threatened him?'

'In a way,' I admitted. 'This was the second time I saw him. He had forced his way into Jill's apartment. She asked him to leave. He refused. When I approached him, he tried jabbing me with his forefinger. I grabbed it and gave it a little twist, and warned him if he didn't leave of his own accord he'd be leaving in pieces.'

'Did you mean that?'

'At the time, yes. His forefinger could very well have left before the rest of him.'

If the detective was at all surprised by my candor, he didn't show it. 'Were you in contact with Mr Kensil at all after that day?'

'No.'

'You never called him to arrange a meeting?'

'No.'

'Where were you the night of September twenty-sixth?'

My kind isn't used to using calendars, so I was trying to recall which day that would've been when the detective mentioned that he was asking about a week ago from Saturday.

I nodded as if I were recalling that night. 'I was staying at Jill's apartment, and I spent the night quietly reading before going to bed.'

'Can anyone verify that?'

'I'm sorry, but no.'

He grunted as if he expected that answer. He squinted again at his notepad, and asked, 'Were you upset when you found out that Mr Kensil had assaulted Ms Zemler at a nightclub? In fact, assaulted her violently enough to send her to the emergency room with a shoulder injury?'

'Of course I was upset that Jill was hurt. I was very upset.'

'Yet you convinced Ms Zemler not to file charges against Mr Kensil?'

I laughed at that. 'That's what Brittany told you? No, that's not what I did. I supported Jill's decision, just as I'll support any decision Jill wants to make.'

This time he seemed surprised by what I said, at least enough to raise his eyebrows. He closed his notepad. 'Why do you suppose Ms Hennessey called us about you?'

I shrugged. 'I can't say. All I can tell you is that Brittany didn't like it when Jill dated Ethan, and she doesn't like it any better that Jill's now dating me.'

'She thinks you might've buried his remains somewhere in New Hampshire.'

'I know. She barged in on Jill and me last night, and made the same bizarre accusation. Detective, I can promise you I didn't do that. If Ethan's ended up buried somewhere in New Hampshire, he wasn't buried there by me.'

His attitude toward me had changed from aloof to apologetic, maybe even somewhat friendly, as if he understood the kind of trouble having an enemy like Brittany can bring.

'Mr Husk, I hope you understand why I had to speak with you. With a case like this we have to follow up on all leads, but I'm sorry for wasting your time. If you want me to talk to your boss and make sure he understands the situation, I'd be happy to do so.'

'No need to bother with that.'

We shook hands, and on my way back to my work I explained to Carl that the police detective's visit was a misunderstanding and nothing more.

'You're not in any trouble?'

'No, just a misunderstanding. The detective apologized for wasting my time.'

I went back to finishing the wall I was building, and as I did so I wondered how much more trouble Brittany was going to try to cause me. A short time later, Carl came to me again, this time to tell me that a beautiful young girl wanted to speak to me and said it was urgent.

I met Jill outside the chain-link fence surrounding the construction site. She looked tense as she stood absently pulling the fingers on her left hand.

'I would've gotten here sooner, but I was in the middle of teaching my freshman class and couldn't leave campus until fifteen minutes ago. The same police detective who spoke with me called wanting to know where he could find you.'

'I know. We talked a few minutes ago. Everything's fine.'

'Why did he want to speak to you?'

'Brittany called the police and said I murdered Ethan, so the detective had to speak with me. I didn't kill Ethan, the detective knows that, and he also knows why Brittany said what she did.'

A white-hot anger burned in Jill's face as she processed what I'd told her, which was nothing more than what she already suspected.

'She's nuts,' she said. 'Certifiable. I'm so sorry, Charlie.'

I smiled at her and told her it was OK, and we made plans for later.

THIRTY-NINE

The clerk finished gift-wrapping the box. She smiled at me. 'It's a beautiful necklace,' she said.

I agreed. I knew little about jewelry, but when I saw it a week ago I wanted to buy it for Jill. It just seemed perfect for her. Delicate like her, also. The freshwater pearls had this pinkish hue to them that reminded me of the color of her skin when we made love, and the flower-shaped gold pendant seemed so finely crafted.

'Is this for a special occasion?' the clerk asked.

'The two-month anniversary of when we officially started dating.'

She laughed at that. 'Were you *unofficially* dating before then?'

'In a way.'

She handed me the box. 'Your girlfriend's going to love this.'

I smiled at her and said I hoped she was right. Even a month ago, I would never have done that. It was nearly unimaginable how much my life had changed. Most nights Jill and I slept together, either at her apartment or at mine. The cravings had completely gone, and have been for seven weeks now. I know it hasn't been very long since I left the clan, but whenever I think about how my life used to be, that just doesn't seem possible. Almost as if it was just a bad nightmare I dreamed. Something unreal that never really happened. I try hard not to think about it.

Sometimes when my thoughts drift, I find myself wondering about the cravings. I still didn't know whether they were the result of mass hysteria and were never real, or whether they were an actual physical disease that I managed to recover from. It was possible that smoking the weed cigarettes allowed me to relax enough so that the exercises I concentrated on were able to work. Or it could be that there is some chemical in the weed I smoked that cured me. Sometimes I find myself thinking about going back to my clan and letting them know there's another way, but I stop myself whenever I realize I'm doing this, because I know they would never listen to me. Or rather, the elders would never let them listen to me. They're too content with their lot. They especially like feeling as if they're the top of the food chain, and that the rest of humanity exists only to be hunted by them and to serve only one purpose.

I don't look at anyone as *them* anymore. I haven't for almost six weeks, and I know I never will again. Along with the cravings disappearing, my bestial self – or what I used to think of as my true self – has vanished. I no longer have anything to mask when I'm around people. What I've always shown Jill, and now show the rest of the world, is my true self.

It sickens me when I think about how I used to see people, and even more so when I think about all the innocents I collected for my clan. But I try hard not to think about that. I was a different person. A different breed. In my heart, I know that's true. That my past life doesn't exist for me anymore. I keep telling myself this whenever my thoughts drift.

I'm happier now than I ever would've thought possible, and I know Jill is mostly, too. There's a sadness, though, that I know weighs on her at times. She can't forgive Brittany for sending the police after me, and refuses to have anything to do with her. I know that's not good for her, and as much as I'd like to never see Brittany again, I've decided to try to reconcile the two of them.

The only thing that worries me these days is that clan in Brooklyn, although not as much as you might think. It's more that I know I have to be cautious about them. Five weeks ago, they spotted me while I was working and later I saw them waiting for me. They thought they could follow me and see where I was living, but they were in their truck so it was easy enough to lose them by taking the subway. They showed up the next day also, and like the previous day I lost them easily. They didn't show up after that, probably because they realized it was pointless. I saw them another time, a week later, driving near *The Cultured Cannibal* – I have no interest in that restaurant anymore, and was simply walking past it on my way to meet Jill at her college – but I'm almost sure that was just a coincidence and I don't think they saw me. But if they were looking for me in Queens, I wonder whether Jill and I should move, especially since we're talking about living together once my sublet finishes next month? I would like to move from Queens entirely, but that's not possible because of Jill's college.

I should've been more alert as I walked to my apartment, but I was distracted, thinking about the wine and flowers I wanted to buy before I met up with Jill. This has to be why I didn't immediately notice the van parked in front of my building, and why I thought only vaguely about how familiar it looked. I realized too late whose van it was and why it was there, even though it was from a different lifetime ago.

Before I could react, something very hard hit me on the side of my head, and I was swallowed up by a sea of blackness.

FORTY

I don't know how long I was unconscious. When I started to come to, my thinking was too muddled for me to make sense of anything. At some level, I knew how badly my head was throbbing. My hands were tied behind my back and I'd been gagged, but I didn't connect that with what had happened. Then I remembered the van that had been parked waiting for me and felt even sicker inside, knowing what I would see once I opened my eyes.

It took a while before I was able to force my eyes open a crack. At first my vision was too blurry to make out much, other than a soft haze of light in the midst of darkness. As my vision cleared, I realized that the haze of light came from an electric lamp, which gave just enough light for me to see that my brother Daniel was sitting across from me. Of course, I was in the back of the van. Even while I'd been mostly out of it, I'd felt the bumps in the road and the sensation of traveling.

'I've been waiting for you to wake,' Daniel said. 'Only reason you ain't in a sack is the elders didn't want you put in one. Otherwise you'd be in that pile with the rest of them. Only reason you ain't dead is the elders told me to bring you back alive.'

I didn't need to look at the burlap sacks piled up in the back to know they were filled. I could hear a soft moaning coming from inside them, and I could sense them quivering as those trussed up inside tried fruitlessly to wriggle free.

Daniel watched me for a long moment. For what, I don't know, since I couldn't speak because of the gag in my mouth. After several minutes of only road noise breaking the silence, he told me that 'she' was in one of the sacks.

'She was easy to get,' he said. 'That little one with the yellow hair. We knew where she lived so we waited, Clement and me, and we took her easy. I made sure not to hit her too hard. Elders wanted her alive, but me and Clement wanted that even more.'

I'd been trying to prepare myself for what he was saying, because I'd expected it. Daniel and Clement knew where to find me because the Brooklyn clan had spied on me and had gotten word back to my clan. And to do that, they must've also spied on Jill. The elders were such a mean-spirited bunch I had no doubt that if they knew about Jill, they would order her to be picked up along with myself.

Even though I had expected what Daniel said, the pain which welled up in my chest was so great all I wanted to do was die. But I fought against that feeling, and fought even harder to keep from sobbing, because I could see the hate burning in Daniel's eyes. He was clutching a brick – most likely the one he'd clobbered me with – and if I had cried out or shown any tears at what he said, his hatred toward me would've gotten the better of him and he would've beaten me to death with the brick. As much as I wanted to, I couldn't let myself die. The only chance Jill had was if I stayed alive.

The full moon was large and bright in the night sky. Daniel and Clement both carried sacks over their shoulders, while I plodded along ahead of them helpless to do anything. When Clement untied the ropes binding my ankles together, I'd seen that the hatred burning in his eyes was every bit as intense as the hatred in Daniel's, so it didn't surprise me that he had left me gagged and with my hands bound behind my back.

I'd forgotten how quiet the nights could be in the New Hampshire wilderness, especially in late November when the insects are mostly gone. There was a biting chill in the air, but snow hadn't fallen yet and a carpeting of leaves and pine needles covered the path. In the gloom of the night, the wilderness we trekked through seemed more like a godforsaken wasteland than a land I used to think of as home.

My head was still woozy from Daniel clobbering me with that brick, and as they padded behind me he and Clement were so quiet that at times I found myself imagining this was just a bad dream and none of it had actually happened. But the path we walked on was overgrown with thorn bushes and overhanging tree branches, and you had to be careful walking along it. Whenever I began imagining none of this was real, I'd get careless and soon afterwards be brought out of my daydreaming by a tree branch or overhang of thorns whipping me across the face.

As we hiked toward the clan's homestead, the cold night air helped clear the fog in my head and I was able to concentrate better. I tried to think only about what was going to be happening soon, and what I might be able to do to save Jill.

In half an hour we would arrive back at the homestead, and some of my kin would trek back to the van to bring back the other sacks. The elders wouldn't wait long to commence the slaughtering rituals. Would they keep me gagged and my hands tied behind my back as a way to further shame me? Or would my nightmare from months ago turn out to be a prophecy? I had to hope it would be the latter – because if I was handed the truncheon to strike the silencing blow, I would use it instead to kill as many of the elders as I could. And I would use the slicing knife to cut Jill free, and I would fight off the rest of my kin for as long as I could. They'd overcome me soon enough, but I hoped I could fight them off long enough for Jill to escape. I had to hope that would happen. That was all I had left. As long as they cut my hands free, I'd have a chance to save Jill.

As we approached the homestead the clearing became wider, and in the twilight I could see wreckage where I had built one of the houses. Soon I could see that all the houses I built had been reduced to rubble. The generators and other equipment I brought back to the clan had also been smashed. Daniel saw me noticing this, and he told me with self-righteousness filling his voice that all the books had been burned also. 'Nothin' from their world is goin' to poison us like it did you.'

As we entered the homestead, I was surprised to see others of my kin waiting outside for us. They were there because they wanted to see me in my humiliation. The elders stood with them, but I didn't see my ma and pa with them. Nor my baby sister Olive, although, since she was only twelve, it was unlikely she would've been married off to another clan during my absence.

None of my kin said anything as I was marched through the homestead. Daniel and Clement dropped their sacks by the sacred hall, and then took me to my parents' shack. My ma and pa were waiting for me there, too ashamed to have joined the rest of my kin outside. My pa stared at me with stony contempt, but I was surprised by the worry and compassion I saw wrecking my ma's face. I never thought I'd see that from her. I stumbled toward the hearth, my head bowed.

'Sit yerself down,' my ma ordered. 'I need to cut that rope.'

I fell to my knees. My pa continued to stare stonily at me as my ma used a knife to fray the rope. Daniel had wrapped several loops of rope around my wrist and tied the knot as tightly as he could manage, so it took my ma a while sawing the knife back and forth before she was able to fray the rope enough for me to pull it apart. With my hands freed, I took the gag out of my mouth and proceeded to rub the numbness out of my arms.

'Pa, it doesn't have to be like this,' I said, imploringly.

His lips curled with disgust and continued to stare at me in that same stony manner.

'The cravings can be cured. I cured them in myself. We don't have to live apart like this.'

The look on his face made it clear that he didn't care what I had to say. All at once I started sobbing uncontrollably. I couldn't help it. I'd made the mistake of letting myself imagine what Jill was going through, and the pain flooding through me had become unbearable. As I sobbed, I tried pleading with him, telling him how important Jill was to me, but even as I did this, I knew I was only disgracing myself further in his eyes. Still, I couldn't help myself, and when I reached for his hand to further implore him, he stepped forward and struck me a hard blow above my ear that drove me to the dirt floor and left me lying on my face.

'You either one of us or one of *them*,' my pa said to me, his voice filled with disgust. I didn't look up, but when I heard my ma start to cry I knew he had left the shack.

FORTY-ONE

None of my kin wanted to stand near me in the sacred hall. That was for the best. The more they kept their distance from me, the better. If the elders didn't call on me to deliver the silencing blow, I would have to fight my way through them to wrestle the truncheon away from whichever elder was holding it. So the further they kept away from me, the better chance I'd have of doing that.

I made sure not to look at the elders. I didn't want them knowing what I was thinking. I wanted them to believe I was standing there chastened and ashamed.

There was movement off to the side of the hall, and I knew the first of the victims was being brought out. More of my kin moved to the front to watch this person being tied up. I felt my heart ready to explode. I'd caught glimpses of this person's muddy hair and slight stature, and knew it had to be Jill. The elders had chosen her to be first. This didn't surprise me. I braced myself for what was going to be happening.

They had finished tying Jill up. All I could see were glimpses of her, thanks to my kin mostly obscuring my view. I looked at the elders beseechingly, pleading silently for them to spare her. This was genuine on my part but also intentional, as I hoped this would spur them on to order me to deliver the silencing blow. And it worked. The elders really are bastards, every single goddamned one of them! The elder holding the truncheon stepped forward, and ordered me to deliver the silencing blow.

Those of my kin standing in front of me parted and I could now clearly see that her yellow hair had been turned muddy brown, just as it had in my dream. As with all the others who had been slaughtered, she'd been tied so her toes barely touched the ground. As she saw me she started to cry, her eyes pleading, begging me. One of my kin hissed as I rushed forward and took the truncheon from the elder. Before she could stop crying long enough to utter a word, I struck her on the side of the head with the truncheon. Then I took the slicing knife from the elder and, after pulling open her slack jaw, I cut out her tongue.

I stepped away from her and moved to the back of the hall. I had hit her too hard – the silencing blow had knocked her unconscious instead of simply stunning her – and several of the women kinfolk were slapping her to wake her. The victims had to be awake for the slaughtering ritual.

This rush of activity kept the rest of my kin from noticing how I was shaking. By the time the womenfolk had wakened her, I had gotten myself under control. It wasn't hard to imagine how it had happened. Daniel and Clement would have seen Brittany and Jill as the same – as one of *them* who was small and yellow-haired. Even if they'd had a photograph of Jill, they wouldn't have been able to tell the two of them apart. All I could imagine was that Brittany must've gone to Jill's apartment to try to make amends, and Daniel and Clement had grabbed her before she could knock on Jill's door.

I felt truly sorry for Brittany as I watched her suffer the horrors of the slaughtering ritual. Even though she had been nothing but a thorn in my side, I would've saved her if I could. But I never had a chance, just like I wouldn't have had a chance of saving her if it had been Jill. I had been deluding myself. Even if I had succeeded in cutting her down, which was unlikely, my kin would've caught up with her before she had a chance to leave the homestead.

The moment I saw it was Brittany, I knew I had to silence her before she saw me and said anything to let my clan know she wasn't the one they wanted. I was sorry my women kinfolk were able to wake her, though.

As I watched her being slaughtered, I realized that the elders were soon going to discover she wasn't Jill. They'd know, once Daniel and Clement looked through the belongings they'd collected and found Brittany's pocketbook. Even if they didn't discover it was Brittany, I had little doubt the Brooklyn clan would. And if the Brooklyn clan didn't grab Jill for themselves, they would send word to the elders.

The slaughtering rituals soon became little more than background noise as a glimmer of an idea came to me. And before long, I had a plan.

FORTY-TWO

The slaughtering rituals ended at sunset. Even though it disgusted me, I sat in the sacred hall and ate the stew I was offered without complaining. I couldn't afford to make my kin any more suspicious of me than they already were. Since my own home had been destroyed, along with the other houses I built, when the slaughtering ritual ended I went to my parents' shack, where my ma made me a bed by the hearth. Before retiring for the night, my pa grudgingly nodded at me, as if I'd made amends of sorts by striking a decisive silencing blow.

I waited until midnight before sneaking out. My kin had destroyed all the power tools I brought to the clan, but I was able to find a small cache of hand tools they'd missed and took a screwdriver from it. Stealthily I headed toward the path that would take me to the van. I moved quickly, sometimes running, sometimes walking briskly, and covered the four miles in less than half an hour. I was out of breath by the time I reached the clearing where the van was kept. I collapsed forward with my hands on my knees as I tried to slow down my breathing and my heart. It was only then, in the moonlight, I noticed Daniel and Clement sitting by the van. They both stood up. Daniel was holding a hatchet, Clement a crowbar.

'You might've fooled those others, but you ain't fooled us,' Daniel said. 'But that's because we learnt that yellow-haired girl was the wrong one. We learnt that when we went through what she was carrying. But you didn't say nothin' about that. That's how we knew you'd be coming here.'

They both stepped toward me, murderous intent shining in their eyes. They'd easily have been able to explain to the elders why they needed to kill me. But what they didn't understand was that while they had hate driving them, I had the desperation of trying to save the woman I loved. That was something they would never understand.

I flew at Daniel. He swung the hatchet, aiming to bury it in my head, but I ducked low and swung my fist into his testicles. My kind don't fight like that. It's considered an unmanly low blow and disgraceful, but then my kind don't usually fight to save the ones they love.

My blow sent Daniel reeling, clutching his groin. Clement hit me hard across my shoulders with the crowbar. The pain knocked me down on all fours, but before Clement could cave my skull in with another blow, I rolled away and grabbed the hatchet that Daniel had dropped. From my knees, I whipped the hatched at Clement. He tried to block it with the crowbar, but the blade dug into his forearm. That didn't stop him, but it slowed him down, and when I tackled him the pain and added weight of the hatchet kept him from swinging the crowbar hard enough to hurt me.

I crawled on top of him and pinned him down with my knees. Clement was always a feisty one, but he was thinner and smaller than me, and he couldn't buck me off of him. I brought my fist back and punched him in the nose, and kept doing that until I knocked him out.

Daniel had gotten back on his feet. His face chalky white in the moonlight, outrage over my low blow glinting in his eyes. He charged me, ignoring the fact that I now had Clement's crowbar. I swung for the fences the same way I'd watched baseball players swing a baseball bat weeks ago in the World Series, and connected solidly enough with his jaw to make a satisfying 'Thunk!' noise. There was no doubt that I had shattered it. He was out well before he hit the ground.

I found the van's keys in his pocket, and also my wallet that he had taken from me earlier. It was still stuffed with money. He and Clement must've been planning to head back to New York to snatch Jill right after they killed me. I tossed away the screwdriver I'd taken, since I no longer needed to get at the ignition wires.

I dumped all the burlap sacks and rope from the back of the van. Then after a moment's thought trussed up Daniel and Clement and put them both in sacks. Maybe the clan would discover them in a few days, or maybe it would take a week. They could both die before that happened. I didn't much care.

I drove off in the van, and kept driving until I reached Massachusetts. As much as I longed to, I couldn't go back to Jill right away. There was something I had to do first, something I wouldn't be able to start until the morning. I found a motel situated off the main road.

That was two days ago. I've been writing this nonstop since buying the necessary notebooks and pens at a convenience store. The motel I checked into has a coffeemaker in the room that's been useful – the coffee I've been drinking has been instrumental in allowing me to write this as quickly as I have. I've tried to be as honest as I can with what I've written, and I've tried my hardest to remember everything that has happened since I first saw Jill back on Labor Day. It's important that people realize this is an accurate accounting of the events that occurred.

I'm planning to figure out a way for this document to be sent to the police and the newspapers, maybe even to a book publisher, if anything ever happens to Jill or myself. Also, I'll be including maps and directions to every hidden clan I know about, and will be giving a copy of all this to the Brooklyn clan to read and to deliver to my clan in New Hampshire. They can take the van back to them if they want to. I don't care.

Last night I called Jill and I told her as much of the truth as I could. That two of my relatives came to New York to kidnap me. That they knocked me out, tied me up, gagged me, and drove me to the family compound without my being able to do anything about it. It broke my heart a little when I heard her whisper 'Oh my God!', and from her voice I was able to imagine how stricken she must've been right then.

I tried joking, telling Jill that the worst part of it was that I lost the present I'd bought her for our two-month 'Officially Dating' anniversary.

'The necklace was freshwater pearls with a gold pendant shaped like a lily. It just seemed so perfect for you, and now you're not even going to believe I bought you anything.'

'Charlie, what they did to you is just so awful! Are you hurt?'

'My head hurts,' I admitted. 'My shoulders and back also.
But I'll be OK.'

'When am I going to see you again?'

'I'll be back in New York in two days, maybe three. I
wish I could see you tonight, but there's something important
I need to do first.' I tried joking again, although it really wasn't
a joke, but rather something I'd been dreading asking her.
'Assuming that you still want to see me, and I'd understand if
you don't given how backward and demented my family is—'

'Charlie, of course I want to see you. I'm not going to
blame you for your family. But you need to call the police.
You have to!'

'I can't,' I said. 'I hope you can trust me regarding this, but
it's best if I don't tell anyone but you about this. My family
will never bother me again. They understand that now.'

That last part was a white lie. But they will understand
once the Brooklyn clan brings them a copy of this document.
If they hurt either of us, they'll be dooming not only themselves but all the other clans too.

As long as they leave us alone, nobody will ever read this.

ACKNOWLEDGEMENTS

This novel wouldn't exist if it wasn't for Dana Kabel. A few years back Dana invited me to contribute a story to an anthology titled 'Kannibal Cookbook', and while that story ended up being almost the polar opposite of what HUSK became, writing it got the creative juices flowing for this novel. I'd like to thank Paul Tremblay for reading an early draft when it had the working title 'American Cannibal: A Love Story', and for providing his blurb. In memoriam, I'd like to acknowledge the late Ed Gorman. Ed was a friend and a mentor for almost fifteen years, and during this time provided me constant encouragement, and HUSK was one of my last novels that Ed was able to read. I'd also like to thank my college buddy and unofficial copyeditor Alan Luedeking for all of his help in improving this book, and also my child-hood friend (and best man at my wedding) Jeff Michaels for his feedback. I'd like to further thank Kate Grant for acquiring this book for Severn House and, for better or worse, giving it the light of day, and to Holly Domney for all of her careful editing which required a careful balancing act to both improve the writing but also maintain Charlie Husk's unique voice. Finally, I'd like to thank my wife and best friend, Judy, for all of her support and help with this book.